Seeds of Deception

Sheila Connolly

BERKLEY PRIME CRIME
New York

BERKLEY PRIME CRIME
Published by Berkley
An imprint of Penguin Random House LLC
375 Hudson Street, New York, New York 10014

Copyright © 2016 by Sheila Connolly
Penguin Random House supports copyright. Copyright fuels creativity, encourages
diverse voices, promotes free speech, and creates a vibrant culture. Thank you for buying
an authorized edition of this book and for complying with copyright laws by not
reproducing, scanning, or distributing any part of it in any form without permission.
You are supporting writers and allowing Penguin Random House to continue to
publish books for every reader.

BERKLEY is a registered trademark and BERKLEY PRIME CRIME and the B colophon
are trademarks of Penguin Random House LLC.

ISBN: 9780425275825

First Edition: October 2016

Printed in the United States of America
3 5 7 9 10 8 6 4 2

Cover art by Mary Ann Lasher
Book design by Laura K. Corless

To John Bartram, Thomas Jefferson,
and John Chapman (aka Johnny Appleseed),
who each played an important role in the cultivation
and spread of orchards in America

Acknowledgments

The Orchard Mysteries are firmly rooted in small-town New England, but for this book, the tenth in the series, I thought it would be fun to get my main characters, Meg and Seth, out of their hometown. After all, they just got married, and they deserve a honeymoon. They didn't count on having to help solve a murder in New Jersey, but with their track record they shouldn't have been surprised when that happened.

It appears that Meg Corey grew up in a town in northern New Jersey that looks quite a bit like the one where I grew up. I haven't kept in touch with many people from those days (and those I've encountered on social media have scattered far and wide), but if I have inadvertently insulted or misrepresented any businesses or individuals there, past or present, I apologize. I do have fond memories of the town (and I think there's a significant reunion coming up soon).

It takes a lot of people to bring a book to fruition (pun intended), and I want to thank my editor, Tom Colgan at Berkley Prime Crime, and his able assistants for seeing this through. I also want to thank my agent, Jessica Faust of BookEnds, who has nudged and prodded this series all along the way. And as always, the support and professional insights provided by Sisters in Crime (and my local chapter, New England Sisters in Crime), the amazing SinC Guppies, and Mystery Writers of America, have been essential. It is an ongoing pleasure to be part of the writers' community, and few of us can do it all alone.

1

"Good morning, Mrs. Chapin."

Meg was awakened by the sound of Seth's voice, followed quickly by the smell of coffee.

"And good morning to you, Mr. Chapin." Meg pried her eyes open.

Seth set the coffee mug down on the table next to Meg, then settled himself beside her on the bed, plumping several pillows behind him. "How're you feeling?" he asked.

"I'm feeling great. Why? Should I be hungover? Or should I be thinking to myself, what have I done? How do I get out of this?"

"I withdraw the question," Seth said hastily, "if that's the way you're thinking."

"Don't worry. I never drink too much, and we're both mature adults and we had plenty of time to think about what we were doing when we decided to get married. We've got plenty of time to regret it later."

"I guess that's encouraging. So, what now?"

Meg pulled herself up to the same level, rearranging her pillows, and took a long swallow of coffee. "Now as in this minute? Today? This week? This month?"

"Any and all of the above. We were so busy trying to plan this wedding, and helping Aaron out of the mess he was in, and worrying about Rachel and the baby, that we kind of ignored something obvious."

"And that would be?" Meg asked, although she had a pretty good idea what he was talking about.

"A honeymoon."

She was right. "Ah yes, that. Do we want one?"

"Don't you?" Seth asked, almost plaintively.

She reflected. Some time alone with just Seth? No chores that needed to be attended to in the orchard. No family demands (although she was quite fond of her new mother-in-law). No interruptions. It was tempting. "I guess I do. Did you have something in mind?"

"Well, I've pretty much rejected a glitzy package in Las Vegas."

"Good thinking—that's not our style."

Seth rolled over to face her. "Look, we've got a week or two free from our own work. Okay, it's winter, and that's not the best time of year for sightseeing. But on the other hand, there are fewer annoying tourists around, and it's easier to book places. We'll just wear a lot of warm clothes."

"So no tropical islands? Foreign countries?"

"Uh, no? Why? Is that what you want?"

"No! My skin doesn't handle sunbathing on beaches

well. And foreign travel, much as I love it, is just too complicated right now. Hold that thought for some later time."

"Okay," Seth said amiably. "So we've decided to stay in this country and not on a beach. Fly or drive?"

"Flying's complicated, too. But do you know, we've never taken a long road trip together? Unless you count Vermont, and that was only a couple of hours."

"Did I meet your standards?"

"For a couple of hours," Meg said, smiling. "Beyond that I can't say. What's your limit?"

"If we want to enjoy ourselves and see something other than highways? Maybe two hours at a stretch. Four or five over a day, if it's broken up in the middle. You want me to drive? You want to drive? You want to split it?"

"I call navigator," Meg replied. "I love reading maps."

"You do know they invented the GPS," Seth reminded her.

"Yes, I've heard of that," she shot back, "but it's not the same as following where you are on a page. And I've known GPS to be wrong."

"So you trust my driving—that's progress. Do you want to go skiing?"

"What's this, Twenty Questions? I don't ski, or at least, not downhill. I've been known to go cross-country skiing, but not lately. May I remind you that it's winter? And we live in New England?"

"What are you saying? That you don't like snow?"

"I love snow, when I can admire it outside my window while I sit in front of a roaring fire and don't have to go anywhere."

"Got it. One veto for going north, where there's bound to be more snow, ice, sleet, et cetera. So, east, west, or south?

Or maybe I should ask first, city or country? Boston would be east."

"I've done Boston, remember?" Meg had lived there for several years, but while she had enjoyed her time there, she felt little need to revisit the place, and she didn't feel compelled to share it with Seth. "And while I think New York or Washington, D.C., could be wonderful, somehow I don't want to spend my honeymoon running around a city trying to fit in all the touristy sites. It's supposed to be time for *us*."

"Agreed. Scratch cities, at least for now."

They both lapsed into silence. Meg sipped her coffee and wondered what she did want. Alone time with Seth would be a luxury, even if they were holed up in a cabin in the woods. As long as there was heat, food, and good coffee, she amended. Was there someplace she wanted to visit, something she wanted to see, that she hadn't had the time or the opportunity for until now? "May I make a suggestion?"

"Of course you may, Meg. I'm all ears."

"We both love history. You like old houses; I like apples and I want to know more about them. I know it's not the best season to look at either, but can we somehow follow our interests? That would give us a sense of purpose as we roam around the country in a car, avoiding cities and snow."

"You, Mrs. Chapin, are a genius. Of course we can. Monticello?"

"Exactly! I've always wanted to see that, but I don't think I've ever been that far south. And it's got both architecture and apples!"

"Okay, that goes on the list. What else?"

"Have you ever heard of Bartram's Garden?"

"Can't say that I have. What is it?"

"It's a place outside of Philadelphia. The Bartram family distributed one of the earliest plant catalogs in the American colonies—and they had lots of apples."

"Excellent. How about Mystic Seaport? Have you been there? No apples that I recall, but it's really interesting."

"I don't insist on apples everywhere, you know, and no, I've never been to Mystic Seaport. It's reasonably close, isn't it?"

"It is."

Meg was silent for a moment, then said carefully, "If we're headed to Monticello, we could stop in at my folks' house on the way back, and you could see where I grew up."

"All right. Your parents aren't home yet, though, are they?"

"No, they're not. I didn't catch all the details before the wedding—things were a little crazy, as you may recall. I think when they stopped by with the wedding suit, they were on their way to some nice bed-and-breakfast somewhere, but I got the impression that they planned to return to civilization after the wedding, I think in Amherst."

"If I never got a chance to say it, that was a lovely suit you wore."

"What, you noticed? It was such a wonderful idea, wearing something that belonged to my grandmother. Something old *and* something borrowed, if you can borrow something from someone who is no longer living. I'm amazed it fit, though."

"Maybe it was meant to be—your grandmother was looking out for you."

"That would be nice, wouldn't it? In any case, maybe Mother is in Amherst to celebrate—I think she despaired of ever marrying me off."

"Was she pressuring you?"

"No, not at all. You may have noticed that we don't talk about personal stuff like that very often. My parents may live in New Jersey, but they're Yankees through and through."

"So if I'd turned out to have two heads and drooled, she would have breathed a sigh of relief that *someone* wanted her spinster daughter?"

Meg swatted his shoulder. "Hey, she came of age in that last big wave of feminism. She would never insist that every woman had to be married. I think she was worried that I'd lead a lonely life."

"So of course she sent you to Granford, where you knew nobody."

"Well, that wasn't supposed to be permanent—just long enough for me to get my feet back on the ground and figure out what I wanted to do, while at the same time fixing up the house to sell it. I think that part was supposed to be therapeutic, but obviously my mother has never tried her hand at home repair. I could say that meeting you changed everything, but as I recall, you didn't like me much when you first met me."

"True, but I was an idiot. I apologize, if I haven't already. But in my defense, it did get kind of messy when you accused my brother of murder. Is your father okay with me?"

"You mean, would he be happier if you wore a suit every day and went to an office in a high-rise? Maybe, but he just wants me to be happy."

"And are you?"

"Yes, Mr. Chapin, I do believe I am."

He leaned over to kiss her, and the kiss kind of kept going. It was a while before they pulled themselves apart.

"You know, I could get used to this," Seth said.

"You mean, not having to get up at dawn and go deal with late deliveries and reluctant pickers? I second that. But this won't last."

"That wasn't the part I was talking about, but you're right. All the more reason we should throw together a plan for this honeymoon. The day is still young—we could be in Mystic by mid-afternoon."

"What, you want to leave today?"

"Why not? Any reason why we can't?"

Meg reflected. "Well, no, I guess not. I'm just more used to planning things ahead of time."

"So let's be spontaneous. Gas up the car and take off. Bree can keep an eye on the animals. Who knows—it could snow tomorrow. Why wait?"

"Mister measure twice and cut once, being spontaneous? You're full of surprises today. But can we check the weather report first, please? Much as I enjoy your company, I don't want to get stuck in a snowdrift on a highway somewhere."

Seth grinned at her. "Spoilsport. Have you no sense of adventure? And I've already checked the forecast—looks fine for the rest of the week, at least for most of the Eastern Seaboard. And I had my car tuned up recently. Unless you want to take yours?"

"No, yours is fine."

Seth jumped quickly off the bed. "All right! I'll go down and work on breakfast, and you can find all the maps in the house, and then we'll sit down and figure out where we're going."

Seth left the room before Meg could answer, and she lay back and wondered what had just happened. Seth seemed positively giddy. Staid, responsible Seth? Was this what marriage did to people?

She got up more slowly and ambled down the hall to take a shower. By the time she was dressed and downstairs, her orchard manager, Bree, was seated at the table, and Seth was whistling as he flipped pancakes.

"Mornin'," Bree said. "I cleared out last night, in case you wanted some privacy."

"Very thoughtful of you, Bree," Meg said, trying to mute her sarcasm. Seth had been a constant feature of the house she and Bree shared for quite some time, so she must have been used to his presence by now. Had she expected some different kind of behavior from them, now that they were legally wed? She tried to imagine what might scandalize Bree and came up blank.

"The wedding breakfast, ladies," Seth said, depositing a platter of pancakes on the table between them. "Syrup coming up." He turned and collected the maple syrup—locally made, of course, at the Parker farm a few miles away—and the coffeepot, then set both on the table. "Enjoy!"

"Did you have a good time at the party, Bree?" Meg asked. It had been kind of a hodgepodge event, with family members and friends from the area. The ceremony and the party after had both taken place in Gran's, a restaurant in the heart of Granford, and one that Meg had helped to create by convincing the local farmers to become shareholders as they provided locally sourced food. There had been so little time or energy to make plans, for either Meg or Seth, and the whole thing had been thrown together when there was time, which wasn't often. But from what she could remember of the night before, people had looked happy, the food had been excellent, and the place had looked lovely in the December twilight.

"Yeah, it was nice," Bree said, as she dug into her pancakes. "Good food. People looked like they were enjoying it. You have any complaints?"

"Nope. It was exactly what I wanted. Small and personal. Although I think my mother was a bit bewildered by the whole thing." Meg glanced at Seth. "Seth and I were talking about taking a honeymoon."

"Really? You mean, actually leave Granford?" Bree said in mock amazement.

"Hey, we once went all the way to Vermont!" Seth protested.

"That was only a couple of hours away," Bree pointed out.

Seth smiled. "We were considering going a little farther this time."

"You mean, like two states away instead of only one? You better leave a trail of bread crumbs, or you'll never find your way back," Bree said, forking up a large wedge of pancake dripping with butter and syrup.

"That settles it—we're getting out of Dodge," Meg said firmly. "Bree, Seth suggested we drive south and check out some historical sites, like Monticello. You mind feeding Max and Lolly and the goats while we're gone? And walking Max? Lolly's low maintenance."

"Of course not. I'm not planning to go anywhere. How long?"

"We haven't decided."

"When you leaving?"

"We don't know yet. Soon."

"Well, obviously you have the planning thing under control. Let me know when you make up your minds. I can handle the animals."

"Thank you, Bree," Meg said formally, with a smile. "Look, Seth, we have Bree's permission to take a honeymoon. There's no stopping us now!"

2

Of course, after that nothing was quite as easy, Meg found quickly.

"Can we leave today?" Seth asked, after they'd finished eating breakfast and cleaned up. Bree had vanished up to her room over the kitchen.

"Seth, it's going to take me a couple of hours to sort out the laundry," Meg protested. "That's one of those things I'd been putting off because of the wedding." And the end of the harvest. And trying to help solve an old crime. "Can we leave in the morning tomorrow?"

"All right. If you insist." He tried to look aggrieved, but Meg suspected that leaving the next day had been his intention all along. He certainly should know there were limits to her spontaneity, and she wasn't about to take off for a week or more without clean clothes.

"How long would you like to take?" she asked.

"You're serious about Monticello?" he asked.

"Yes. I've always wanted to see it, even more now that I know about Jefferson's orchards."

"Okay. I figure round-trip to Monticello and back is maybe fifteen hundred miles, all in. Maybe more if we make any side trips. If we drive about four hours a day, figuring an average rate of sixty miles per hour, allowing for a combination of highway and local roads, that would be . . . eight to ten days. That sound all right?"

Four hours a day in a car sounded reasonable. At least he wasn't one of those guys who insisted on driving all day. "Did you really just figure all this out in your head?" When Seth nodded, Meg added, "That sounds like it would work. I can't remember the last time I was away from the orchard and the house for that long."

"Meg, I think the place will survive without your presence for a week or two. It's not like anything's happening with either of our jobs. Your trees are all dormant, and it's too cold for me to do any kind of serious construction. The indoor projects can wait, and most people aren't in a hurry to tear up their houses when they can't get away from the mess. And Christmas isn't that far off. Relax, our schedules are clear."

"Excellent points, sir. I must really need a break if I feel guilty about going somewhere for a week."

"Meg, this is our honeymoon. Please tell me I'm more important to you than your trees are," Seth said.

"You are. Maybe ten percent more. Okay, twenty. Should we book ahead?"

"I don't think it's essential—this isn't exactly prime travel season for most people, what with the holidays and kids in school and stuff. I might have some ideas . . . but I'd rather surprise you."

"Ooh, nice," Meg said. It was kind of fun to see a different side of Seth. Usually he was so . . . dependable. Predictable. The idea of just taking off without a detailed plan was surprising, coming from him.

"I should call Mom and let her know what we're planning. You going to call your parents?"

"No need. We just saw them yesterday, right? They're off having fun on their own. We can call once we know when we might show up at their house. You know, it's encouraging that they still enjoy vacationing together. Gives us hope, doesn't it?"

"We haven't taken our first one yet."

"Well, yes, that's true. Are you worried that we'll be at each other's throats by the end of it?" Meg asked.

"I don't know. Do you kibitz when somebody else is driving? Do you insist on stopping every two hours like clockwork for a potty break?"

"A potty break?" Meg started laughing. "I am not six years old. I don't get carsick. I don't whine that I'm bored, nor do I ask 'are we there yet' starting five miles from home. I am a reasonable adult person. I will read your maps, and I will hand you change if need be—you don't happen to have E-ZPass, do you?"

"Shoot, no. I seldom go anywhere by highway so I don't think about it. Should we cancel the whole trip?"

"No, of course not. Most tollbooths still take money, or at least one of them does at each toll plaza—usually the most inconvenient one all the way at the end. Although even that may not last long. Or maybe they scan your license plate and send you a bill."

"Ain't modern technology grand? Well, then, do you eat a lot of junk food and leave crumbs and empty bags in the car?"

Meg cocked her head at him. "You sure you know who you're married to?"

"I think so, but this is uncharted territory."

"Uh-huh." Meg took their coffee mugs to the sink and washed them. If she was leaving for a week, she didn't want to leave dirty dishes sitting around. Make sure there was enough cat food and dog food for a couple of weeks. Ask Bree if she planned to stay in the house or whether she expected to spend time with her boyfriend, Michael, in Amherst. Remind Bree to turn down the thermostat if she was going to be out of the house for long. Find her spare charger for her cell phone. Find her AAA card, in case something went wrong on the road. Empty her wallet of seldom-used credit cards—no need to tempt fate.

"Meg?" Seth's voice interrupted her mental merry-go-round.

"Yes?"

"Relax. This is supposed to be fun. You aren't planning the invasion of Normandy."

"Hmm. How many planes do you think I'll need? What about ammo supplies?"

"You are kidding, aren't you?" Seth asked.

"Of course I am. But you're right—I'm overthinking this. See? You do know me well. Go call your mother so we can check one thing off the to-do list."

"Yes, ma'am!" Seth located his cell phone and strode off to the front of the house to talk to his mother.

He came back five minutes later with a peculiar expression on his face. "Everything all right?" Meg asked.

"Apparently. She applauds our decision to leave town and says she'll be happy to walk Max if Bree doesn't want to do it every day."

"Then why the odd look?"

"Christopher was there."

Christopher was by now an old friend: Meg's mentor for her orchard enterprise, Bree's former university professor, officiator at the wedding by special license, and an all-around delightful person. And . . . Meg finally put two and two together: early in the morning, Christopher was at Lydia's house. Oh-ho.

"Well, good for them. Okay, I know, she's your mother, but they're both lovely people and both unattached, so why not? Tell me you're actually surprised."

Seth was honest enough to look sheepish. "Uh, no, I guess not. But I was doing my best not to think about it."

"Looks like you'd better get over it. See what weddings do to people? Is she going to tell Rachel about the honeymoon, or should we call her?"

"I'm sure they'll have lots to talk about—let Mom have that pleasure. Is that everyone who needs to know?"

"I'd better update Bree. I don't think she has any plans, but she doesn't always share when she does. And I'd better get started on that laundry!"

Meg made her way upstairs and started collecting what needed washing. She really had been neglecting that chore, because her basket overflowed before she was half-finished. She set it down, wondering how much was really necessary for their excursion. They'd probably be gone for at least a week. Better to be prepared.

But before she started the long trek to the basement, she went down the hall and rapped on Bree's door. "Bree?"

The door opened quickly. "You need something?" Bree asked.

"I just wanted to fill you in on our brand-new plans. We think we're leaving tomorrow morning, but it's still not clear how long we'll be gone—probably at least a week, maybe longer. Seth talked to his mother, and she says she can help out with Max if you're busy, or if you just want a break. Just be sure the goats have enough feed and the water line doesn't freeze up, okay?"

"Yeah, yeah. We've kept them going this long, so I think they can survive another couple of weeks. Listen, I—" Bree started, then stopped herself. "No, it can wait. While you're gone I'll run the final numbers on the orchard income for this year, maybe get a head start on taxes. Catch up on all the paperwork and stuff."

"That would be terrific, Bree," Meg said, and meant it. The business side of running the orchard was an ongoing source of friction between the two of them, and it was great to hear Bree volunteering to get started without any nagging. She had definitely matured professionally in the two years she'd been working for Meg. Or Meg had been working for her—it wasn't quite clear. When she had begun, Bree had the technical expertise and knowledge to manage an orchard, but little to no experience. Meg had had neither, so she had willingly followed Bree's instructions. Her first solo effort had been to open up a new section of orchard, using a piece of Seth's adjoining land and choosing trees that were a mix of dependable producers and some less common heirloom varieties that were appealing to local foodies. They wouldn't be bearing fruit for a couple of years, but it made Meg feel good that they were planning for a future, not just lurching from crisis to crisis.

"Nice party," Bree commented, and Meg wondered if she was deflecting Meg's praise. "Not too fussy."

"That's what I wanted. I could never see myself walking down the aisle in a poofy white dress, watched by a couple hundred of my parents' dearest friends, who I'd never even met. I think it worked out, didn't it?"

"I thought so. Lydia and Christopher seemed to be hitting it off."

Bree was more observant than Meg usually gave her credit for. "You okay with that? I mean, you don't think it's weird? He was your professor, after all."

"Sure. Why wouldn't I be? I think it's great. They're both good people. Was there anything else?"

"No, that's all I wanted to say right now. I've still got the rest of the day to nag you."

"I wondered if you'd go somewhere, after," Bree said. "You were acting like everything stopped once you threw that party."

"Well, in our own defense, there were a couple of distractions."

"Yeah, like Aaron Eastman and his problems. But you got them worked out in good time. He looked a lot better, too, last night."

"I agree. I hope things will work out for him. Anyway, I guess planning a honeymoon wasn't high on our list of things to do. Is that odd?"

"You're asking me? I've got zero experience. But I'm guessing going someplace is different from just sitting around here making gooey eyes at each other."

"We don't do that!" Meg protested.

"Now and then you do," Bree countered, smiling. "Not too much. But being stuck with each other in a car for hours at a time isn't the same. Tell me there aren't things you haven't talked about."

"Well, I guess. We'll just have to figure it out."

Meg left by the hall door to sort out laundry in the bedroom. Bree hadn't even mentioned that Seth had managed to install not one but two new bathrooms in the house in the days leading up to the wedding, on schedule. She herself hadn't even had time to get used to the fact they existed.

As she sorted laundry, Meg reviewed the past twenty-four hours in her mind. It had been a nice party. Nicky Czarnecki had done a terrific job with the food, using local products—not easy to do in December. The restaurant, a former house, had looked lovely. Christopher had managed the service with dignity and warmth, not an easy combination to pull off. It had seemed like half the town was there, which was altogether possible, since the town wasn't very big and Seth had lived here all his life. Even better, she had recognized most of the people at the wedding, and had been able to greet them by name. Of course, Seth had helped her out when she'd drawn a blank on a few. There hadn't been many unfamiliar faces, but even if they had been crashers, it was a community celebration as much as a personal one, and she wasn't going to begrudge anyone a meal and some human company on a winter's evening.

She had finished sorting the laundry into towering piles on the floor when her cell phone rang. To her amazement she found it quickly, and saw her mother's number.

"Hi, Mother," she said.

"Hello, darling. I just wanted to say what a lovely event your wedding turned out to be."

Had she been surprised? Meg wondered. "I thought so, too. I didn't want anything too fancy—I wanted everyone to feel welcome. I'm glad you enjoyed it. When are you headed home?"

"In a couple of days—no rush. Phillip cleared his work schedule so we could take our time and enjoy ourselves. Are you and Seth doing anything?"

"Do you know, we were so caught up in sorting out the wedding and all that we never even thought about a honeymoon. We were kicking ideas around this morning, and I think we've decided to take a road trip, with Monticello as the end point. It combines history, architecture, and apples—what more could we ask?"

"That sounds perfect." Elizabeth Corey hesitated, which was unlike her. "Would you like to have dinner with us tonight? Please say no if you'd rather have the time to yourselves. But we see you so rarely these days. Oh, drat, listen to me! I promised myself years ago that I'd never be a whiny parent, or worse, an in-law. If you'd like to get together, we'd love it, but if you have other plans, I won't guilt-trip you."

Meg laughed. "Mother, so far the only plan I've made is to get the laundry done before we take off tomorrow morning. Of course, I should confer with my husband"—and how odd was it to say that!—"but I don't think he'll have a problem with it."

"That's wonderful! Listen, we're staying at the Lord Jeffery in Amherst. You could meet us there. Our treat, of course."

"Fine. But let's keep it an early night. Say, seven?"

"I'll tell Phillip to make reservations. It will be wonderful to see you both again, and so soon! And I promise that we'll get out of your hair after that."

"See you later!"

It might be an odd way to start a honeymoon, spending the evening with your parents, but Elizabeth was right: they had seen very little of each other in recent years, and it was a shame to waste the opportunity. And it wasn't like they had anything else planned for the evening.

She dumped the clothes in the laundry baskets and picked one up to carry downstairs. She found Seth still in the kitchen, reading the Sunday paper, and realized how odd it was to find him just sitting—he always had multiple projects going. She deposited the basket by the door to the cellar, where the washer and dryer lurked, and dropped into a chair across from him.

"I talked to my mother. She invited us to have dinner with the two of them at the Lord Jeffery in Amherst this evening. Is that all right?"

"I'm going to assume you said yes, but sure, that's fine. All I really need to do is to find a suitcase. I can't remember the last time I needed one."

"Well, you have most of the day to do it. I have faith in your ability to track down the errant valise. For our first ever road trip."

3

Somehow they passed the day. Bree stayed out of sight, giving Meg and Seth some space. Which seemed kind of silly to Meg, since they'd all been living cheek by jowl in the house for months, but it was thoughtful of her. Seth did guy things, like checking all the fluid levels in the car, even though he said he'd already done just that. Still, better safe than sorry. He had decided that they would take his car, which was fine with her, since his was newer and sturdier than hers. He even installed new wiper blades and vacuumed the interior. He disappeared for an hour or two to check the attic of his own house just over the hill, currently unoccupied, to see if he could find a suitcase. Meg washed all the clothes she had collected, and then started in on sheets and towels, for reasons she didn't quite understand. They were leaving;

why make things tidy now? But it kept her busy. *I am a wife, and I am doing wifely things.* She giggled.

She had not realized how accustomed she had become to being busy. The orchard was a demanding mistress much of the year. There was always something that needed to be done: fertilizing, pruning, spraying (in an ecologically responsible manner!), watering in dry years, contracting with vendors who would buy the crop, planning to replace trees that had been damaged or were no longer producing, and keeping an eye on finances. In what little spare time she had, she had delved into her family's genealogy, which made a nice change of pace and didn't demand a lot of exercise, except on those occasions when she went searching for one or another of her ancestors in a distant cemetery. She tried to remember the last time she had read a book cover to cover. Usually she could manage to finish a single chapter before she fell asleep at night, and that was with lighter, more entertaining books, not serious historical or philosophical tomes. She had a stack of those next to the bed as well—collecting dust.

Somehow she thought it would be a bit rude to take a book, frivolous or serious, on her honeymoon. Of course, there was always her laptop . . .

Was it an accident that she had ended up with Seth? They were both morning people, and both industrious and hardworking. They both enjoyed the company of others— Seth more than she, and he'd been involved in community affairs for years. They were both intelligent, and capable of carrying on a reasonably informed conversation. And they both had a peculiar ability to get sucked into crime-solving, through no desire or effort of their own. She had no clue why that kept happening. Maybe they also shared an innate desire to make things right.

She hadn't probed deeply into his politics, but from what she'd seen they were more or less on the same page. He had both male and female friends, and he was kind to his mother. Obviously he was the perfect man. Unless, of course, she discovered that he loved to drive really fast, and to curse out other drivers while going eighty on interstate highways. Or he insisted on cranking up country music in the car to an earsplitting level. That would certainly kill any conversation.

There were in fact a lot of things they had never talked about. What to do with his house was at the top of the list. He didn't want to sell it, and she could understand that—it had been in the Chapin family since it was built over two hundred years earlier, as had the one near it that his mother lived in. But Meg wanted to live in her house (technically her mother's), and he seemed to agree with that, and he'd added the bathrooms by his own choice (although maybe he was looking ahead at possible sale value?). Finances: she had little idea how much he earned annually, and she had never asked. Of course, after two harvest seasons she had only a vague handle on what she was earning from the orchard, and she had to pay the pickers and Bree out of that. Neither she nor Seth was extravagant in their spending, but surely there should be some discussion about where their money went, whether separately or pooled? Was he helping to support his mother? Were they going to share medical insurance? Car insurance? Had they really not discussed any of this, floating in a rosy cloud in the months leading up to the wedding, interrupted by the occasional foray into crime-solving?

And then there was the bigger question of kids. They hadn't come anywhere near that topic. She'd seen Seth with his sister Rachel's children, and he was great: he didn't condescend to them, and he appeared to sincerely enjoy their company. He even handled Rachel's new baby, Meg's namesake, Maggie, with relaxed competence. Probably more than she possessed, since she'd spent little time around children since she had earned pocket money as a babysitter in high school. Seth deserved to have kids, although he'd never said he wanted them, in so many words. But Meg wasn't so sure what she felt. She shoved that whole idea firmly on a high shelf in her mind: they needed to know each other a lot better before they made any major life decisions like having children. They'd known each other for less than two years, and for the first part of that Seth hadn't exactly liked her. There was plenty of time. Wasn't there?

She realized that she'd been sitting on the stripped bed staring into space only when Seth returned from whatever errand he'd been on and sat next to her. "You look like you're a million miles away. Please tell me you're not worrying about trip details?"

Meg laughed. "Actually, no. I'm just trying to figure out what to do when I don't *have* to do anything. I'm out of practice. What have you been up to?"

"I was scouting out places to stay, online, on my office computer. One important point: Mystic Seaport is open only until four tomorrow, and not at all the day after, so if we want to see it all we need to get started early."

"No problem. Have you checked the weather forecast?"

"Yes, for the third time. It's fine, at least for the next few days. Are you worried about getting snowed in with me somewhere?"

"Actually, that might be kind of nice, especially if we find a place with a working fireplace and tea and scones at four o'clock."

"I'll work on that. So, are you the grand hotel type? Or highway motels?"

Meg made a face at him. "Neither of us can afford grand hotels. Highway motels tend to be not too clean, and they often reek of cigarette smoke, no matter what the management says."

Seth threw himself back onto the bed and stared at the ceiling. "Do you speak from experience?"

"Oh, right, like I've spent a lot of time in ratty hotels." She lay down next to him, propped up on one elbow. "When I used to travel for work, which wasn't very often, I usually stayed in mid-priced big chain hotels. I couldn't tell them apart. If I get a choice, I'd rather have something with a little more character, but it doesn't have to be expensive."

"Of course you have a choice, Meg. I want you to be happy."

"Trust me, I am." She leaned toward him to kiss him, and then one thing led to another . . . well, it was their honeymoon, and they had plenty of time . . .

The Lord Jeffery hotel looked welcoming when Meg and Seth drove up to it. It was not yet seven, but daylight didn't last much past five in December. On a Saturday night, it was doing good business, and Seth ended up parking in the lot across the street from the hotel's main parking area behind the building. At least it hadn't snowed much yet this year, so they wouldn't have to scramble over snowbanks to reach the hotel entrance. Meg felt a pang; they hadn't told Rachel that they would be in Amherst. But this was an evening that Meg didn't want to share. These were her parents, and they had little time together.

When they walked into the lobby, Phillip and Elizabeth Corey were settled on a settee in front of a fireplace with a real fire, although Meg suspected it was gas-fed. They stood quickly when they saw Meg and Seth.

"Hello, darling. You look radiant." Elizabeth's eyes twinkled.

"Hello, Mother. I hope you're being sarcastic. Or maybe six loads of laundry brings out the best in me. Hi, Daddy."

Phillip greeted them warmly. "Meg, Seth, I'm glad you could join us on such short notice. I took the liberty of making a reservation at a small place down the street recommended by the management here. I hope you don't mind."

"Of course not. Everywhere I've eaten in this town has been great," Meg told him.

"It's within easy walking distance, but I think we should get over there. I don't want to keep you two out too late."

Phillip and Elizabeth pulled on their coats, and they all went out the front door. Phillip led the way, with Seth at his side. Meg and Elizabeth trailed behind. "I thought you and Daddy were planning to stay out in the country somewhere."

"That was the original plan, but Phillip thought it would be easier to leave for home from here. Besides, I've heard good things about this hotel, and I read online that they remodeled it recently. It's kept its New England character, but everything works very well. So, you've survived your first day of married life?"

"Were you worried?" Meg countered.

"No. I've seen you together before, you know. I really do like Seth, and you suit each other."

An unusually personal remark, coming from my mother, Meg thought. She had always made a point of keeping her distance from Meg's personal decisions. Which had been both good and bad: Meg had grown up to be an independent person, but she'd always felt kind of neglected. In the end she settled for saying, "I'm glad you think so."

The men had stopped in the middle of the next block, waiting for them to catch up. "We cross here," Phillip said. They followed him dutifully toward the restaurant. On the other side of the street they climbed the low stairs and stepped into a warm, dark room that smelled wonderful. Meg's mouth started watering immediately. The manager led them to a table halfway back, and Phillip took their coats before they all sat.

After they were seated and a waiter had brought them menus, Phillip said, "Meg, how are your plans for the grand tour coming?"

"We're working on it. I realized that Seth and I have never been outside of Massachusetts together, except for a quick trip to Vermont, and I thought I'd better find out if he turns into a pumpkin when he crosses the state line."

"Do you two have a plan, or are you going to go where the wind takes you?"

"Yes and no, sir," Seth told him. "Our primary goal is Monticello, a place I've wanted to see for years, for its architecture and all the great details Jefferson incorporated. And Meg wants to see the orchards there. We haven't worked out what we'll do along the way."

"It's a luxury to have control of your own time, isn't

it?" Phillip said, and the talk turned to places visited and happy memories, along with a few disasters that were easy to laugh at now that plenty of time had passed. A bottle of good wine appeared, and they ordered an assortment of dishes, all of which were delicious. It was a relaxed and pleasant meal, and after a couple hours Phillip asked, "Dessert? Coffee?"

"I think coffee's a good idea," Seth said. "I'll pass on dessert."

"I won't," Meg said promptly. "Mother, you want to split one?"

"I think I can manage that," Elizabeth said, smiling.

After they'd ordered, Meg said, "Mother tells me the hotel is lovely. I've heard very nice things about it."

"It's very pleasant. No restaurant, though—mostly bar food," Phillip said grudgingly.

"Daddy, this is foodie country—I can't tell you how many restaurants there are here in the center of town, and then there's always Northampton, which has even more. I wish Seth and I had more time to explore them all. You two can, if you're staying around."

"We're planning to leave tomorrow," Phillip told her. "I'd like to get back—it's already been a week. We'll push straight through to New Jersey and be home in time for dinner."

Meg looked briefly at her mother, who didn't comment. Then she glanced at Seth. "You know, we were thinking we might stop by and see you on our way back from Virginia. If that's convenient."

"Well of course it is!" Elizabeth said quickly. "And you can show Seth where you grew up!"

Meg held up one hand. "Mother, please don't start

calling all my childhood friends—or their parents! I'm happy to introduce Seth to New Jersey, or vice versa, but I don't think I have much to say to the people I knew in high school. And those few I've kept in touch with, mainly on Facebook, they don't live in the area anymore."

"Whatever you like, darling. This is your trip. We will be delighted to see you. Won't we, Phillip?"

Phillip Corey appeared to have been woolgathering. "What? Oh yes, of course, Meg, we would love to see you any time you like. I've been cutting back on my law practice of late, which gives me plenty of free time to do the things I enjoy. Like come to your wedding. And take a little time with your mother." He smiled at Elizabeth.

Meg wondered when that had begun. Her father had always been very wrapped up in his practice, leaving her mother to fill her time with volunteer functions. How did she feel about this change of heart? "Are you thinking of retiring, Daddy?"

"No, no, nothing like that, not yet anyway," he blustered. "Just being a bit more selective about the cases I choose to take on. And I do want some time to smell the roses." He reached out and took Elizabeth's hand, and she twined her fingers with his and smiled back at him.

What had happened to her parents? Meg couldn't remember the last time she'd seen them be this demonstrative in a public place.

But now was not the time to ask. The coffee arrived, along with one dessert and four forks, and they made short work of it. Finally Elizabeth said, "Phillip, perhaps we should call it a night? Particularly now that we know we can look forward to seeing Meg and Seth again soon."

"You're right, my dear." Phillip made a subtle gesture

and the check miraculously appeared and was settled
quickly. They gathered up their coats and moved toward
the door. The restaurant was now nearly empty, although
it appeared that many of the patrons had migrated to the
bar, which was still noisy. Once outside, Phillip inhaled
deeply. "Nothing like New England air on a winter's night
to clear the head. Maybe a nightcap at the hotel bar?"

Meg looked at Seth, who somehow conveyed that it was
her decision. "A short one, maybe. We've still got to get
back and pack for tomorrow. We want to get an early start."

The walk back to the hotel didn't take long, and when
they entered the spacious bar, there was yet another fire
burning in a fireplace. Definitely a winter-friendly place.
Phillip looked happy to be there, rubbing his hands together
in anticipation. "What would you all like?"

They settled on drinks: Meg opted for an Irish coffee,
while Seth settled for plain coffee. Meg checked the time
and was surprised to find it was approaching ten. But the
ride back to Granford would take them the better part of
half an hour, and there were still things to be done . . .

"Meg?" her mother's voice interrupted her. "Are you
still with us?"

"Oh, sorry. Just thinking. It's been a long couple of
weeks."

"Then we should let you go, especially now that we'll
be seeing you again."

"I'll get this," Seth volunteered, and went over to the
bar to settle the tab.

When Seth returned, Phillip asked, "Where are you
two parked?"

"Out back, sir," Seth informed him.

"Seth, please drop the 'sir.' You make me feel ancient, and anyway, you're family now. I'm Phillip. But never Phil, please. We'll walk you out—that is, if you don't mind, Elizabeth?"

"That's fine. A bit of air will help me sleep." Feigning secrecy, she leaned toward Meg and said in a loud whisper, "He really only wants an excuse to smoke a cigar."

"Daddy! I thought you quit smoking years ago!"

"I allow myself the occasional cigar after a fine meal, my dear. And I like the aroma—I don't inhale."

It wasn't worth arguing about, Meg decided. "Well, I'm glad you put tonight's dinner in the 'fine meal' category. Thank you for asking us."

They retrieved their coats once again, and left by the side entrance to go around back. Phillip was occupied with the arcane cigar ritual that Meg remembered from her childhood when Elizabeth said, tugging at her husband's coat sleeve, "Phillip, we may have a problem."

Phillip turned to follow her gaze, toward the back of the parking lot. Their car was parked away from any lights, but even in the near-dark Meg could tell that the back bumper was crumpled.

"Oh, dear. That can't be good," Meg said, trying to suppress childhood memories of some of her father's more memorable rages.

Phillip didn't speak immediately, but even by the dim light in the parking lot Meg could see that his face darkened. She could almost visualize smoke coming from his ears. But when he spoke, his voice was tightly controlled. "Elizabeth, why don't we go back inside so I can have a word with the management? Since this is their lot, they must share some responsibility. Meg, Seth, you two go on home—you have a busy few days ahead of you. We can take care of this."

"Are you sure, Phillip?" Seth said. "I know some good mechanics around here, if you need to find one quickly."

Phillip replied curtly, "Seth, don't trouble yourself. I'm sure we can work things out. Go! Yesterday was your wedding, and I'm sure you have better things to do than talk to auto repair shops."

Elizabeth nodded. "We'll handle it. Meg, Seth, it was wonderful spending this time together, and we'll look forward to seeing you in a week or so. Just give us a ring when you know what your plans are. Now, shoo!"

They all exchanged hugs, then Seth led Meg back across the street to where his car was parked, now almost alone in the other lot. He paused and turned back to the hotel's parking lot.

"What?" Meg asked.

"I wonder if there were any cameras on the lot that might have seen who ran into your father's car. I don't see any."

"The hotel will take care of things, won't they?" Meg said. "They have an excellent reputation."

"How much of a fuss will your father make?"

Meg considered how to answer that. Seth had spent only a few hours total in her father's company, so he didn't know Phillip well. She didn't want to prejudice him. "He's a lawyer, remember? He'll know what to do. By the time he's done, the hotel may offer to replace the entire car. He thrives on that kind of thing."

Seth ignored her comment. "There are a couple windows overlooking the lot—maybe someone noticed when something hit the car."

"Seth? It's regrettable, but it's not our problem. Can we go now?"

Seth seemed to come back to the present situation. "Oh, sorry. Of course."

As Meg climbed into the car she saw her mother and father still looking at the damaged car, and her father was shaking his head, and looking up at the hotel much as Seth had.

4

Sunday morning Meg awoke before the sun was up and started running mentally through lists—and realized there really was nothing essential left to do. It had simply become a habit. There were clean clothes in suitcases; credit cards were sorted; the car was tuned up; the weather was cooperating (as if she could control the weather!). They could leave any time after they'd eaten breakfast, and after assuring Lolly and Max that, yes, they would be back, after some unimaginable length of cat or dog time.

Meg turned to Seth to see him watching her. He smiled. She smiled. Then she asked, "Do you think Mother and Daddy will be all right?"

"Without us to hold their hands? I think so, Meg. They're adults, and they've survived this long without our help—well, maybe with one exception—and they're not exactly decrepit. Why on earth are you worrying about them at this moment?"

"Because I can't find anything else to worry about? I know. That sounds completely ridiculous. And you and I are going to go see interesting things and play. Maybe it's all my Puritan ancestors insisting that enjoying oneself was immoral."

"And that's why you're torturing yourself? You're right; that is ridiculous."

"Yes, and I know it. It'll pass, I'm sure. Let's go make coffee."

They were finishing up breakfast, and the sun had finally risen over the horizon, when Bree stumbled into the kitchen. "You haven't left yet?"

"Almost ready," Meg replied. "We were fortifying ourselves for the journey. I've left you a list of things that need to be done . . ."

Bree filled a mug with coffee and dropped into a chair. "Meg, I am neither an idiot nor a child. I think I can keep the place going for a week or two. Please, feel free to take two weeks. Have fun. See the sights. The orchard will still be here when you get back."

"I know. I guess I'm just keyed up. Seth, are you ready?"

"I am. Is your suitcase closed?"

"No. Let me check it one last time, and then I can put it in the car."

"Go!"

Packing really and truly finished, Meg checked to be sure she had her tablet and her maps in her roomy bag, and took one final look around the bedroom. Everything looked fine. Why did she feel as though she was setting off on an expedition to the North Pole? Heck, they were headed toward warmer weather, and they were going to see things she'd been hoping to see for half her life. Time to hit the road.

Downstairs, Seth was waiting for her in the kitchen, leaning against the wall. "Ready?"

"I hope so. We're aiming to get to Mystic before lunch, right?"

"Yes. Do not decide you need to pack a complete lunch in case we get hopelessly lost in the wilderness that is Connecticut. You do have your cell phone, right?"

"Yes, and the charger. And the backup charger."

"You have enough warm clothes, in case the next ice age arrives fast?"

"I do. Jackets of three different down ratings in the backseat."

"Then may we please get going?"

As if on cue, Bree came down the back stairs. "What he said. Go! Now!"

"Yes, ma'am," Meg said meekly and followed Seth out the door.

Once they were settled in the car, luggage safely stowed, Seth pulled out of the driveway and headed toward the back route that led to the turnpike. "It's not too late to change your mind."

"About what? Marrying you? Driving halfway down the East Coast?"

"Take your pick. You're acting kind of weird."

"I'm excited. And maybe nervous, I guess. I remember taking road trips with my father when I was about ten or twelve. He was always an impatient driver. He would lecture the other drivers on the road, not that they could hear him, telling them what they were doing wrong, and then he'd whip around them, which half the time scared the other people to death. He had some weird theory about efficient gas consumption."

"No accidents?"

"No. He was either careful or lucky. Or both. Anyway, my mother would make soothing noises, but that was about all. I sat in the backseat and kept my mouth shut and tried to pretend I didn't know either one of them."

"Your mother never drove?"

"Nope. No doubt Daddy would have lectured *her* on what she was doing wrong, and that would have been even worse."

"May I point out that I am not your father, Meg?"

"So I've noticed. Two hours to Mystic?"

"About that. You've got the map."

"So I do." And a sheaf of printed directions, which gave the details for local roads once they got off the main highways. She carefully unfolded and refolded the appropriate map so she could follow their progress. "I told you, I love maps. I like to follow where we've been, and what distance we've covered. A GPS is not the same, and that voice keeps yelling at me that I've done something wrong and it has to recalculate. I don't like to be judged by my electronics."

"Seriously?" Seth said.

"Yes. Anyway, do you know where you're going? Or should I prompt you?"

"Only in time to get off at the right exit."

"Do we know where we're staying tonight?"

"I made a reservation. Should I have consulted you first?"

"Not necessary. I trust your judgment. What are we going to see?"

"Ships?"

"I think I could have figured that out myself. It's probably called a seaport for a reason. More than one ship?"

"So I'm told. Quite a few, actually."

"Anything else?"

"A re-created nineteenth-century village, but with more sea-oriented shops than Sturbridge. You want more?"

"No, that sounds good. I like stepping back in time, and I like boats."

"Do you know much about boats?"

"Not big ones. More about the smaller ones—we used to take sailing lessons when we went on vacation at the Jersey Shore. And my father likes fishing, as you know. He took me out a time or two, but it really wasn't my thing."

"Was it the worms?"

"No, it was getting the poor wriggling fish off the hook." She shivered at the memory. "And I don't hunt, either, but neither does my father."

"But you like the ocean?" Seth asked.

"Yes, I do, although I have to watch out for sunburn. But I like swimming, not sitting on the beach pretending to read and getting sand in my hair. You have seen an ocean, right?" she ended dubiously. One more thing she had never asked.

"Of course, but not often. One year my father had a little extra cash, so he took the family on a weekend trip to Cape Cod. We stayed in the cheapest motel he could find and he still grumbled about the cost. And I also went to the Cape in college with some of my friends, when I wasn't working for Dad. Although my memories of that trip are rather fuzzy—I believe there was a certain amount of drinking involved."

"I'll keep an eye on your consumption on this trip. So you really are a novice at vacationing?"

"Looks like it."

Meg laughed. "What a pair we are! We have no clue how to relax. Oh, and since we're both self-employed and small business owners, if we look at apples and old buildings, does that mean this trip will be tax deductible?"

"I won't say no. You're the financial genius—you tell me."

"I'll make a mental note of it, to consider come April. So we'd better pay attention and take lots of pictures to show what we did in case the IRS wants proof."

The first—and shortest—leg of the trip passed quickly. The highways were all but empty on a Sunday afternoon in winter. They had no trouble locating Seaport, and the grounds weren't crowded, either. Seth hadn't been kidding about the ships, which ranged from whalers to tugboats to schooners to lobster boats and more. Many were in working order, although there wasn't time to take a quick sail. Meg made another mental note to think about that for a later date, maybe in the summer, now that she knew how easy it was to get to the place. Seth looked like a little boy, almost drooling over the wooden timbers in the earlier ships and how all the structural pieces were fitted together, running his hands along planes and over joints when he could. Meg hoped he wouldn't decide to start building a boat out in the barn.

They stopped for a quick bite to eat, then strolled companionably through the re-created village. Meg was fascinated by the ropewalk. "I never thought about what went into making rope, but they must have needed a lot of it, right?"

"You saw the ships," Seth reminded her. "All that rigging?"

"Yes, of course. But what I don't understand is why rope stays twisted at all. Why doesn't it come apart?"

"Think of it as very large yarn. You know how to knit, right?"

"I can do it, but badly. You're saying knitting yarn and rope are the same structure, but on a different scale?"

"More or less. You take your fibers, which once were hemp but later manila because it was more durable, and you twist them together to make yarn. Then you take multiple lengths of yarn and twist them together to make a strand. And *then* you take three strands and twist them together in the opposite direction, which creates a tension that holds the rope together—the bits are trying to unwind but in different directions. This ropewalk is only a part of the original, which could have been a thousand feet long, because the rope makers had to do their twisting in a straight line to make it work."

"Wow! And why is it you know all this, Seth?"

"I like to know how things work, and this was basically a simple process, just large. Interesting, isn't it?"

"It is. And thanks for the explanation. I'll never look at rope—well, natural fiber rope—in the same way again."

Arm in arm they strolled past the other structures. They knew they had limited time before the place closed, but neither of them felt compelled to see everything, for which Meg was grateful. She had never enjoyed manic sightseeing, and was glad that Seth didn't seem to, either.

As four o'clock neared, Meg was beginning to feel chilled, as the wind blew in from the water. Seth was quick to notice. "Seen enough?"

"I think so. I'd like to come back someday, now that I know how close it is."

"That could be arranged. Let's head for the hotel."

Settled in the car, Meg turned up the heat. Seth seemed to know where he was going, so she didn't volunteer any directions. It took him only a few minutes to pull into the parking lot behind a handsome hotel near the center of town. "This is where we're staying?"

"I've booked a room. Unless you hate it on sight?"

"Not at all—I think it's lovely."

The inside proved as charming as the outside; their room had sweeping views of the river—and a fireplace for warmth. Once they'd dropped their luggage, Meg was drawn to the windows: the sun was sinking, and the river looked like polished pewter. Seth came up behind her and wrapped his arms around her shoulders. "This is nice," he said quietly.

Meg smiled to herself. "Which part? The room? The view?"

"Being here with you. Do you realize, this is the first time we've spent a night together in a place that wasn't home?"

"It feels kind of illicit, doesn't it?" Meg said.

"Kind of. Even though we're completely legal, not that it matters much these days."

"It matters to me." Meg pivoted in his arms so that she faced him. "Thank you."

"For what?"

"For existing. For being unflappable under pressure. For knowing what I need even when I don't. For loving me."

"The last one's the easiest part."

Their kiss started slowly but then picked up steam, and

when they pulled apart after some unknowable interval, Meg said, "I should call my parents."

Seth looked at her incredulously, then burst out laughing. "*That's* what you're thinking about at a moment like this? I am mortally offended."

"Don't be. I thought I'd call them so they don't interrupt us later, when we might be, uh, busy."

"Well, in that case, call them and be done with it. Then we can go searching for food and drink, before we get too busy."

"I'll do that." Reluctantly Meg peeled herself away from Seth and went to retrieve her phone from her bag. She hit the speed dial for her mother's number.

Elizabeth answered quickly. "Meg? Everything all right?"

"Everything is just fine. Why wouldn't it be?"

"Because you're calling me on your honeymoon, darling. Don't you have better things to do than talk to your mother? I did give you the birds-and-the-bees lecture a while ago, didn't I?"

"Yes, you did. I just wanted to make sure you got the car business worked out."

"More or less. As you might guess, it was hard to find a shop that was open on Sunday, and when we did, with the help of the hotel, it didn't have all the parts in stock, so they have to order them, which they can't do until tomorrow morning. We're still in Massachusetts, but I think we're going to rent a car tomorrow, if the parts don't arrive, and drive home and let them find a way to ship the car to us. But don't worry about us. You and Seth have a lovely time. You'll call us later in the week if it looks like you'll be stopping in New Jersey? Not that you have to, if something better turns up."

Meg could all but hear her father fuming at the delay, and her mother trying to smooth things over. "We'll play it by ear, but we're still planning on seeing you. Say hi to Daddy for me. We're off to find something to eat."

After turning off her phone, Meg turned back to Seth. "Now, where were we?"

5

When Meg woke up the next morning—well past dawn, for a change—she stretched like a cat and smiled. So this was what a vacation was like; it was hard to remember the feeling. Extending one hand, she added, *this is what a husband feels like*. She giggled. She'd been doing a lot of giggling over the last couple of days. Very immature of her, no doubt, but it felt good.

Day three of married life. The wide-open road ahead of them. But a hotel breakfast first. Then get out the maps and plot their next move. Luckily they were taking major highways for much of the trip, so there wasn't a lot of decision-making required. This was Monday, right? No way they could make it to Monticello in one day, or more accurately, only if they wanted to spend the entire day driving. That didn't sound like fun, even with Seth. There were plenty of interesting things to be seen between here and there, including one in particular she felt she needed to investigate.

"You want to shower first?" Seth's voice interrupted her thinking.

"Okay. Unless there's room for the two of us in there?"

"Regrettably, no. But I like the way you think."

Meg sighed dramatically. "Ah, well. There will be other showers—although we didn't exactly lay out the one back home for two."

"There wasn't room, if you recall. But the new old bathtub has potential."

"That it does." Meg stood up. "I won't be long. Is breakfast included with the room?"

"I do believe it is."

"Good, because I'm hungry."

Clean and dressed, they took their time getting to the dining room, which also overlooked the river. There were only a few other couples, but Meg didn't mind. She wasn't there to make friends, she was there to enjoy her new husband's company. They filled their plates from the breakfast buffet, topped up their coffee, and settled comfortably at a table overlooking the water.

But before she started eating, Meg felt the urge to say something. "Seth, I might as well say this now and get it out of the way. I know you haven't changed since last week, but every time I look at you I see the word *HUSBAND* in big letters."

He smiled. "On my chest? Floating over my head? What?"

"Nothing so specific. It's just that I didn't expect it to make a difference. We've been together for a while now, so we know each other. But somehow going through a fifteen-minute ceremony seems to have made a psychological difference to me."

"Hmm," Seth said. "Is that good or bad?"

"I really don't know. I know that overall things are kind of in flux about where marriage fits in our society today, but I think we're both old enough that we brought along some of our parents' baggage, if you know what I mean. We were brought up with the old model. There might have been some rebels back in their day, but still, a lot more couples got married when they were in their twenties back then than do today. You and I, we had a choice: we could go on just the way we were, which was nice, or we could buy into the whole ceremonial thing, which we did, at least in a low-key way. But we've got that piece of paper, and somehow, to me at least, it does make a difference. Do you feel anything like that?"

Seth pushed the food around his plate, giving himself time to think. "My folks got married fairly early, and stayed married, even when there were difficult times." He looked up at Meg. "Is that what you mean? That's the old model?"

"In a way," she told him. "Being married, and staying married, meant something to them. Just being unhappy wasn't enough reason to break up a couple, because they'd made a commitment. If you don't mind my asking, what did you expect when you married Nancy?" She wasn't sure it was appropriate to bring up Seth's first wife over breakfast three days after their wedding, but she wanted to get everything out in the open sooner rather than later.

"Ask away, Meg. We're not supposed to have secrets.

At least, I don't want to. Nancy and I got married almost ten years ago. We were in love, or we believed we were. As I've told you before, she had expectations about where our lives would lead, and she felt I kind of let her down by taking over the family business. She assumed I'd be a hotshot academic. She didn't plan to live with a plumber. The problem was, we'd never really laid out those expectations, on either side."

"Would it have made a difference, talking about it all, if she had really loved you?"

Seth sat back in his chair and met her gaze. "Meg, I can't say. I was a different person then. I think she and I started out on the same page, but then my father died and things changed. I had to think about my family, and paying the bills, because my father never did manage to save any money. I did what I thought I had to do, but Nancy didn't like the way things went. And that was that."

Based on what few comments Lydia Chapin had let slip, and what Seth said now and then, for years Seth had watched his mother put up with a man who was not particularly successful and resented it, and who might have taken his anger out on his wife and children. Not a pretty picture. "Seth, please don't think I'm judging. I don't have a great track record with relationships myself, not that I've walked away from any significant ones." *Probably because I was too afraid to get into one in the first place.* The only model I've ever really known was my parents', and you've seen them together. I think they have a good marriage, and it's lasted, but there is a certain formality between them, and there always has been. There are things they don't discuss, and certainly didn't in front of me. It's worked fine for them, so I guess you could say they were on the same page. But if you have a problem, with me or anything else, I want to know about it. Good or bad. Is that all right with you?"

"Of course it is. No secrets. We talk things out—together. If we can stay awake long enough."

"Well, we're awake now. Plus we have several hundred miles of driving ahead of us, and that makes you a captive audience."

"Is that a threat?" Seth asked, his smile back.

"Or a promise. And of course you can ask anything about me."

"Deal. Let's start with what we're doing today, though, can we?"

"Of course. You wanted to get as far as Delaware, maybe, before stopping? Do we have a place for the night?"

"We do, but it's a surprise. The drive to Wilmington, Delaware, should take between four and five hours, depending on what kind of traffic we run into. And about the same from Wilmington to Charlottesville. Any stops or detours you want to make along the way? We did veto Philadelphia, didn't we?"

"Yes, for the city," Meg said firmly. "No cities. I like cities, but not right now. But I do have a request."

Seth quirked one eyebrow. "Which is?"

"Remember I told you about Bartram's Garden? It's south of the city, and not far from the interstate and the airport, so we'd go right by it on the way to Wilmington."

"Refresh my memory: what is it?"

"Aha! I've stumped you. It is both historic and agricultural. John Bartram was the colony's first botanist, and he was a dedicated collector. He explored the wilderness in this country and gathered seeds, and he sent a lot of them back to England. That became his business, and it extended over three generations of Bartrams. He developed one of the first seed catalogs, both handwritten and printed as circulars. The 1785 catalog, from the third generation to manage the business, is one of the earliest botanical lists of North American plants. His 1760 greenhouse survives on the site, one of what became many. Actually a few years ago the place started selling plants again, but it's not practical for us to get any if we're traveling. I've read that there's some replanting of the orchard going on. Although I don't think he sold a lot of apple trees. He was much more interested in the seeds."

· "All right, you've sold me," Seth said. "Just tell me where we're going."

"Take Interstate 95 past Philadelphia—as I said, it's near the airport."

They managed to avoid most Monday morning traffic around New York and Philadelphia. Meg already knew that Seth was a steady and competent driver—so unlike her impatient father!—so she could relax and enjoy the scenery. Following Interstate 95 was not necessarily the prettiest route, but it was the most efficient; they were facing a drive of four hours to their destination, and they wanted to allow a little daylight time to see what remained of the historic garden. They didn't talk much, but the silence was not uncomfortable. There was something soothing about the hum of tires on the road, the steady flow of changing landscape to look at going by—inlets, houses, patches of trees, cities of varying size that grew as they approached, then trickled away behind them. Meg could feel her tension unwinding. Maybe she should take more road trips. With Seth, of course.

They arrived at Bartram's Garden shortly after one. When she had said it was close to the airport, she hadn't realized that it was practically *in* the airport. It took only a few turns once they'd passed the airport exit and they were there. Meg looked at the parking lot dubiously. "There doesn't seem to be much happening here," she said.

"On the plus side, it doesn't look like Disneyland," Seth said cheerfully. "Oh, by the way, how do you feel about zoos?"

"Zoos?" Meg laughed. "I've seen a few. I always feel bad about the captive animals, and then I have to think that if they weren't in the zoos, they wouldn't survive at all. So I guess I have mixed feelings. Were we planning to visit a zoo?"

"No. Just checking, for future reference. Are we going in?"

"Well, we're here. I gather that the Welcome Center is closed today, but since it's December there's not much to see in the way of plants, or at least, I wouldn't recognize them without leaves. I really wanted to get a sense of the history of the place."

They followed a well-marked path, leaving the near-empty parking lot behind. Once they were on the property, Meg could see the Delaware River in the distance. "The Bartram family owned over a hundred acres, down to the river there, and lived in the midst of it. As I was telling you, at their peak they had ten greenhouses, and literally thousands of species of native and exotic plants. This place is a landmark in horticultural history."

"I'm impressed, Meg." Seth came up behind her and put his arms around her shoulders. "Seriously. Two years ago you were a financial analyst who happened to inherit an orchard. You probably couldn't have named more than ten apple varieties, the ones that you'd seen in grocery stores. Look at how far you've come."

"I was planning to walk away . . ." Meg said, almost to herself. Then in a stronger voice she added, "But then I figured, if I was going to stay, I was going to do it right. I knew I had a lot to learn."

Seth sighed melodramatically. "And here I thought it was my charms that kept you in Granford."

She turned and punched his shoulder. "That came later, remember? All my life, I'd been the good girl—worked hard, got high grades, went to a good college, found a relatively stable job. When the nice safe path I'd chosen suddenly crumbled beneath my feet, I figured maybe the universe was trying to send me a message. So instead of sulking, I embraced the change. And here we are."

"Well, if there's a god of random events, I'd like to send an offering to him."

"Why do you think it's a he?"

"Because women are more organized than men. I'll give you a goddess of order if you want."

"That works for me," Meg said cheerfully. "Shall we see what there is to see before it gets dark?"

"Lead the way. You don't happen to have a map of the place do you?"

"Nope. But as I pointed out earlier, most of the vegetation is dead, so it's no great loss if we miss it. Nice view of the city." Meg pointed toward the skyline of Philadelphia, visible in the distance.

"Just remember it wouldn't have looked like that in your John Bartram's day."

"Yes and no," Meg countered. "He might have seen the

smoke of cooking fires and such, maybe some ships headed for the city port. The city, or at least the waterfront, pre-dates this place. And I have now just about exhausted everything I know about this region, so I'll shut up."

They wandered through the grounds, admiring the solid stone house, the layout, the views, and what few plants they could identify. Meg was glad she had brought a down jacket along, because the wind from the river was biting. That was probably what had discouraged many sightseers, although there were a few intrepid walkers and bikers who passed them quickly.

"Seen enough?" Seth asked after a while.

"I guess so. I told you, there isn't much to see. It's the principle of the thing. I wonder if John Chapman and one or another of the Bartrams ever crossed paths? They were in the same business, sort of, and Johnny Appleseed did spend some time in Pennsylvania, although not around here, from what I've read. Of course, one of the Bartrams could have run across him in their plant collecting expeditions."

"Could be. I gather there were limited roads back in the day, so if they were on the move, they didn't have a lot of choices. Let's head back to the car."

"All right. How far are we from our mysterious destination?"

"Under half an hour. Speak now if there's anything else in this neighborhood that you want to see. I understand there are other significant historic sites, although a lot of them seem to be battlefields."

"I'll pass. I'm getting cold, and the light is going. We can think about it for the trip back."

"Then we will move on to our next stop."

"Which is?"

"The nicest hotel in Wilmington, the Hotel du Pont. I figured we deserved one splurge."

"Ooh, lovely! Maybe they'll have a high tea."

"They do. We have a reservation."

Meg hugged him. "Another reason why I love you."

6

By the time they left the Garden's grounds, the sun was halfway down the sky. The wind hadn't dropped off, and Meg was getting cold. When they got into the car, Seth turned on the heat while they sat for a bit.

"Do you know where you're going from here?" Meg asked.

"Near enough," he said. "Wilmington's not that big a city, but it is the next one near this highway."

"Have you ever been there?"

"Only passing through by train. I took myself off to Washington once, a long time ago, because I thought I should see the place."

"What did you think?"

"It was interesting. A bit unreal, almost stagy, if you know what I mean. But that's what it was supposed to be—designed to impress the rest of the world. I didn't have the time to explore the museums or the rest of the area. Mostly I walked around. You've seen it?"

"Yes, on a high school field trip, a long time ago. How well do you know Boston?"

"Not very. Sure, I've been there, but it's not the same as knowing a place. Same with New York. I could say something corny like, 'I'm a country boy at heart.'"

"A country boy with an education from one of the best small liberal arts colleges in the country," Meg shot back. "So you're not exactly ignorant of the rest of the country, or the world. Did you ever want to go to Europe?"

"It crossed my mind, but I couldn't leave the business that long, even if I'd had the money. You?"

"I took a trip with a friend the summer after I graduated from college. We didn't have a plan, or a lot of money— mostly we went where we felt like it and stayed in places we could afford. We spent some time in London and Paris, and then we rented a car and saw some of the countryside. It seems a long time ago now. Can we put it on our bucket list for some future date?"

"Sure. As long as it isn't during growing season."

"Good point. But there'd be fewer tourists in winter, and it can't be any colder there than in Massachusetts. Should we start an official bucket list?"

"Like, in writing? Why not?" Seth said. "Ready to go?"

"I am. I can feel my toes again."

As Seth had promised, it was a short drive to downtown Wilmington. Apparently the hotel was one of the larger buildings in the city, and rather impossible to miss. When they reached the entrance, Meg was already feeling tongue-tied. "Oh, my. Can we afford this?"

"It's our honeymoon, Meg. We should have a few experiences worth remembering, shouldn't we? This is our well-deserved indulgence."

"Well, I love it. It's gorgeous."

She sat back and let Seth manage things: valet parking, and a liveried doorman to collect their luggage and escort them to the front door, in case they were incapable of finding it on their own. The lobby was everything she would have imagined: high ceilinged, with gilt everywhere. The reception staff was efficient and courteous, and within a couple of minutes they found themselves in a spacious room—where there was no gilt. Meg suppressed a giggle—again—wondering where they could have added gold to a standard hotel room. Maybe the toilet seat . . .

"Tea awaits us. If you're willing," Seth reminded her.

"I'd hate to waste the reservation. Will there be finger sandwiches? *Petits fours?*"

"I'm supposed to know?" Seth replied. "Why don't we go find out?"

They descended once again in the opulent elevator, and were directed to the Green Room. It was laid out for a small army of tea-drinkers, although there were not many people in the room, and Meg and Seth had their choice of seats. Meg picked up a small menu, which on one side was printed the entire history of afternoon tea, with notes on etiquette. "Good grief, I've blown it already. My purse is supposed to go on my lap—obviously they've never seen my purse. The rest of the formal details I think I can manage. Oh joy, there are tea sandwiches *and* pastries! Wait—are we supposed to eat dinner tonight?"

"We can eat late, if you stuff yourself now," Seth said, smiling.

"That's rude. I shall limit myself to only one of everything. Unless it's really, *really* good."

High tea in an elegant room in an historic hotel. Was this how she had envisioned her honeymoon? In truth, she'd never given it much thought. She'd never been close to marriage with anyone. At times she'd wondered if there was something wrong with her, but mostly she'd been comfortable with her life—her job, her friends, her activities. She hadn't been actively seeking a man, and she was ashamed to admit that at an earlier time in her life she wouldn't have looked twice at Seth Chapin. They hadn't "met cute." In fact, they'd met ugly, if there was such a thing. She'd been thrust into the middle of his life under unpleasant circumstances, and as she had said more than once, she had always planned to leave Granford as soon as she had dealt with her mother's house, even without some unexpected complications. Like a murder. And now, less than two years later, here she was, sitting in Delaware with her new husband. She realized that Seth was watching her—how long had she been silent? "What are you thinking?" she asked.

"How unlikely it is that we would be sitting here like this. Married," Seth replied.

"Funny—that's exactly what I was thinking. Apparently planning your life is highly overrated. Things only got interesting after I stopped trying."

"I agree. Who was it who said, life is what happens when you're making plans?"

"The revered American philosopher Sheryl Crow, among others." Meg looked around the room. "I don't know if I brought anything fancy enough for dinner in this place."

"Well, there's always room service."

"There is that," Meg agreed. "But if this is just the room where they serve tea, I'd really like to see the main dining room."

"Up to you. More tea?"

"No, my kidneys are floating. And I could use a nap."

"That can be arranged."

In the end they did settle for room service, which was a treat in itself. The fabulous tea had been marvelous, but Meg could feel her frugal New England ancestors glaring their disapproval at her over the centuries at the idea of eating another self-indulgent meal in the lap of luxury—on the same day! Maybe there'd be something to splurge on in Virginia. Like a tree. No, that wouldn't work—it was too late to plant one this year, since the ground was frozen, and besides, they'd be hauling it around the countryside for days. She had to laugh at the idea of dragging a small tree with them, and carefully bringing it in each night so it wouldn't freeze. Almost like a pet. With some regret Meg gave up the idea of having one of Thomas Jefferson's trees—well, at least one he would have approved of—on her own property. But then, she could probably order one by mail. Would Thomas Jefferson be satisfied with that?

They both woke early the next morning, after retiring before ten the night before, and took advantage of the lavish breakfast, having in a moment of weakness agreed that ordering room service again was a good idea.

"How far to Monticello?" Meg asked, enjoying some excellent French toast.

"I thought you were the navigator. Anyway, it's about four hours, door to door."

"So we'll be there by lunchtime?"

"Thereabouts. Are you hungry already? You haven't finished breakfast."

"Just thinking ahead. Do we have a place to stay?"

"Yes. I thought you'd given up on planning?"

"That's for the big things in life. I can still obsess with the little things, can't I?"

"If you insist. Yes, we have a reservation at a respectable motel not far from Monticello. I doubt it will meet the standards of our present accommodations, though."

"What could? Besides, I wouldn't want to muddle the memories—one fabulous hotel is plenty."

"I'm glad to hear that. My bank account thanks you."

"Hey, this honeymoon belongs to both of us—you've got to let me chip in financially."

"I won't argue," Seth said amiably. "So, are you ready to hit the road again?"

Meg drained her coffee cup. "I am now."

Meg felt a pang of regret as they pulled away from the hotel, but she was looking forward to Monticello. They headed toward Interstate 95 south, and skirted Baltimore, then took the beltway to avoid Washington, abandoning the interstate and aiming for Charlottesville, Virginia. As Seth had predicted, it was almost exactly four hours later that they arrived at their destination. They hadn't stopped along the way.

The approach to Monticello was not what she had expected. Maybe she had assumed there would be a tacky strip mall with neon lights advertising TJ's favorite ale. She shook herself: why should she think that? Jefferson was respected, even beloved, for his role in American history. But as she knew too well, that didn't always translate into treating memories with good taste.

They drove partway up a hill and parked near the visitor center. "Do you want to take the tour?" Seth asked.

"I think we'd better—I can't say I know much about the building, apart from the fact that Jefferson liked to think up ingenious ways of doing things. Do you mind?"

"Of course not. We can tour the grounds after the tour of the house."

"With maybe a quick stop at the café in between?"

"Sure."

They bought tickets and joined a group gathered under the portico on the far side of the building, overlooking the gently rolling Virginia countryside. The docent began by explaining the intricate sundial-clock under the portico, apparently designed by Jefferson, but the group of visitors did not linger long—even in Virginia it was cold in winter, and there was much, much more to see inside. Meg marveled at Jefferson's clever wine elevator, and puzzled over the bed that spanned the space between two adjoining rooms. She'd always heard that Jefferson was a tall man, over six feet, and it seemed unlikely that he could have fit in the bed, unless he had slept sitting up. But mostly Meg enjoyed watching Seth in his element. He understood the intricacies of both design and assembly, and he looked like a boy in a candy store—or would that be a comic book store these days? Coming to this place had been a good decision.

They finished the interior tour at the back of the house, and Meg and Seth peeled off from the tour group. "Food now?" Meg asked.

"Sure. But humor me—let's walk down to the end of the lawn here."

Mystified, Meg followed him along the perimeter path. At the far end he stopped and turned her around, and she burst out laughing. "It's the view from the nickel! Although I guess I should say the old nickel. It really does look like the coin, or vice versa. I just hadn't put this place together with the coin. Wow."

"It does. The café's back in the visitor center, but we'll have to walk down to see the orchard anyway."

"Lead on, since you seem to have done your homework."

They ate sandwiches quickly, reluctant to waste the daylight, then climbed partway up the hill again to visit the orchards and other plantings. This was Meg's territory. "So, there's the vegetable garden," she said, pointing, "and then there are two orchards, plus vineyards. The South Orchard is right below the vegetable garden, and has the widest variety of fruit trees."

"You've been doing your homework, too," Seth said.

"When it comes to the apples, yes, I have. Did you realize that Jefferson planted his orchard before he began building the house? Did you know that this hill, or small mountain, is high enough that warm air rises to the top of it, which protects blooming trees in the spring? Which was good for the more sensitive plants like peaches and grapes, but not so good for apple varieties. He had to pick mostly ones that thrived in the South, which limited his options."

"I never thought about that. Too bad we can't take advantage of that for our orchard."

"We've got plenty of northern apples that can tolerate the cold. Anyway, Jefferson planted over a thousand fruit trees in the South Orchard, on a grid pattern, with eighteen varieties of apples. Peaches did best, plums not so well. Jefferson concentrated on cider apples and a couple of dessert or eating apples—the Newtown Pippin and Esopus

Spitzenburg, which actually originated in New York. A lot of the Pippins were shipped to England. And that, sir, is just about all I know."

"Well done. Do we have any of those?"

"No, but I'd like to add a couple, more for sentiment than because they're in high demand. At least now—I think the market for the less common heirlooms is still growing. I should order trees now, if I want to plant them in the spring."

They wandered through the gardens. As Meg had feared, there was little growing, but the layout and orientation of the various beds were clear. Near the bottom of the hill they came upon the cemetery. After a few silent moments she said, "It seems that not only is Jefferson buried here, but lineal descendants may also be buried here, even now."

"I did not know that. So there's an element of genealogy, too. But I doubt that either of us has any ancestors here."

"Not likely."

For several long moments they stood silently in front of the largest monument, which Meg guessed was not the one that had originally graced Jefferson's burial place. "He really loved this place, didn't he?" she said softly.

"He did, I'd say," Seth replied as quietly. "It was his home, in the best sense of the word."

Meg moved closer. "I'm glad we came."

Seth put his arm around her. "So am I."

7

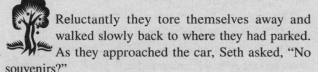Reluctantly they tore themselves away and walked slowly back to where they had parked. As they approached the car, Seth asked, "No souvenirs?"

"I'd rather wait and get a tree later—then I'll think of this place every time I see it."

"I like that idea." Seth started the car and pointed it down the hill.

Partway down there was another historic marker in front of a modest nineteenth-century building. "What's that?" Meg asked.

Seth slowed to read the sign. "It's the former estate of James Monroe."

"I didn't know he had one. Not much of a place, is it? For a former president, I mean."

"The contrast with what we've just seen is rather striking, I must say. And Monroe was also governor of Virginia, secretary of state under President Madison, and president for two terms."

"And you know all this why?" Meg demanded.

"I like history." Then he grinned. "I cheated and looked at a guidebook."

"Well, I for one feel sorry for Monroe, having Jefferson looking down on him in his humble home."

"I'm sure he'd appreciate your sentiment, although I always thought he sounded like a rather cranky man. I think he once sued the government for reimbursement for his presidential expenses. Motel now?"

"Fine. I'm sure there are other things worth seeing in this area, like the University of Virginia, but I don't feel compelled to investigate. I am enjoying *not* feeling obligated to play the diligent tourist."

This time Seth had selected a conveniently close, modest motel. "Sorry it's not up to last night's standard," he said.

"Hey, it's clean, relatively quiet, and has all the necessities, like a bed and running water. It's fine," Meg assured him. "And it makes last night all the more memorable. Is it time for dinner yet?"

"Didn't you just eat?" Seth demanded.

"It's been at least two hours. I'm just thinking ahead. There seems to be a restaurant here."

Seth sighed melodramatically. "All right. Let's get checked in, and then we can eat."

Check-in took little time, since on a Tuesday in December there were few tourists. As Meg had assumed, the room was clean and functional, and the fixtures worked. Maybe it wasn't up to her parents' standards, but she had no complaints.

They took their time over dinner, starting with a leisurely glass of wine. They were halfway through a pleasant if not noteworthy meal when Meg's cell phone rang in the depths of her purse. She'd forgotten to turn it off, and it took her a few moments to retrieve it. She was surprised to see her mother's number on the screen. "Hi, Mother. We were going to call you in the morning. What's up?"

"Sorry to disturb you again so soon, Meg, but I need to talk to you about your visit. It might be better if you didn't come right now."

Her mother's voice sounded curiously uncertain, and Meg's senses went on high alert. "Is something wrong? You're sick? Daddy's sick?" She glanced at Seth.

"We're fine, dear, but there's been a little trouble at the house."

Meg's imagination leapt to worst-case scenarios: it had burned down, it had been burgled and/or ransacked, there had been a tornado (in Montclair, New Jersey? In December?). "What is it?"

"Well, the repair shop couldn't get the parts they needed soon enough to suit your father, so yesterday your father rented a car and we drove home. We'll deal with our car later."

This rambling and evasive story was very unlike her mother, and Meg was becoming increasingly concerned. "And? The house was in ruins when you got home?"

"No, it was fine. Well, more or less. So we parked the car in the driveway and went inside, and got a bite to eat, and went to bed."

Elizabeth was still waffling about something, Meg thought. "Mother, will you please get to the point? What did you call to tell me?" Meg looked at Seth across the table and shrugged in frustration.

"Well, you know the Hagens across the street? This morning they saw the unfamiliar car parked in our driveway and they were concerned, since they knew we had been away for your wedding, so they called the police to check the house. When the police arrived they were being cautious, so they checked the outside before they tried the door. And they found something."

"What?" Meg had to work hard not to scream into the phone.

"A body. In the backyard."

That brought Meg to a screeching halt. "What?" she all but whispered. Now Seth was looking at her with real concern. She swallowed. "This was last night? What have you been doing since then?"

"Well, of course we had to go to the police station and make a statement about where we were."

"Wait—why? You're respectable citizens, and a simple call to the hotel in Amherst would establish that you've been there all along, right? And Daddy's a lawyer, for God's sake."

"Well, yes, but there was a little trouble with an arrest of the police chief's son a while back that involved your father, so the chief wasn't in a very generous mood. But the police let us come home this morning."

"Who was the . . . body? Someone you knew?"

"Actually, yes. He's the handyman we hire to do small jobs around the property—you know, mow the lawn, or shovel snow, or watch out for ice dams. I don't recall if you've met him, but we've been using him for years. Enrique Rodriguez, that's—that was—his name. When we knew we'd be away for a bit, we asked him to stop by once a day to make sure that everything was all right. Take in the mail, that kind of thing."

"How long . . ." No. Meg stopped herself. She wasn't about to interrogate her mother over the phone—she'd already had a hard day. "We'll be there by lunchtime tomorrow—it's only about six hours." She looked at Seth for confirmation, and he nodded.

"Meg, darling"—her mother started to protest—"you don't need . . ."

"Yes, I do. You want me to stand by and just call now and then to see how the murder investigation of someone you knew is going? Wait, the man was murdered, wasn't he? He didn't have a stroke or a heart attack in your back-yard, did he?"

"No, dear." Her mother sighed. "It was the traditional blunt force object, in this case a loose brick from the patio."

"And he didn't happen to fall and hit his head?"

"Not possible, according to the medical examiner."

"Are you all right, Mother? And Daddy?"

"We're . . . coping. Your father is angry, both that this happened and that the police treated him shabbily, or so he believes. I'm just . . . tired."

"Then I'll let you go now. See you tomorrow in time for lunch." Meg cut off the call before her mother could protest. No matter what Elizabeth said, Meg was pretty sure that she wouldn't have called unless she was looking for some support from Meg. Who also happened to have experience in murder investigations, although not in New Jersey.

She jammed her phone back in her bag and looked up to see Seth watching her. "What's the story?"

"Handyman-slash-caretaker found dead in the backyard from a blow to the head with a brick. Neighbor saw the rental car at the house and got worried, so called the cops.

The local cops are not inclined to look kindly on my father due to some conflict over the police chief's son." And no doubt her father had only made things worse when he was dragged to the police station and kept there far too long. He'd have been tired after driving half the day, and already ticked off about the car troubles. "You heard what I told Mother. Are you okay with going up there tomorrow?"

"Of course I am. This is family."

"Thank you. So at least we can finish eating, and use that hotel room." Although Meg wasn't sure how much sleep she'd be able to get. Was this some kind of weird karma following her around? "I didn't want to make you drive all that way at night, and I doubt there's anything we could do tonight, anyway. I'm sorry."

"For what?" Seth asked. "You didn't arrange this murder just to mess up our honeymoon, did you?"

"No, of course not. But we do seem to keep stumbling over bodies."

An hour later she was lying in bed, staring at the ceiling, trying to make sense of what her mother had told her. The man—who she could not remember meeting—had been doing his rounds, making sure the place was locked up. Someone had come up—behind him?—and whacked him with a brick, and he'd died. Had the blow killed him? Wait, when had he been killed? Earlier in the week? Then the exposure could have killed him once he was unconscious? How long had he lain there behind the house? It was unlikely anyone could have seen him from the street or from either side—her father believed in privacy, which he achieved through high privet hedges rather than fences. It could have been one night, or it could have been days. Wait—how had he gotten there? Probably a truck, if he was doing odd jobs.

Wouldn't the snoopy neighbor have noticed his truck parked there overnight? If it wasn't there, where was it?

Her mother hadn't said that the house had been broken into, or that anything was missing. The garage? Her mother's car? What kind of problem had her father had with the police chief that could cause so much hostility? Was that recent, or an old grudge? Anyway, her father should have a more than ample alibi, what with hotel and meal receipts, gas receipts, car rental agreement, and the like. Assuming he didn't have a fit and refuse to submit any of his corroborating evidence, operating under some misguided principle that his word should be enough. Unfortunately she could see him doing that, and Meg wasn't sure her mother could talk him out of it.

"Meg," Seth whispered in her ear, "get some sleep. You can't do anything right now, and if you don't sleep you'll be useless tomorrow. We'll sort things out when we get there."

Meg rolled over so she was facing him, and he put his arms around her. "Why does this keep happening? Am I cursed? Is it contagious?"

"I will pretend to consider that suggestion seriously, if it makes you happy. What kind of law does your father practice?"

"Criminal, but mostly white-collar, corporate stuff. Which is why I wonder how the police chief butted heads with him."

"You can ask that tomorrow. What else?"

"Was the intent robbery? Did the poor man interrupt the robber on the way in or the way out? Mother didn't say anything about a theft, but she wasn't exactly herself."

"You can ask that tomorrow," Seth repeated, in hypnotically low tones.

"They have a good alarm system in that house, and I'm sure they left it on, even with the guy keeping an eye on things."

"Tell me what the house is like," Seth said soothingly.

"Nice. Fieldstone colonial, built in the 1920s. Too big for them, of course, but it makes a statement. I mean, seriously, the front hall has to be fifteen or twenty feet across. Who needs a hall like that?"

"We don't. Much of a lot?"

"No, well under an acre. Nice neighborhood, mostly older people who've been there a while. Train to New York for the commuters . . ." And Meg faded into sleep.

Seth was already showered and dressed when Meg woke up the next morning. "What time is it?" she asked.

"Seven."

Meg sat bolt upright in bed. "Shoot, it's six hours to Montclair. We should be on the road by now."

"Don't worry. I doubt anything is happening fast. Take a shower. I'll go get some food and you can eat in the car. All right?"

"Yes. Good. Thank you." She bounded out of bed, planted a kiss on him, and ducked into the bathroom.

By the time Meg had showered and dressed, and thrown what little she had unpacked back into her bag, Seth was waiting for her with large coffees in Styrofoam cups and an assortment of muffins. Meg thanked the stars once again that she had been lucky enough to find a man who knew exactly what to do in a crisis, and then did it quickly and well, without fuss.

They settled themselves in the car and lodged the coffee cups into stable cup holders. "Which way do we go?" Seth asked.

"North," Meg said. "Seriously, go back and find Interstate 95, take that to the New Jersey Turnpike, get onto the Garden State Parkway when you come to it, then get off on Exit 151—Watchung Avenue—and I can take it from there."

"Remind me once we get to the area, will you? So, six hours. That should be about enough time to fill me in on your entire childhood history, and how your parents could have found a body in their backyard."

8

Once they were on the main highway, Seth said, "You know, you've never told me much about your childhood."

Meg was startled out of her reverie—or maybe it was more like a funk, she mused. "You're right. No, I'm not hiding any deep dark secrets. It's just that you and I kind of skipped over the 'getting to know you' phase when we got together. I have to say I know a lot more about you and your background than you do about mine."

"That's because you've been living in the middle of it all. My history is an open book. So tell me. We have plenty of time."

"All right." Meg took a moment to collect her thoughts—she wasn't used to talking about herself. "You know my folks met in Cambridge, back in the wild seventies?"

"Yes, I think that came up when your mother visited. Then what?"

"They got married right after he got his law degree from Harvard, and my father joined a Boston law firm right away. It wasn't one of the big-name firms, but a small solid one. He worked there for five or six years, then he was recruited by a bigger New York firm, Blackwell, Hyzy, and Cates. You probably don't recognize the name, but they were important. Anyway, he jumped at the chance—I was about four at the time, so I don't remember all this, only snatches of it. I don't know if he was worried about making partner in Boston, or if he just wanted a bigger playing field."

"So he and your mother moved to New York?"

"Not exactly. I'm not sure if it was because they didn't want to raise a family in the city, but for whatever reason they looked at the bedroom communities with commuter lines in northern New Jersey. And found something they could afford in Madison."

Seth shook his head. "Never heard of it."

"No reason why you should have. It was, and still is, a nice town with about fifteen thousand people. One high school. A real town center. One of the first malls in the area was only a short ride away. It was a nice place to grow up."

"But they don't live there now. When did they move?"

"After I left for college. Daddy worked for Blackwell, Hyzy for close to fifteen years, all through my high school years, and after. I really never saw much of him back then. You know, lawyers work long hours, plus he was commuting, so he left early in the morning and was lucky to make it home by dinner."

"How did your mother feel about that?" Seth asked carefully. "That was a long stretch of her life."

"She didn't complain, at least not to me. She never held down a paying job, but she did a lot of volunteer work, first at my elementary school, and later at the library and the high school PTA and for a few other worthy causes. And she and I did all the nice things in New York—museums, plays. Sometimes after a matinee we'd have dinner with Daddy in the city. We never talked about it, but I had the feeling that she knew what she was signing on for when she married Daddy. She wanted a successful lawyer for a husband, and that's what she got, even if it meant sacrifices. Sorry—that makes her sound kind of cold, and I don't mean it that way. She was always a fairly independent person, and she had her own life."

"So how did the move to Montclair come about?"

"I left for college in 2000. They moved during that year. The two towns are less than twenty miles apart, but the commute was easier for Daddy. And to be honest, Montclair was a swankier address—more prestige, more money in town. I guess they figured that with me out of the house, they could move on—or up."

"Is he still with that firm? We've never really talked about what they do professionally," Seth said.

"No. After twenty-odd years working in New York, Daddy decided he wanted a different environment, or maybe he just wanted to slow down after all those years of working so hard, so he left them and opened his own law firm in 2010, in Montclair. He brought along a colleague from the old firm—Arthur Ackerman. I've never met him, but I think they're about the same age. They focus on white-collar issues—they still have New York contacts, but a lot of the business leaders have homes outside the city, or their companies have moved to the suburbs, so it's more convenient for everyone. I graduated from college and then I got an MBA and started working, so I didn't get home much, mainly for holidays, now and then, and my grandparents' funerals. I never got to know Montclair, so I can't tell you much about it."

"Why there?" Seth asked.

"Status, I think. Bigger, more impressive house, better address for business purposes."

"So you never knew this caretaker?"

"No. Why would I? I was rarely there, and I don't think they were worried about keeping the lawn trimmed when I was visiting."

"Did they have any other help in the house?"

Meg leaned back and regarded him. "Listen to you! Is this how you think the rich folk live?"

"I'm just asking," Seth told her. "I'm trying to figure out who else knows the house, if they had access to it, if they knew the dead man. Where was he from, do you know? Mexico? South America?"

"Seth, how am I supposed to know that? I haven't lived in the state for years. Even if I had met him, which I didn't, I couldn't have told you. I can't even answer that question for Hispanic residents of Massachusetts. Maybe for the Jamaican population. Can you?"

"No, I can't. I retract the question."

"Are you trying to connect my father to Colombian drug lords or something?" Meg asked, not sure whether she was joking.

"No. Is it possible, though?"

Meg considered being insulted by Seth's question, but realized how little she knew about what her father really did—and with whom. "Shoot, I don't know. Daddy and I don't talk about his work. Seth, I know what New Jersey used to be like, when I was growing up. I have very little idea what it's like now. I will say that towns like Madison and Montclair don't change much, except to get more expensive. I'll bet there are fewer kids in my high school now than there were when I went there, because a lot of parents can't afford to live there. And I doubt there's a whole lot of diversity."

"You don't have to jump all over me. My question was simply, was the handyman—Enrique—involved in something that got him killed, or did he just happen to be in the wrong place at the wrong time?"

"And I can't tell you that. I think Mother mentioned at some point that she had a cleaning woman come in once a week, or every other week, but I've never seen her, either. And Mother does do most of her own housework. Heck, how do you think I learned how to do it?"

"The same way I did—from my mother. Okay, obviously there's a lot we don't know, and we shouldn't theorize ahead of our data. We can spin stories all we like, but we don't have much to work with."

"I know. That's why I'm frustrated."

"And what do you think you can do once we get there?"

"Give my mother some moral support, I guess. Seth, you didn't hear her on the phone. You've met her, more than once, and she's always very controlled, very together. But last night she sounded really rattled. This is serious."

"Of course it is. A body in your yard is serious stuff. But your father must have all sorts of contacts in the area. He can figure this out, can't he?"

"You're saying I shouldn't be there? That we don't need to shove ourselves into the middle of this?"

"No, I'm not. As I said at the beginning, this is your *family*. Family is important. If I'm in the way, just tell me and I'll clear out and let you deal with your parents."

"No!" Meg said, more loudly than she intended. "No, please don't. You're family, too, now, and I think we can all use an outsider's perspective. Especially from someone who has some passing experience with suspicious deaths."

"I wish we didn't," Seth said.

"But we might never have met, otherwise," Meg replied.

"There is that."

Six hours in a car was a long time, even with someone you liked, and who was also a careful driver. They stopped only briefly, to use the restrooms and stock up on munchies and water. The original time estimate proved to be accurate, and Meg guided Seth through her parents' residential neighborhood before two o'clock. She noticed that Seth was driving slowly, not so much because it was unfamiliar territory for him but because he was scoping out the houses and the lawns and shrubbery that surrounded them. "It's the next one on the right," she told him.

He pulled up in front of the house, leaving the engine running.

"You can use the driveway, you know," Meg said.

"I'm just looking. I see what you mean about privacy. From the street you can't see much of anything. Which neighbors were the ones who reported the car?"

"Those, I think. I've heard the name but I've never met them." Meg pointed to a house not directly across the street, but offset so that it had a direct view up the driveway toward the garage. "They would have seen the rental car from there."

"Right." Seth pulled forward and made the turn into the driveway. The house was set on a low hill, so the drive sloped upward to the two-car garage, where both doors were shut. The rental car was still there, so Seth pulled into the space next to it and turned off the engine. "Do we have to go in the front door?"

"Of course not. We can go in the kitchen door. Yes, there's a doorbell—no doubt for the peasants who brought their humble offerings to the lord of the manor."

"You're being sarcastic," Seth commented.

"Yes, I am. I guess I'm nervous, because I don't know what we're going to find. If they'd found the killer, wouldn't Mother or Daddy have called while we were on the way?"

"I would think so."

The interior door opened, and Meg's mother appeared behind the storm door. Her face lit up when she saw them in the driveway. She had reached the car before Meg and Seth had managed to extricate themselves from it. "Darling, I'm so glad you're here. Hello again, Seth, and welcome to our home. Come in, come in, before you freeze."

Meg hugged her mother, who held on a few beats longer than usual. "Anything new?"

"No, not really. No suspects, or at least, not that anyone has told us. Certainly no arrests. It's nerve-racking, not knowing anything."

"How's Daddy holding up?" Meg asked.

"Angry. Frustrated. He's spent a lot of the day barking at people in Amherst, trying to get the car brought down here. I think it's only his way of blowing off steam. Please, come in. Have you eaten?"

"Just snacks. We figured we should get here as quickly as we could."

"That was very sweet of you, although I don't know that there's anything you can do."

"Help if we can. Hold your hand if we can't."

"I'll take it. Come on in. Your father's upstairs in the office—you two can have the big room overlooking the yard. The one you used to use."

"That's fine. I assume . . . Enrique is no longer there? Is there police tape?"

"No, he's gone," Elizabeth answered. "The medical examiner's office did what they had to do and took him away last night. Earlier today there was a herd of people with latex gloves on rummaging around and taking pictures, but they left and haven't returned. Besides which, he was found close to the house, and you couldn't see that from the upstairs room anyway."

"Which way . . . no, we can talk about that later. You said something about food?"

"Yes. I made soup, since I couldn't figure out what else to do. There's some good bread—that was in the freezer. We haven't done any shopping yet."

"Maybe we can do that later, together."

"That would be nice. Were you planning on staying long?"

Meg glanced at Seth. "We hadn't really decided anything, even before this happened. There's nothing urgent we have to be back for. The animals are taken care of. We can play it by ear."

"I'm sure you have better things to do on your honeymoon than hang around here waiting for the police to do their jobs." Elizabeth turned to the stove, where a kettle was simmering on a back burner. Meg looked enviously at the appliance: six burners and two ovens. She could feed an army with that. Not that there was room in her Colonial-sized kitchen for such a giant appliance.

Seth, too, was taking in the room. "Big kitchen you have here, Elizabeth."

"Yes, it is. It's ridiculously big for the two of us, unless we were planning some serious dinner parties, which we never have. Sit down in the alcove there and I'll dish up."

"There is also a breakfast room adjoining the kitchen," Meg informed him, "and the formal dining room beyond it, in the front of the house."

"Before you ask," Elizabeth said, carrying two steaming bowls of soup over to the table, "I have no idea how anyone decided where to eat when this place was built. I'm guessing it was the servants who ate in here, or maybe the children, and the family ate breakfast in the aptly named breakfast room, which is also where the china storage cupboards are. Somewhere Emily Post may have rules for all of this, but I've never found them."

"There are two rooms for servants on the third floor," Meg added, "and there are back stairs so no one would see the hired help. And the stairs near the back door where we came in lead down to the laundry room."

"Not at all like our houses, right?" Seth said. "Pre-Depression, I take it, Elizabeth?"

"Yes, mid 1920s. To quote a cliché, they don't make them like this anymore."

They were startled to hear the sound of someone—Phillip, obviously—stomping his way down the front stairs, muttering curses along the way. Elizabeth looked anxious, which in turn made Seth look wary. Meg decided to take the bull by the horns, and went to greet her father at the kitchen door. "Hi, Daddy. We made it!"

"Hey, little girl." He grabbed her in a bear hug, but released her quickly. "Seth." He nodded. "Elizabeth, those idiots got the parts on yesterday, but they claim they can't get my car down here until tomorrow at the earliest. I'm almost tempted to fly back and get it myself. It would be faster."

"Phillip, I think you need to be here, in case . . ." Elizabeth protested.

"In case what?" Phillip demanded sharply. "Those incompetent detectives manage to figure out who killed Gonzalez? And why he was left there in the yard? The killer could have simply taken him away—then we'd never have noticed, and most likely the police wouldn't have, either."

"Phillip, I'd like you to be here," Elizabeth said firmly. "And the children are here. You don't need your car really, do you? You can use mine."

Phillip sat down at the table, still grumbling. "Sorry to break up your honeymoon like this, kids. We're happy to see you again. I just wish it was under better circumstances. Now, tell me about Monticello. What's it like?"

The subject of the late Enrique Gonzalez was closed.

9

Having devoted the day to driving to New Jersey, now that she had arrived Meg had no idea what to do. She was out of her element. While she might have grown up in the state, she hadn't spent any serious time in it for years, and she was sure things had changed. Unlike in Granford, she couldn't call up a friend on the local police force and ask about what was going on, even if it did relate to her family. She could confirm for them her parents' presence in Massachusetts when Enrique was presumably killed, but so could impersonal credit card receipts. She'd come to offer her support without even questioning her motives. Her parents hadn't asked for her help, nor were they likely to, unless it was to request assistance in selecting the best apple for a dish. Both her parents had encouraged her to be independent, and as a result, no one in the family seemed to know how to ask for help.

She was free to leave at any time, and Seth wouldn't question her decision. Was there anything to be done if they stayed? Was there anything to be gained? Still, she knew she couldn't leave without the answers to quite a few questions.

When they'd finished eating, Phillip disappeared back into his study while Meg and Elizabeth cleaned up the kitchen, which didn't take much effort. Seth sat silently, watching, and Meg wondered what he was thinking. Once the dishes had been dried, Elizabeth said, in an artificial tone, "I really should do some shopping. You will be staying for dinner, won't you?" She plastered on a shallow smile, trying valiantly to pretend that this was a purely social visit.

"Mother, we'll stay as long as you want us to. If you tell us to go, well, that's diffcrent. I think I want some answers before we head home."

Elizabeth's smile melted quickly. "I'll make some tea." She turned her back on Meg to fill a kettle.

Meg took a chair next to Seth and reached for his hand. "You're quiet," she said. "What are you thinking?"

Seth glanced at Elizabeth's back before answering. "I think I agree with you. There's something going on here that doesn't make sense. Elizabeth, what is it you're not telling us?"

Elizabeth stopped fiddling with tea bags and turned to face them. "Why do you think I'm hiding anything?"

"Because you're not acting like yourself," Seth said quietly.

"Seth, you've spent less than twenty-four hours with me in your life," Elizabeth protested. "How do you know what my normal is?"

"Sometimes someone who doesn't know you can see more clearly. And Meg's too worried to notice details."

"Seth, that's not true!" Meg told him.

"Isn't it? Your father is wandering around like a caged bear, growling. Is that normal for him?"

"Well, no," Meg admitted, "but he's never had to worry about a murdered employee."

"Exactly. Murdered."

The word hung in the air between them. Elizabeth turned abruptly and filled the teapot, slapped a cozy over it, then sat down at the table facing them. "What do you mean?"

"I mean, you told Meg yourself that the man didn't die a natural death. He was hit over the head from behind. Correct?"

Elizabeth nodded once, her eyes not leaving Seth's face.

"I'm going to assume that this is a low crime area, at least in this neighborhood. I'm guessing someone keeps an eye on it? The police drive through? There's a community watch?"

"The former," Elizabeth said.

"They would have known about Enrique's comings and goings, but there had to be someone else here. Unless you suspect one of your neighbors?"

Elizabeth gave a short bark of a laugh. "That's ridiculous. Most of them are our age, and I can't imagine any of them wanting Enrique dead."

"Did he work for any of them?"

"I think so. We used his services only occasionally, and we would have recommended him to anyone who asked."

"How much did you know about him as a person?"

"He turned up when he said he would, he worked hard while he was here, he charged a fair rate by local standards, he cleaned up after himself. He was clean and polite and courteous."

"Do you know anything about his personal life?"

Elizabeth cocked her head at Seth. "Seth, why are you doing this? The police covered most of these questions. We answered. We knew very little about the man. He came to us recommended by a family who no longer lives in this neighborhood, back when we first moved here and Phillip was too busy to mow the lawn. We've never had any complaints. Do we socialize with him? No. The closest we've come is when we've shared an iced tea on the patio on a hot day after he'd finished mowing. I think he mentioned a wife and children, but I have no idea where he lived."

"You paid him off the books?" Meg asked, surprised. "What about taxes? Social Security? Was he here illegally?"

"Meg, he was an independent contractor—he didn't work for a company or service. I handed him a check once a month, based on the work he had provided the prior month, which varied. I assumed he was dealing with his own taxes and licenses and such. Of course we checked his residency status, but we certainly didn't interrogate him about his business practices. But the short answer is, no, we never had a home address for him because we never needed one. Is that a problem for you?"

"I didn't mean to imply that, Mother. But knowing so little about the man doesn't get us very far, or explain why he's dead and why he died here."

"Meg, isn't that for the police to find out?"

Meg smiled ruefully. "I suppose it is, unless you're under suspicion. Are you?"

Elizabeth didn't answer immediately. Then she said, "I don't think so."

"Elizabeth, you don't sound very sure," Seth said. "Is there something more?"

"I . . . don't know. I may be imagining things."

"Such as?" Meg asked.

"Well, for one thing, when the car was damaged in Amherst. There was plenty of maneuvering room in that parking lot. It was reasonably well lit, although not glaringly bright because I'm sure some of the guests would have complained. I'm guessing that the police in Amherst have assumed that it was someone who had had a bit too much to drink and missed his turn or couldn't focus well enough to see where he was going," Elizabeth finished tentatively.

"You don't believe that?" Meg demanded.

"I believe it's possible, but I'm still troubled. The vehicle hit our car hard enough to do some significant damage, and that means he was going fairly fast in a small parking lot. And he didn't just clip the back bumper, he hit head-on a few feet closer to the front of the car. It must have made some noise, but so far no guests have come forward to say they saw or heard anything that evening. It wasn't even all that late."

"All right, there are some things that don't seem quite right. You're not suggesting that the Amherst police are trying to cover anything up?" Seth asked.

"No, nothing like that. But what I'm envisioning is a single driver who was not drunk, who wanted to hit our car and do some damage, and who left in a big hurry."

"His car would have been damaged, too," Seth said.

"Yes, but it was dark, and maybe he knew how to get out of sight quickly. Or maybe it was already damaged. Or maybe it was stolen and he abandoned it fast. My fear is that the police don't think it's important enough to follow up on."

"Be that as it may," Seth said, "you're leaving out one important point: *why* would he do this? What's the point? Did this person simply feel like bashing something to hear the bang, or did he know whose car he was hitting?"

"Seth, I don't know," Elizabeth all but whispered.

Seth reflected for a moment. "I don't want to sound like I'm bullying you. I'm just trying to get as much information as possible. Let me ask you this: You seem to have jumped quickly to the idea that this could have been a deliberate act. Do you have some reason to believe that? Have there been other incidents like this?"

"I'm . . . not sure." Elizabeth stood up suddenly and went to get mugs and sugar and milk.

Meg joined her and carried the teapot to the table. She added spoons, then waited until Elizabeth had settled herself again at the table. "All right, Mother. What else have you noticed?"

Elizabeth concentrated on filling her mug. "Maybe I should start at the end and work backward. We told the police that this house hadn't been broken into and nothing was missing."

"So you said. Have you changed your mind?"

Elizabeth seemed to be choosing her words carefully. "There was no break-in, but Enrique did have a key, so if he was killed, then the person would have had time to enter the house and go through it, and let himself out again."

"What about the alarm?" Seth asked.

"Enrique might have disabled it temporarily—we did ask him to check inside the house, in case the furnace was acting up or a pipe had burst. The . . . other person could have entered then."

"Say he got in," Meg said. "Nothing was taken? Or even disturbed?"

"'Disturbed' is kind of a relative term, Meg. I know I've always laughed when I've seen this kind of thing on a television show, but it felt as though someone had been in the house. Not Enrique—he was always very respectful of the place, and he rarely came past the kitchen, where I'd offer him something to drink. But I had the sense that someone had walked through, touching things, moving them half an inch this way or that. I know; it sounds paranoid. I'll admit your father and I were tired after a day's drive, and already keyed up because of the problems with the car, so it's possible that I could have been imagining things. That's why I haven't mentioned it to your father. There's nothing I can put a finger on, but something feels wrong."

"I suppose you haven't checked all your paper or computer files, to be sure nothing is missing?" Seth said.

"No, of course not. I probably wouldn't even know what I was looking for. Phillip keeps his work files at his office, so they're safe."

"An intruder might not know that," Meg pointed out.

"True, but there's no way I can sort that out."

"What if this person wanted to leave something *in* the house, rather than remove it?" Seth asked.

"You mean, like a camera, or a recording device? Or a bomb? Incriminating evidence? What? Seth, if you're trying to help, so far all you've done is make me feel more upset."

"I apologize, Elizabeth. I don't want to do that. If you're

right about someone being in the house, and I'm not doubting your word, there had to have been a reason. And if it's true, it shifts the focus to you and Phillip rather than Enrique. Once this person got in, Enrique was an inconvenience, not a target. But maybe this person wanted no more than to walk through your home and lay hands on your possessions. Which implies that it wasn't about the money, because I assume you have jewelry and other items that he could have taken and sold easily enough."

"We do, but nothing extremely valuable."

"Someone looking for money for his next fix wouldn't care—anything he could sell would do."

Meg laid a hand on his arm. "Seth, a junkie wouldn't have had the patience to plan and execute this so carefully. He'd be more likely to smash things and run."

"Good point. But say someone chose this house for a reason, and planned ahead. Maybe he slipped in behind Enrique and waited until he was gone, but Enrique forgot something and came back unexpectedly and messed up all his planning. And he had to be silenced."

They were quiet for a minute or more, each lost in their own thoughts, sipping the cooling tea.

Meg didn't have any reason to doubt her mother's observations. She knew Elizabeth was meticulous about what she displayed and where she placed it, so if something had been disturbed she would have known, consciously or maybe subconsciously. But for someone to break in and not take anything was just plain creepy. An underwear-sniffer, maybe? Had Elizabeth inventoried her underwear drawer? Meg wasn't about to ask such an absurd question. How about someone scoping the place out for a later heist? But she had to admit her mother was right: she had nice things but none that were particularly valuable or rare. Surely there were better targets if someone was going to go to the trouble to plan a burglary.

Planting a listening device or a motion-activated camera? Possible, but why? There was nothing about Elizabeth's life that the world couldn't or shouldn't see. Which left her father. How much did she really know about what her father did? Who he represented? He'd always been careful about drawing the line: his clients and anything pertaining to them stayed at work. He never talked about his cases at home, and the cases he took on seldom if ever appeared on the news. That was his job: to keep them *off* the news. So *if* he was willing to concede that there was something going on, he'd have to break that code, at least to her and Seth. Was he really prepared to blow all this off, ignore his wife's concerns, pretend the death of the handyman was an unfortunate random act? Did he really believe that?

She looked at Seth, trying to read his mind, but he didn't give anything away. She turned back to Elizabeth. "Mother, you said you needed to go food shopping if we're going to eat. Want me and Seth to come along and help?"

Elizabeth looked momentarily startled at the change of subject, then smiled and said, "That would be lovely, dear. You can tell me what you'd enjoy eating. Why don't we go now?"

"That's fine." *Interrogation deferred*, Meg thought, but the break should give all of them time to digest what they'd heard and decide what they should do next.

10

They finished the shopping in under an hour. Elizabeth let Seth drive to the store, directing him to an upscale market a few miles from the house. Once inside, she took a cart but rambled aimlessly up and down the aisles, picking things up and putting them down, clearly distracted. Finally Meg got frustrated and said, "Why don't I make dinner tonight?" Before Elizabeth could protest, Meg started grabbing things she thought she could use, and added some staples like milk and eggs. Seth was pushing the cart, and he cocked his eyebrow at her with a half-smile, as if he had figured out what she was doing.

"Is anybody on a diet?" Meg asked as they neared the end of the shelves. She didn't wait for an answer but laid some cookies and a small frosted cake on the pile in the cart. She and Seth would eat them if nobody else would, but she thought they could all use a treat, and she was in no mood to bake. Elizabeth didn't appear to notice. They cleared the checkout line quickly, and Elizabeth didn't even make a token effort to pay—again, unlike her, Meg thought. Her mother had very clear standards regarding hospitality: a guest did not buy the groceries and make their own dinner. Therefore, Meg deduced, Elizabeth was more upset than she was willing to admit.

When they arrived back at the house, Meg said, "Seth, can you help Mother put away the groceries? I want to have a word with Daddy. Is he upstairs, Mother?"

Elizabeth seemed to come back from some distant place to focus on Meg. "I suppose. He was using my car and it's in the drive, and he spends most of his time up there."

Meg went upstairs to his home office, which was adjacent to the master bedroom at the front of the house. When she peered in he was seated at his antique kneehole desk, with papers spread in front of him, but he was staring blankly into space. She rapped on the open door. "Daddy?"

He jumped, startled, then turned to her with a quickly mustered smile. "Meg. What have you all been up to?"

"We were talking in the kitchen for a while, and then we went food shopping, since you were pretty much out of everything. I volunteered to cook dinner."

"Sweetheart, you didn't have to do that. I'd be happy to take you all out tonight."

"Daddy, I think that would be wasted on us right now. We're all tired and on edge. We need to talk. And don't you dare say, 'about what?' Something's wrong."

"I agree. Enrique's death, for one thing."

"Yes, there's that. Mother says he was a hard worker—dependable. Why is he dead?"

"I've been wondering the same thing. The best I can figure is that he startled an intruder, who lashed out with the first weapon he could lay his hands on—a loose brick. Sadly, I'd asked him to replace a few in the patio, but he said it was too cold to do it now."

"Do you get a lot of intruders in this neighborhood?"

"Well, no."

He'd barely finished answering when Meg pressed on. "When was the last murder here?"

"Not in our time here. I can't speak to before that, but in general there is little crime in this particular neighborhood. What are you getting at?"

"Do you believe that Enrique's death was a random event?"

Phillip didn't answer immediately, staring at her bleakly. Finally he said, "No."

Meg felt a small sense of triumph, mixed with dismay. Would she have believed him if he had said yes? "Why?"

Her father smiled without humor. "It's a shame you didn't want to become a lawyer. Or maybe you've changed recently. You're doing a good job of getting right to the point."

"Thank you. That's not an answer. You do know that Mother is worried?"

"She hasn't said anything to me."

Were all men so clueless, or was he making a deliberate effort not to see? "Well, she is. I think she didn't want to bother you, since you were already upset about your car. But she thinks there might have been someone in the house."

"Why would she think that?" Phillip looked startled. "Nothing's been taken."

"Small details, things out of place." Meg wasn't about to say it was her mother's "feeling" because she was pretty sure that her father would laugh at that. "Have you noticed anything?"

"I . . ." he began, then stopped himself. "All right, I'll admit I wondered if perhaps some papers on my desk here had been moved, but nothing was missing, and it had been more than a week since we'd been here. I could have forgotten exactly where things were. I didn't think it was important."

Meg pushed away from the door where she'd been leaning and dropped into a straight chair close to the desk. It was a chair she'd always hated as a child, because it had a handsome but slippery leather seat rimmed with domed brass tacks, and she was always afraid that she would slide off it onto the floor. "All right. Say there was someone in the house. Why would anyone sneak in and not take anything?"

"That I can't tell you," her father said, looking her in the eye.

"Have you butted heads with any clients lately? Are you in debt up to your eyeballs to the casinos? Do you have a stalker?"

"No to all of the above, my dear. My clients are no more contentious than they have ever been, we are financially solvent, and I haven't noticed anyone skulking around and following me."

"Are you holding any valuable items or documents on behalf of one of your clients?"

"Of course not. Anything of significance or value I would take to a bank for safekeeping. Meg, what are you getting at?"

She ignored his question. "Do you have any reason to believe that the accident in Amherst is related to Enrique's death and the hypothetical break-in here?"

"Why for all that's holy would I think that?"

"I don't know. But that's two incidents that may have been directed toward you in a short span of time. Don't you find that odd?"

"Coincidence."

"Really?"

"Meg, what do you want from me? Are you bored with your marriage already and looking to create a little excitement?"

Meg had to stifle a laugh. That was the furthest thing from her mind. "Good heavens, no. Seth and I were looking forward to a little self-indulgent downtime, away from both work and crimes. But does that mean we should just dismiss Enrique's death as an unfortunate accident and walk away?"

"Not if the facts indicate otherwise. I taught you well, didn't I?"

"I paid attention."

"What is it you're suggesting?" Phillip asked, now looking slightly amused.

"For now, we just talk about what's happened, between ourselves. If we can eliminate any doubts, then we drop the whole thing and life goes on. What's your problem with the local police?"

"That was a fast switch. It's a long story."

"Hey, I've got a couple of days clear. Tell me about it. Wait—does Mother know the details?"

"Yes and no. She knows there's some hostility there, but she doesn't know the details, at least not from me. Some of her local friends might have filled in some of the blanks."

"She gets together with people around here?" Had

Elizabeth ever mentioned any activities? Had she ever asked her mother what she did with herself all day? Was she still volunteering anywhere now? Meg felt a pang of guilt: had she really meant to shut her mother out of her life? Not that she did a better job of staying in touch with her father, for that matter.

"Of course she does, Meg. She's an intelligent, active woman. What did you expect?"

Meg didn't want to answer his question. "Is she involved in anything that might prompt someone to stalk her? Anything that touches on criminal activity? Even volunteering at a shelter could trigger something, although she might not know it."

He stared at Meg, looking troubled. "I really don't know," he said, in a curiously flat voice.

It made Meg sad that her father had little idea what her mother did all day while he was at his office. She took a deep breath. "Daddy, here's what I think we need to do— the four of us, together. We should sit down and go over everything you and I have touched on here. No polite evasions, no pooh-poohing any ideas. Just lay it all out on the table. It might not lead anywhere. Or something might surprise us. And, much as I hate to say it, we should all be alert to anything else odd that happens, just in case. It could be nothing, but wouldn't you rather be safe than sorry?"

"You're right. So when do you suggest we hold this free-for-all family summit?"

"Sooner rather than later? Tonight, after dinner?"

"Very well. But right now I could use a Scotch."

"First you tell me what happened with the police chief."

"Oh," Phillip said. *Had he hoped she would forget?* Meg wondered. "I thought it was a minor mix-up at the time.

Not long after we'd moved here, while I was still working in New York, the son of one of the police captains—he wasn't chief then—got into some trouble, and since I'd met the officer socially, he came to me and asked if I'd represent the boy. It wasn't a capital crime, but it involved some larceny, so it couldn't just be brushed off with a fine and some community service, and the man wanted it handled openly—he was always a good cop. It would be easy for me to take on, and I thought it would be a goodwill gesture in our new community here."

"So what went wrong? He was convicted? His sentence was extreme?"

"Neither of those. While he was being held in the local jail he was involved in an altercation, through no fault of his own, and as a result he suffered some significant head trauma. He's never fully recovered—he still lives with his parents."

"That's a shame, but why does the now-chief hold this against you?"

"He believed then that I should have acted more quickly to get him released on bail, or into his father's custody. It was a reasonable assumption."

"Was he right?"

"Maybe I could have acted more quickly, or maybe not. But he wanted someone to blame, especially since he still has to deal with his son on a daily basis."

Or maybe he's still nursing some guilt that his son was attacked because he was the son of a police officer? "And how does this affect what happens now?"

"I'm not sure it does. From all I've heard, the chief is a good man, and an honest one. But because of what passed between us, he will go by the letter of the law in any dealings he has with me. Hence the prolonged interrogation after we got home the other night. He did nothing wrong, but he could have cut us some slack and didn't. And that's all there is to that."

"All right. Is the boy functional?"

"You mean, is he competent enough to break in here and nose around? Probably. But I have no reason to believe that he bears any grudge against me personally. I'd like to think he knows that his father would not condone such a thing. And he couldn't have been involved in the Amherst incident. He doesn't drive."

"That would take him out of the picture, wouldn't it? I'm sorry that what happened—what, fifteen years ago?— has created problems for you now. I didn't know."

"Sweetheart, it's never been a problem. I regret what happened, but I seriously doubt it has anything to do with what's happening now. And why on earth should you know? This town has never been your home, and you know it no better than I know your Granford."

Meg decided they'd had as much honesty as they could handle in one sitting. She stood up. "As I said, I promised Mother I'd make dinner, and I've left her alone with Seth— or vice versa—for too long. You coming down for that Scotch?"

"Are you worried that Seth will spill all your deepest, darkest secrets to your mother?" her father said, with a more honest smile, as he stood up.

"If he can find any, he's welcome to share them." Meg had the feeling that she knew far more about Seth than her parents had ever known about each other. Was it a generational thing? Or were they just very different people? Seth was both intelligent and a true "people person." He got along well with everyone, but he wasn't a pushover for anyone. She had always been more reserved—more like her mother—but she was working on that. And things for her had changed very quickly—she'd moved to Granford less than two years earlier, and here she was now, a married farmer running a business. Nothing she had ever anticipated.

"Did you ever expect to have a farmer for a daughter, Daddy?"

"I always expected you to be good at whatever you chose to do, sweetheart. If you're happy, then your mother and I are. And we like your young man. I'm not just saying that. I'm glad you waited."

"I kind of like him, too, Daddy."

11

Downstairs Phillip made a beeline for the cabinet in the dining room where the liquor had been kept as long as Meg could remember. Meg joined her mother and Seth in the kitchen, and Phillip entered a moment later holding a bottle that Meg recognized as a single-malt Scotch she had never tasted—too expensive. "Anybody want to join me?" he asked, holding up the bottle.

"A small one," Seth said, surprising Meg—he seldom drank hard liquor. Maybe it was a guy thing.

"Meg," Elizabeth said, "I have a bottle of white wine in the refrigerator. Would you prefer that?"

"That sounds nice."

Phillip gave Meg a challenging look and said, "Our daughter here thinks we should have a family conference about what may or may not have been happening here. And in Amherst."

"Daddy!" Meg protested. "I only said that we should talk about it and pool any information we might have. It may all turn out to be the product of our overactive imaginations."

"Meg, Enrique died," her mother reminded her gently.

Meg turned to her quickly. "I know that, Mother, and I take that seriously, believe me. But we need to determine if this family is involved somehow. If we decide we had nothing to do with it, we'll let the police go on about their business. Is that fair?"

There followed a complicated exchange of glances. Phillip and Elizabeth made some wordless communication, but Meg was pretty sure that there were things that neither had shared with the other. Seth cocked an eyebrow at Meg, but she tried to reassure him without saying anything, which proved to be challenging. Finally she said, "Just sit, everyone, will you? I was going to suggest doing this after dinner, but we may all be too wiped out by then to think straight. I said I'd make dinner, and I'd like to have a little time to do that, so maybe we can get this out of the way first?"

Elizabeth fetched two wineglasses and the bottle from the refrigerator and set them on the table before taking a seat in the nook in the kitchen. Phillip found two highball glasses and added Scotch to them—more to one glass than the other. "Seth, if you haven't tried this before, I recommend adding just a splash of water—it brings out the subtleties of the flavor. Never ice."

Seth tolerated Phillip's condescension with grace. "Duly noted. I'll let you add the right amount."

Meg and Elizabeth waited while Phillip added what he believed was just the right amount of water, then returned to find their own seats. Meg was vaguely amused that they'd chosen to settle round what was probably the smallest table in the house, but at least it forced them into close contact. She tried to retrieve a Sherlock Holmes quote about gathering everyone together, but gave up. "Thank you. Mother, Daddy, I've talked to both of you about what happened when you arrived home, and Daddy has filled me in on the issues regarding the police chief, so I think we're all at a common starting point. Agreed?"

Nods all around. Her father seemed to be enjoying the show Meg was putting on, and she hoped he realized that she was serious. His expertise lay in white-collar crime; she was pretty sure she knew more of the gritty details of murder investigations. She took a sip of wine and cleared her throat. "I think we all agree that you had no problems with Enrique Gonzalez? That he was an occasional employee and you were on polite terms and nothing more?"

"That about covers it," Phillip said. "He seemed to be a good and decent man, but we were never close in any sense." Elizabeth nodded her agreement.

"So let's assume he was an unintended victim," Meg continued, "who happened to be in the wrong place at the wrong time. Daddy, was it your impression that the police agreed with that?"

"I think it's fair to say that. They asked a lot of questions, and we answered them."

"Did they talk to you together?" Meg asked her parents.

"At first, and then separately. As I told you, all by the book. I assume they were recording our conversations—

doesn't everyone these days? They were polite and business-like. There was no bullying, no empty threats. Would you agree, Elizabeth?"

"I think they were fair and impersonal. I might have seen one or another officer around town here, but I'd never had a conversation with any of them, so we didn't know each other. There were no unexpected questions. Have you turned over our trip receipts, Phillip, dear?"

"I did—I e-mailed them copies earlier today."

"Did you get a police report on the car, Daddy?" Meg asked.

"Not yet. I did get the mechanic's bill"—Phillip grimaced—"but that doesn't address cause, just the damage. Let me note for the record that the car is one renowned for its quality of workmanship, so it took some effort to do as much harm as was inflicted."

"Which suggests it was not a careless sideswipe in the dark," Seth commented, speaking for the first time.

Phillip turned to him and nodded. "Precisely. Unless someone in that parking lot had a very heavy foot."

"Have you ever represented anyone from that part of Massachusetts?" Seth asked.

"Not that I can recall. But when you've been practicing as long as I have, you tend to forget some of those smaller details. I have never appeared in court in that part of Massachusetts, if that's any help. Of course I've participated in the Boston area, if not lately."

"So, to the best of your shared knowledge, there is no one in the western part of Massachusetts who holds any kind of grudge against either of you?" Meg asked.

Phillip and Elizabeth shared another glance, and then each of them shook their head no.

"Then let's set that end of things aside for now. What about here in New Jersey?"

"You're asking if there's anyone here who would want to do me harm?" Phillip asked. When Meg nodded he said, "Of course over the years I've antagonized some people. I don't win every case, you know. In fact, many of my cases never go to trial—we often settle out of court. Is there anyone who was angry enough about the outcome to pursue me personally? Not that I can think of."

A thought struck Meg. "Has anything like this happened before? Not murder, of course, but minor annoyances, small harassments?"

Elizabeth chose to answer that question. "I can't speak for Phillip's workplace, but I don't recall anything like that here at home. Beyond the occasional Mischief Night non-sense around Halloween, and most of that has been inno-cent enough—eggs and toilet paper, that sort of thing. No serious damage."

"You've lived here, what, fifteen years?" Meg asked.

"About that," Elizabeth agreed.

"What about before that, when you were still in Madi-son?" Meg pressed.

"That's ancient history," Phillip said firmly. "And I think you would have been aware of any incidents that took place there—you were still living at home."

"True, although you might have tried to shield me from them," Meg said, "and I probably wasn't paying attention." She recalled her childhood and youth as both typical and idyllic, unsullied by nasty things like vandalism. But maybe her parents had tried to cushion her from unpleasantness— or maybe she'd just been oblivious. Something she should reexamine now.

"Meg, what are you getting at?" Seth asked.

"I'm trying to identify anyone who might have any reason to harm either of my parents. Don't lawyers always make enemies, Daddy?"

"Of course, but those enemies seldom resort to violence, and certainly not carefully considered revenge, long after the original trial."

Meg checked the time on the kitchen clock. "If we want to eat dinner at a decent hour, I should start cooking. I think we've defined the problem here, and I want you two to think about anything that stands out in the past few years. Or if you've ever seen anyone else with Enrique—did he always work alone?"

"It would be a relief if we could lay this at an outsider's feet," Phillip admitted.

Meg nodded her encouragement. "So think about it, both of you," she repeated. "Did the police say they would want to talk to you again?"

Phillip shook his head. "We told them everything we know. If they've verified our alibis, they have no reason to call us back. We couldn't possibly be suspects in Enrique's killing."

"They could think you have enough money to hire someone to kill him," Meg tossed out.

"Darling, that's ridiculous!" Elizabeth said. "Why would we want to do that?"

"Maybe he was smuggling drugs in the potted plants he brought and using your address as a distribution point. Maybe he was the son of a Colombian drug lord. Maybe he was an undercover FBI agent keeping an eye on you."

Phillip smiled. "You are kidding, aren't you, Meg?"

"I don't know. Am I?"

Her father sat up straighter in his seat. "Meg, while I can't say we are perfect, I'd like to think your mother and I have led relatively blameless lives. We have engaged in no criminal activity. We have harmed no one, beyond the usual range of human interactions. We are decent people. But I understand why you're asking these questions." He stood up. "Elizabeth, why don't we adjourn to the living room and let Meg and Seth deal with dinner?"

"Certainly. Meg, will you be able to find what you need?"

"Mother, I think I can manage. Shoo, you two."

After a final uncertain glance at her daughter, Elizabeth followed Phillip out of the kitchen. When they were out of hearing range, Seth said, "Meg, what was that about?"

"You have a problem with it?" Meg said, more harshly than she had intended.

"No. They're your parents, and you're trying to help. Not that they've asked for help."

"Of course they haven't—I'm their little girl. And I think they're both very good at denial."

"You think they're hiding something? One or the other?"

"Not necessarily." Although Elizabeth had handed her a few surprises on her last visit to Granford, Meg recalled. "I think they want to see themselves as nice people. Dirty things like crime don't happen to nice people. If they could wish dead Enrique away, they would."

"But they can't, obviously," Seth said. "Still, Meg, your father is an accomplished lawyer. Can't he handle this on his own?"

"Probably. Why do *you* think I'm doing this?"

He came closer and pulled her into his arms. "Because you want to help. Because they're your parents. Maybe you're the one who doesn't want to see any blot on their lives, so you can hold on to your image of a perfect childhood."

Meg snorted. "Perfect? Daddy was at work for most of my young life. Mother devoted a lot of energy to keeping him happy. I just kept my head down and hoped they'd ignore me and let me go on with my own life."

"Sounds a touch defensive to me. Your father doesn't seem like a bad guy."

"He's not. But he's a dinosaur, a throwback. He believed that the man should rule the roost, and the woman was there to make things easier for him. I'm glad he acknowledges that Mother has a brain in her head, but I wonder how long it took for that to sink in."

"Meg, you sound angry," Seth said.

"Well, maybe I am!" she snapped. "Not at you. But this was supposed to be our honeymoon—*our* time. I'd love to think I could swoop in and figure this out in a day and hand them the solution with bows on it and be done with it."

"Well, we only arrived after lunch today. You've still got time."

Meg's anger evaporated as quickly as it had come. She leaned her head on Seth's chest. "Seth, I don't want us to end up like them. There's a kind of distance between them, and that's kind of how I was raised. They did everything right as parents—they were thoughtful and responsible, and they followed the Good Parent playbook. But I'm trying to remember when we had fun—just honest, spontaneous fun. And that's what I mean about being oblivious: they could have angered someone without even noticing, because they don't really connect well with other people."

"And that's come back to bite them now? Why?"

"I don't know, because I don't know who or why, and

maybe they don't know, either. Or maybe I'm making this whole thing up in my head as a way to vent my own frustrations. Please tell me you won't think of me as your personal maidservant, and that you'll share problems with me and that you'll treat me like an equal partner?"

"Do you really have to ask?"

"No," she said into his chest. "Call it post-wedding jitters. We didn't have time for pre-wedding jitters."

They stood like that for a while, just leaning against each other, until they were interrupted by Elizabeth's voice. "I didn't hear much cooking noise, so I thought I'd check if you two were all right. It looks like you're just fine."

Meg peeled herself away from Seth and smiled at her mother. "We are. And we're going to make you fine, too. But first we're going to make dinner."

12

Dinner was some kind of chicken thing that Meg improvised, with onions and random vegetables and whatever spices she could find, her mind elsewhere. No one complained. It was an odd meal, Meg reflected, watching her family eat. Back in the day there had been a rule in the household that one did not discuss anything at the dinner table that might upset one's digestion. Murder would certainly be on that list, not that it had ever been a remote possibility. At some point the conversation landed on Seth's occupation as a safe topic.

"You took over your father's business, didn't you, Seth?" Meg's father fired the first shot across the bow.

"I did. He was a plumber, but he passed away at a fairly young age. I was just finishing college, but somebody had to pay the bills, so I stepped up."

Meg thought about speaking out in defense of plumbers—a noble and useful profession—but decided to let Seth fight his own battles. He seemed comfortable enough, and she knew that whatever issues he might have had with his occupation, he had long since come to terms with them.

"But now I'm getting more involved with home restoration," he went on, "which seems a natural segue from plumbing. I know a lot about the innards of older construction, you might say."

"And how do you differentiate between restoration and renovation?" Phillip asked.

"It's a sliding scale, but I try to maintain or replicate as much of the original structure and detail of a building as possible," Seth told him. "If someone comes to me and asks me to gut the interior so they can go with Scandinavian Modern, I turn them down politely. I love historic buildings, even what goes on behind the walls. I hate to see them destroyed or muddled up."

"Do you have a cutoff date for your definition of historic?"

"Probably World War Two. Construction styles and materials changed significantly after the war, and I'm simply less interested in more modern buildings. But as you have probably noticed, there are plenty of older buildings in Granford and the surrounding area that need work, and plenty of people who respect the structure but have no idea how to repair or maintain it."

"What about this house?" Elizabeth asked suddenly.

"I think it's representative of an era. Good quality, handsome proportions."

"And rather too large for the two of us," Elizabeth said. Phillip shot her a glance.

"Are you thinking of moving?" Meg asked.

"Let's say it's on the horizon," Phillip hurried to say.

"Along with retirement?" Meg said.

Phillip smiled. "Meg, my dear, I'm not sure what I would do with myself if I retired. I haven't done enough interesting things in my life to consider writing a memoir. I don't like golf, and I have no hobbies to speak of. Your mother and I play bridge with some other couples on occasion, but I wouldn't miss it if we stopped."

"Phillip!" Elizabeth said. "You never told me you didn't like bridge!"

"I don't dislike it, but it's not a consuming passion. It is nice to socialize with our friends, and it's lovely to spend time with you." He smiled at his wife.

Nice save, Daddy, Meg thought.

Phillip turned to Meg. "What about you? Do you see yourself running an orchard in ten or twenty years?"

Meg glanced briefly at Seth, who pointedly ignored her, examining the pattern on his dinner plate. "It's been such a hectic couple of years that I haven't given it any real thought. We did plant some new trees last year—sort of a joint venture, before we were even talking about marriage. They won't produce a significant crop for a while yet. So I guess you could say I've looked that far ahead. In some ways I still feel like the new kid on the block—I'm still learning. And there is a lot to learn, believe me, from both the agricultural side and the business side. I will say that I like Granford and that part of the state. Maybe Seth and I could open a detective agency."

That got Seth's attention. "Uh, what?"

"Just kidding. Well, maybe in winter, when things are slow for both of us. We could call it *Winter Crimes.* Daddy, you could be our legal consultant, as needed."

"At what billable rate?" he asked, his eyes twinkling.

"We'll negotiate."

"There's cake for dessert," Elizabeth announced. "Store bought, I'm afraid, but the market has a good bakery. Anyone for coffee?"

"Please," Meg said. "I'd like us to have our wits about us."

"Why?" Phillip asked.

"Because we aren't finished with what we were talking about earlier."

Seth sent her a warning glance, then stood and began collecting the plates to take to the kitchen.

"Oh, sweetheart, can't we give it a rest? We've told you everything we know," her mother said.

Meg could understand her mother's reluctance, but waiting would benefit no one. "No. The longer we wait, the less clear details are in anyone's mind. I would concede that maybe your subconscious would kick something to the front of your brain if you gave it a rest overnight, but there are other things to talk about."

Elizabeth sighed, and picked up more plates. "I'll go and make sure Seth is all right, and start the coffee."

"You don't let go, do you, Meg?" Phillip said.

Was he pleased or annoyed? "I'd like to resolve this so Seth and I can go back to enjoying ourselves," Meg told him.

"We never asked you two to do this, you know." Phillip sounded a bit testy.

"I know that. I want to. And four minds are better than two." And Meg wasn't sure the original two had planned to give the problem any thought at all. And at the moment all four minds around the table had been influenced by the consumption of some amount of alcohol. Would that loosen things up?

Elizabeth and Seth returned, with Seth carrying a tray laden with cake, plates, forks, and cups. Elizabeth carried the coffeepot.

Meg waited until everyone was seated again before asking, "Are we all on board with this?"

This time Phillip and Elizabeth exchanged glances of their own, and Phillip shrugged. "If this doesn't produce anything useful, no harm, no foul. Right?"

"Of course. But please be honest. Now, Daddy, tell me all about the clients who have lost cases with you." And Meg sat back and waited.

As Meg could have predicted, Phillip sputtered, "I can't discuss my clients. You know that."

"All right, don't name names. Would you like to play Twenty Questions?"

"What on earth do you mean?"

"I ask a question that requires only a yes or no answer. See? No names."

"Give me an example," Phillip said.

"Have you ever lost a case?"

"Yes."

"Have you lost more than ten cases?"

"Over what time period?"

"Questions aren't usually allowed, but you're new at this. Ever, in your legal career."

"Lost when I was the lead attorney, or lost as part of a team?"

"Daddy, you're complicating things. To make this quicker, let's say lost when you had primary responsibility for the client's welfare."

"Yes, more than ten, then."

"More than a hundred?"

Phillip looked up at the ceiling, presumably counting. Finally he said, "No."

"Did any of those clients threaten you in any way? Physically? Financially?"

"Yes, of course."

That answer surprised Meg. "Do you know where those who threatened you can be found, at this time?"

"No, not all of them."

"Could you find them, if you had to?"

"Probably. Is that a yes answer?"

"Close enough. Are there any in particular that concern you?"

"They hadn't, before all this started this week."

"Have you changed your mind about them?"

"Can I defer that question? Is there such a thing as a 'pass' response?"

"I'll make an exception for you, Daddy. Were any of the cases you lost capital offenses?"

"A few."

"Did the crimes involve violence?"

"In some cases, yes. Not all. And most of those are well in the past."

"Were these clients men or women?"

"That's not a yes-no question, but I'll answer anyway. Primarily men. I've had very few women as clients."

Meg tucked that fact away for future consideration. She tried to figure out what other questions would be helpful. "Have you done any pro bono work?"

"On occasion, yes."

"Were any of those clients among the ones you might take a harder look at now?"

Phillip looked exasperated. "Meg, I understand what

you're doing, but this is not simple. Most of the answers I've given you refer to my earlier days as an attorney, not my current activities. I was a court-appointed attorney for a number of cases. Some of those clients were . . . I'm not sure how to say this without sounding offensive. Black, poor, uneducated, angry? Honestly I cannot recall if any of those clients felt I had let them down and vowed to get back at me for it. I'd have to check my records. And they were all years ago."

"Did the police ask you any of these questions?"

"No."

Meg digested that for a moment. To her it looked as though the police had made up their minds early on that Enrique had interrupted a break-in and paid the price. Her parents were not currently suspects, if they had ever been, although the police chief might have given them a hard time for personal reasons. She looked around at their small circle. Her mother appeared to be dozing off. Seth just looked tired. Neither had said a word.

"Do either of you have anything to add?"

"What?" her mother said, startled out of her doze. "No, dear. I think you're doing a good job. Have you found out what you wanted?"

"Some of it, Mother. Seth? Anything from you?"

"Did any of your clients include members of the Mafia?" Seth spoke up.

Meg struggled to hide a smile. Was Seth serious? Was the first thing that occurred to him the New Jersey Mafia?

She was surprised when her father responded seriously. "What do you know of them, Seth?"

"Only what I've read, and that's not much. Are they still active around here?"

"Perhaps not as much as they once were, but they're still a force to be reckoned with."

"Did you ever represent a known member of that group?" Seth asked.

"Possibly. If so, it was nothing we ever discussed openly. We were careful to stick to terms like 'my business' and 'my colleagues.' An early version of 'don't ask, don't tell.'"

This was something she'd never known about, and she had trouble picturing her staid father dealing with the Mob. But, she had to admit, they were businessmen in their own way. "More than one case?" Meg asked.

"Only one that stands out in my memory," Phillip told her.

"What was the case about?"

"If I recall correctly, it was about a business transaction that went awry. I handle mainly contract law, so that's why this person would have come to me. I believe we prevailed, and as far as I know the two sides settled without further dispute."

"Are both parties still alive?" Seth asked.

"Seth, I really don't know. I don't follow those things anymore, not that I ever did to any great extent. I can't answer yea or nay. Can we wrap this up, Meg? We can always pick it up again tomorrow, if you still have questions."

"Don't you have to be at work?"

"I freed up a couple extra days when I learned that you might visit—one of the perks of working for yourself, as long as there aren't plants or animals depending on you. I am at your disposal."

"Meg, I think taking a break is a good idea," Seth said.

She looked more carefully at him and felt dismayed. He'd gotten up at dawn to drive here, and he'd sat patiently while she'd badgered her mother and father with questions about a crime or crimes that might not even exist, ignoring him. He was a remarkably patient man. Great spouse she was turning out to be. "Of course we can."

"Perhaps tomorrow you could take Seth to Madison, show him where you grew up?" her mother suggested.

Was Elizabeth trying to get them out of the house? Or just break up the inquisition? Either way, it was a reasonable idea. "Sure. That is, if you're interested, Seth."

"I'd enjoy that. You said it's not too far away?"

"It's a half-hour drive. Well, then, it's a plan." She stood up. "Mother, Daddy, I'm sorry if you feel like I've put you through the wringer. I really would like to tie this up and make sure you're in the clear."

"We know, dear," her mother said. She stood quickly, then gave Meg a hug. "I think it's safe to say that this problem will still be here in the morning. Good night, you two."

Meg and Seth carried the dishes to the kitchen and cleaned up after Meg's parents had vanished. Seth washed while Meg dried them. "Am I going about this all wrong, Seth?" she asked, focusing on her dish towel.

Seth didn't look at her. "I'm not sure why you're doing it at all."

"You don't think there's something fishy here?"

"Maybe, but I'm not sure it's our business."

"I guess I feel it became our business if it stretches to Amherst."

"I heard that 'if,' Meg. There's no evidence it's connected to what happened here. Why can't you accept it as an unpleasant coincidence?"

"I don't know. I'm sorry—I'm not being fair to you, I know. This isn't the way either of us planned to use this time."

Seth wiped out the sink and set down the sponge before turning to Meg. "Well, the first part was nice, and it's not over yet. And you're going to show me where little Meg lived in the morning. Do you still know anyone there?"

"Not a soul, as far as I know."

"So it won't be a long trip. Are you ready to go up?"

"Yes. Shoot, I never gave you the grand tour. Did you find the room we're staying in?"

"Yes, because I took our luggage up a while ago. It's kind of hard to get lost in a house, you know."

"I guess you're right. Then let us retire and you can look forward to a stroll through my childhood haunts, which aren't anywhere near as pretty as Granford."

"I'll look forward to it."

13

 "This room is ridiculously big for a bedroom," Meg said the next morning, after making sure Seth's eyes were open.

"My guess would be that it started as two rooms, with the back end a kind of solarium. Hence all the windows," he told her.

"I hadn't thought of that. I like the window seat, though. Too bad that wouldn't fit in our house."

"I have a feeling that the people who built and lived in our house didn't have time to sit in a sunny corner and read a book. Assuming they knew how to read."

"Of course they did—I've seen some diaries, although they don't come from the original builders. But you're right—I doubt they were exactly literary people, Emily Dickinson notwithstanding."

"Isn't it kind of early in the morning for 'notwith-standing'?"

"I, sir, am a literary person. I'm also hungry. Are you still up for touring my childhood turf?"

"This is your turf, so it's up to you to decide. Are you trying to weasel out of it? Are you hiding something there? May I ask, though, how long you want to devote to this task of sorting out Enrique's death?"

"A fair question, and the answer is, I don't know. I've just started. If we were home I'd talk to Art and ask him to see what he could wangle from the state police, but I don't have that kind of access here. Am I making too much of all this, Seth? I mean, Daddy refuses to worry about it, or so he says, and Mother would really rather forget about it. Do I just wait until the next awful thing happens and then sit back and say, 'I told you so'?"

"Meg, I think you're right to look into it. All I wanted to know was how long this might take. Or to take it from the other side, when would you like to get home again?"

"Give me a day or two, okay? If nothing new emerges, we can head back to Granford over the weekend. Deal?"

"Works for me. I'll grab a shower. Are your folks up, do you think? This house is so solidly built, it's hard to hear other people moving around in it."

"Probably. They were always morning people. I'll go down and see what's what while you shower."

Meg ambled down the stairs, which was not a short walk: down a few steps, across a landing that ran the width of the hall below, and down a longer flight. Then back to the kitchen, where she found her mother sitting in the nook with a mug of coffee in her hand, staring into space. Meg could almost see Elizabeth shake herself when Meg walked in.

"Good morning, darling. Did you sleep well?" Elizabeth said brightly.

"Just fine, although I guess I missed all those animal noises, like the goats. Not to mention a cat jumping on me at random intervals. You?" Meg thought her mother didn't look any more rested than she had the night before.

"It always takes a bit to settle down after coming home from a break," her mother said.

That sounded evasive to Meg, but she didn't feel like pushing. Maybe this was her obsession, and there really was nothing going on. Her personal wild-goose chase. "I wouldn't know—I haven't had a lot of opportunities to find out lately."

"I suppose you don't have much opportunity for vacations, do you, dear?"

"Not hardly. It had never occurred to me that raising any kind of crop could be so demanding. I'm glad I didn't decide to try raising milk cows—that never seems to end."

"So I understand. Are you still planning to go to Madison today?"

Meg helped herself to a cup of coffee and a piece of coffee cake. "Yes. I want Seth to see the place, although I don't feel a lot of connection to it anymore. But I live in the midst of many generations of Chapins, so I guess I want to stake out a little ground of my own. Did you keep in touch with anyone there after you moved?"

"Not really. You know, once you were out of school, and then out of the house, there didn't seem to be any reason to keep in touch with people there. That was before our bridge-playing era, though." Elizabeth summoned up a smile. "I forget—do you play?"

"If I say yes, you promise you won't draft me?"

"Of course."

"Then yes, I played some in college—it seems like bridge playing comes and goes in and out of fashion. But I haven't played since. I haven't heard 'bridge' mentioned at all in Granford. If I have spare time, I'd rather use it exploring local history and our family tree. You haven't been bitten by that bug yet, have you?"

Elizabeth shook her head. "No, I'll leave that to you."

Seth appeared, looking cheerful. "Found you—I followed the smell of coffee. Good morning, Elizabeth. Meg, the shower's all yours."

Meg swallowed the last of her coffee cake. "I'll take my coffee with me. Where's Daddy?"

"He said he wanted to look at something at his office—it's not far," her mother answered. "But you two probably won't be back for lunch?"

"I doubt it," Meg told her. "I'm keeping my options open. I won't be long in the shower."

Fifteen minutes later Meg descended again, ready to face dragons. Maybe showing Seth her former hometown would jolt her out of her worries. She tried to remember the last time she'd been there—it must have been close to a decade now.

In the kitchen, Seth and Elizabeth were both chattering happily, and she realized that Seth was making a deliberate effort to cheer her mother up, which was sweet of him. She watched from the doorway for a moment before they

noticed her. Her mother and her husband. She was struck
once again that she had never thought much about the
day-to-day realities of being married. Had she given up
expecting to marry? When had that happened?

Some movement must have caught her mother's eye,
and Elizabeth smiled. "You look ready to go. You know
the way?"

"I think I can find it, Mother. What are your plans for
the day?"

"Unpacking. Laundry. Checking the mail for bills. All
those exciting things."

"You could come with us if you like. You certainly
knew Madison better than I did."

"No, darling, you go and show it to Seth in your own
way. I'd probably be horrified at the things you noticed
that I didn't. Or the things you never told me about."

"Probably. Seth, why don't I drive, since I know the way?"

"No problem." He fished into his pocket and handed
her the car keys. "Elizabeth, we'll see you later."

"I'll give you a call when we know when we'll be back,
Mother," Meg said. "Maybe we could eat out tonight?"

"That sounds lovely, dear," Elizabeth said absently.
"Now go and enjoy yourselves."

Meg retrieved her purse and coat, and she and Seth went
out the back to the car and got in. "I'm glad it's not
snowing—then we'd be stuck in the house."

"You drive in snow all the time," Seth said.

"Yes, but not in places I only half remember, that may
have changed anyway." She started up the car and rolled
slowly backward down the driveway, then pulled out into
the street. "Any overnight epiphanies?"

Seth turned to look at her. "Even though I know what

'epiphany' means, I don't think anything like that popped up overnight. Not even a germ of an idea. I was tired."

"I didn't do any better. I still think Mother looks worried, if not about this, then about something."

"I would agree with that. Any health problems for either one of them?"

"Not that they've shared with me. Thank you so much for giving me something else to worry about."

"That wasn't my intention. But at least you can ask. Wouldn't it be better to know than to worry?"

"I think I'll embroider that saying on a sampler—just as soon as I learn to embroider. In my spare time."

The trip to Madison was indeed short, and there was little traffic. As they approached the town center, Meg launched into an abbreviated summary. "Madison, formerly known as Bottle Hill after a famous—or infamous—tavern whose site we are about to pass. Founded in seventeen-I-don't-know-what. Population about fifteen thousand, and that's been holding steady for years. One main street, one big intersection with a traffic light. Commuter rail line to the City, which always means New York. Borough hall is a pale pink marble pile built by the local lords of the manor, the Dodge family, who also built the train station and gave the land for the high school. The town next door to the school is called Florham Park in honor of Florence and Hamilton Dodge."

"Pink?" was Seth's only comment.

"It's marble, but it really does have a pinkish cast, especially when it's wet. The police department is housed there, and there are a couple of holding cells in the basement—some friends and I got brave in high school and asked to take the tour. If I recall correctly, the police showed us how to take fingerprints, back when they still used ink. There was a nice old library building next to the tracks, a little farther down, but it's a museum now—there's a newer library at the other end of town, but that dates from after my time here. One elementary school, one middle school in what started out as the high school, and one high school."

"Did you like growing up here? Because that's not exactly a warm and fuzzy description."

"I guess I did. It was a nice town—safe, clean, accessible. I had friends. I did well in school, played on the girls' sports teams, took art and guitar lessons for a while."

"But you're not smiling as though you remember all that fondly."

Meg didn't answer Seth's question as she went through the town center and then took the turn toward the high school. "Anthony Wayne was billeted in a house along here during the Revolutionary War. That was when Washington was staying in a grander house over in Morristown." She arrived at the high school and pulled into the deep semicircular driveway that led from the street down to the front entrance, then back to the street. There was a parking lot past the school building, overlooking the football field, and Meg pulled in there and parked. She shut off the engine and turned to Seth.

"Was I happy here? I don't know. I was one of the invisible kids, but there was a nice group of us. I went through the usual teenage angst, but mostly I remember wanting to get out, go to college, and get on with my life. I never dated. I had a couple of close friends—what I guess you'd call 'BFFs' today—but those friendships didn't last. I made new friends in college, and after."

"Tell me, Meg, did you ever have a screaming, knock-down battle with your parents, singly or together?"

Meg looked down her nose at him, which was a challenge since he was taller than she was. "The Coreys do not scream. Neither do they cry. Neither do they air their dirty laundry in public. Stiff upper lip and all that. So the short answer is no."

"Did you feel that when you were growing up here? That there were things you couldn't say or do?"

Meg shrugged. "Every family is different. This was what I knew. If I'd had siblings things might have been different. I knew they both loved me, but they had trouble showing it." She turned away from Seth and looked out at the football field, now brown and barren. She'd gone to every game the last two years of school. So had a lot of the town. "Is that what this is about? My difficulties in showing affection? Or accepting that somebody loves me?"

"Meg, I didn't mean to open a huge can of worms. You know my family history, and it wasn't picture book, either. I never got along with my father, and he resented that I ended up going to what he called a fancy-schmancy college, even if he never had to pay out a dime for it. I hated the way he treated my mother, and I hated the way she let him. My brother, Stephen, you know about. I think Rachel turned out the most normal of all of us. But we did have some pretty blazing battles, although my mother tried to stay out of them."

"So sound and fury equals caring in your book?"

"Maybe. It shows that you care enough about something to fight for it. Assuming, of course, that you're not just a bully."

"Would you like to have a fight and see how it goes?" Meg asked, not sure if she was serious.

"No, not really. Certainly not here and now. Meg, I love you. I hope you know that."

"I do, Seth." She reached over and pulled him close and kissed him, a kiss that went on for a while. When she came up for air she said, "I never thought I'd be necking in my high school parking lot. Chalk up another first." Then she sobered. "Are you saying that I'm trying to prove something to my parents now? Or make them pay attention to me?"

Seth shook his head. "No, because the body of Enrique Gonzalez is undeniably real. Maybe it is irrelevant to your family. Maybe not. You asked the right questions, and to me it looked like they didn't like those questions." He hesitated for a moment before going on. "But having listened to and talked with your parents over the past day, I think there is something going on that either they don't acknowledge or they don't want to think about. Having said that, I don't know that it's up to us to fix that. Leave it to them and to the police."

"The murder and the car event coming so close together does trouble me, and I'd like to be sure it really is just a coincidence. And if something happened to either of them, I'd feel awful."

"I understand that, and I agree that you need to keep trying, at least up to a point." He stopped for a moment, then said, "I'm hungry. Does this town of yours offer anything like lunch?"

So Seth is changing the subject, Meg thought, *but he's probably right to do it.* "Last time I looked, the pizza joint in the center had morphed into a Japanese-French fusion place, which tells you something. But I'm sure we can find some kind of food."

"Then let's go park in town and explore, And then you can show me your old house."

"Deal." Meg started the engine and pulled out of the parking lot, away from her old alma mater. "Hail, Madison High," ran the opening of the school song. But for now, hail and farewell.

14

Parking in the center of town had not improved since Meg's time. There were two choices: one was a narrow slice that ran between the stores on the main street and the railroad tracks behind, accessed through narrow single-lane gaps at either end; the other was on the opposite side of the main street, and it was larger. Meg opted for the smaller one, since it was closer to the things she remembered and wanted to share with Seth. Luckily there were few occupants at the moment, so Meg had no trouble finding a space.

They climbed out of the car and wrapped their scarves more firmly around their necks. "Now where?" Seth asked.

"Let's just go over to the main street and stroll, and see what's survived since my day. I don't know what stores are here anymore, but people have to eat, so I assume there are restaurants. We can walk out the way we drove in, so you can admire the former library." She held out her hand, and Seth took it. They paused on the sidewalk for a minute to look at the nineteenth-century building that had once housed the library, although Meg couldn't remember using it. Then they turned right and walked around the corner and paused again so Meg could explain the layout. "This is—wait for it—Main Street. There is one significant cross street, which goes under the railroad tracks. That's down at the far end of this block. There used to be a decent restaurant on the block beyond that, which I think was an old inn. The cool kids used to hang out at the Friendly's down a mile or so farther. I went in there once with a couple of friends, and we didn't receive what I would call a warm welcome."

"Teenagers are pretty tribal. If you're an outsider, they'll eat you."

"Exactly." Walking slowly down the main street, Meg commented about what was there now and what had been there when she lived in the town. She hadn't spent time in Madison for over fifteen years, and there had been quite a few changes. Mostly for the better: there were more restaurants, and they looked—and smelled—good. Or maybe she was just hungry. They reached the single big intersection and Meg pointed toward the underpass. "The train station is over there toward the left, and across the street from it is town hall. Do you feel a burning need to see either of those?"

"I think I can live without them. Do we walk back on the other side of Main Street?"

"Sure. And I think I remember a fair restaurant there."

They crossed at the corner and located the restaurant

Meg could recall in the middle of the next block. It was still early for lunch, but Meg was happy to see a good range of food choices. Seth was equally happy to see a variety of local craft beers. "I'm not going to be driving, am I?" he asked plaintively.

"No, go ahead and sample. I'll settle for coffee."

Once they were seated and had ordered, Meg asked, "So, what do you think?"

Seth took a swallow of his beer. "Nice town. Not so different from Granford, but more tightly packed. I'm guessing there's more money here. More stores, obviously, and not low-end chains."

"And you'd be right. I haven't looked at property values, but I'd bet a lot of the houses up the hill would be worth seven figures."

Seth whistled. "I guess you can't come home again."

"I never wanted to," Meg told him.

Their food arrived and they devoted appropriate attention to it. Meg didn't think the town had been as much of a gourmet haven when she lived in town, not that she had explored many places as a teenager, but things were definitely looking up. When the food had disappeared, Seth said, "Where to next?"

"You haven't seen enough?"

"You haven't shown me your old house."

"If you insist."

They started walking back to the parking lot, but Meg stopped suddenly in front of one store. "I can't believe this is still open," she said. "Joe's Sporting Goods. This is where all the teams at the high school got their stuff. I had a hockey stick that came from here. Mind if we go in?"

"Go right ahead," Seth said, opening the door for her.

Meg walked toward the center of the stop and halted. "It hasn't changed. It's like a time warp."

"Meg? Meg Corey?" A voice called out from behind the counter at the far side.

Meg turned to see a man of her own age approaching. "Joe? Wow, I'm amazed you remember me. We didn't exactly hang out with the same people."

Joe waved a dismissive hand. "Hey, you were one of the brainiacs. There weren't a lot of them, so you were easy to remember. What goes on in your life?"

"Well, I just got married," she said, belatedly reminding herself that Seth was standing behind her. "This is my husband, Seth Chapin. We live in Massachusetts now. Seth, this is Joe Caffarelli—we went to school together."

"Good to meet you, Seth," Joe said, in a salesman voice. "What do you do?"

"I have a small home-renovation business, mostly historical restorations."

Joe nodded. "Cool." Then he lost interest; Seth was not about to buy a load of sports equipment.

"You own this place, Joe?" Meg asked.

"My father used to—he was the Joe on the sign. You probably didn't know him. He turned it over to me a coupla years ago so he could retire to Florida and fish."

"You married?"

"Sure am. You remember Linda Giordano? We got married a year after graduation. Three kids, all boys. You got kids?"

"Wow, three kids! No to the kids for us—we only got married last week."

"Hey, you guys took your time. Better get started. Your father still practicing law?"

"He is," Meg said nodding. "You've got quite a memory. He has his own practice now, and he and my mother live in Montclair. Why on earth do you remember him?"

"My dad was one of his clients, years back. I was cleaning out the basement just last week and stumbled over the file. Talk about coincidence! Here you are, just a few days later."

"I don't think my father ever mentioned him, but he never talked about his work at home, or maybe I tuned him out. What was that all about?"

Joe shrugged. "I only looked at it long enough to figure out what it was. I think Dad wanted to sue one of his vendors for not delivering, and for inflated billing, and your father helped him out."

"So it all worked out for your father?"

Joe nodded. "Sure did. Like you see, the business is still here."

"I'll tell my father you remembered him, Joe."

"Ah, don't bother. It's been a long time, and I'm sure he's handled plenty of cases since. Good to see you again, Meg. If you ever need any sports equipment, you better think of me. Oh, what is it you do?"

"I run an apple orchard."

That stopped Joe cold for a couple of beats. "Wow! I never would have expected that—Meg Corey, a farmer. I knew you went off to college somewhere else. You like what you're doing?"

"I do, actually. I was as surprised as you are, Joe. Nice talking with you."

When they were outside, Seth said, "Did you know him well?"

"Vaguely. Of course, our class wasn't all that big, so it wasn't hard. As I recall, he was an okay guy. Played on some sports teams, although I can't tell you which ones, since the only games I went to were football. I never did see a high school basketball game."

They retrieved the car, and Meg drove the few miles to the house she had grown up in. "As you can see, it's not exactly close to the center of town. This is 'The Hill,' for obvious reasons. The house itself is on a cul-de-sac, and when I lived there, there were plenty of young kids and very few cars, so it was safe. This is it." Meg pulled up to the curb on the far side of the street and stared. "I think they've done some 'improving'"—Meg made air quotes—"since I lived here, mostly in the direction of pretentious. I don't remember it looking like this."

"You mean all the pillars and stuff? I'd agree. I think the core house was built in the 1940s. Seems nice enough. What's your single favorite memory from this place?"

"What is this, a quiz?" Meg thought for a moment, rifling through her memories. Finally she said, "When I was about four, a bird got into the house and was flying around the living room running into things—it couldn't find a way out. The room had a plate-glass picture window overlooking the back lawn and the bird kept flying at it, thinking it could get through. My father trapped it against the window with a hat—a fedora, I think—and took it outside and released it. I thought that was very heroic."

"Nice."

"It was. I wonder if he remembers it? Oh, and he used to love to plant blue morning glories, over there on an old stump. Where the swimming pool is now. I have no idea why, because he didn't like gardening much. Mother did most of it. It was only that single kind of flower." Meg studied the front of the house one last time. "I could name the kids that lived around the block—we used to go to one another's birthday parties, and go trick-or-treating together, at least for a while. Long time ago." She sighed. "You ready to go? Anything else you want to see? Can I tempt you with Washington's Headquarters in Morristown? Or maybe Fort Nonsense?"

"Are you joking?" Seth asked.

"Nope. Fort Nonsense was an earthworks built in 1777 by Washington's order. It was a good vantage point, and it may have been used for signal fires. And there's nothing much to see there now except the view."

"Will you be mortally offended if I pass on that?" Seth said.

"Of course not. But don't say I didn't offer you up the finest of our local history. You ready to go back to Montclair?"

"I think so." She thought briefly about calling her mother, then decided they'd be home early enough to make any plans for the evening. She was happy to leave, in case there was any afternoon traffic to beat—it had been so long since she had spent any time in the area that she didn't know what the patterns were. And she had seen—and shared— all that she cared to. Madison was her past, and she didn't feel any need to dwell on it. She didn't have any misconceptions about her idyllic youth. It had been fine but not memorable, with few crises and no disasters. She had long since moved on.

Had Seth? Effectively he had never left home. She had

no idea what that would be like, although he seemed content enough. But had he never wanted more?

The ride back to Montclair took less time than Meg had thought, and it was barely three o'clock when they pulled up her parents' driveway and parked. She noticed quickly that her father's car had appeared in the driveway, all visible damage repaired. "That should make Daddy happy," Meg said, pointing. "At least one thing worked out." She turned off the engine, but she found she was in no hurry to get out. "Anything else you want to do or see while we're in the area?" she asked Seth.

"I hate to say it, but I'd really like to leave it. Head home," he said.

"I know. I'm sorry I dragged you into this. I'd like to do that too, so we can get back to our own lives. I'm not usually all that involved in my parents' lives, as no doubt you've noticed by now."

"I'd say that's true. Are you implying I'm too involved with my family?"

She wondered if she had offended him. "No, not at all. You all live in essentially the same community. It would be weird if you weren't involved with them. Besides, I like your family." Except Stephen, of course, but they didn't talk about that, even with Seth's mother, Lydia.

"And you don't like your own?" Seth asked.

"It's not that, exactly. Look, I've had friends whose families were horrible—demanding, domineering, unreasonable, and impossible to please. I have nothing to complain about. We're just not particularly close. That's the way we've always been."

"Well, if I see you shutting me out, I'm going to do something about it."

"I want you to, Seth." Meg leaned against Seth, and he pulled her close.

They sat like that for several minutes, until Meg finally said, "I suppose we should go in. We sort of made vague noises about going out for dinner tonight, as I recall."

"Fine with me. Okay to leave the car here?"

"Sure. If we decide to go out again, we can move it."

Seth climbed out of the car and waited for Meg to join him, then they headed for the back door. *Does anyone use the front door anymore?* Meg wondered. She fished out a key and opened the door, stepping into the back hallway. "Mother?" she called out. She was surprised when her mother didn't answer. She walked through the kitchen toward the main hall. "Mother?" she tried again.

"Maybe she's taking a nap?" Seth suggested.

"She's not a napper. Or I should say, she didn't take naps when I was around, but I guess she is getting older." She decided to check the living room before going upstairs, and was surprised to see her mother sitting on the couch, staring blindly into space. Again. What had happened to her energetic, focused mother? "Mother? Are you all right?"

It took Elizabeth a moment to come back from wherever her mind had wandered, and she turned and looked up at Meg. "No, I don't think so."

Meg quickly sat next to her on the couch. "What's wrong?"

"It's your father," Elizabeth said, then stopped again.

"What—he's sick? Hurt?"

"No, neither. You know he went into his office this morning? He thought he should check in, see if there was anything important he should attend to. He'd given his

secretary time off while he was away, and his partner had
decided to take a vacation too, while he had the chance. It
seems that not many people seek legal help right before
the holidays."

Meg was becoming impatient. "So what's going on?"

"Your father is at the police station. When he arrived
at the office, he found his partner Arthur on the floor there,
unconscious. He wasn't even supposed to be in town."

"Is he all right? Arthur, I mean?" Meg racked her brain
to try to remember if she had ever met Arthur and came
up blank. "Was it a stroke? A heart attack?"

"No, he was attacked. Just like Enrique. By someone
who didn't expect to find him there, apparently."

A string of questions raced through Meg's mind, and
she tried to sort out which were the most important.
"Daddy found him?"

Elizabeth nodded.

"Is Arthur all right?" Meg asked.

"He was still unconscious, the last I heard. Which was
some time ago."

"Why is Daddy at the police station?"

Elizabeth took a deep breath. "When your father found
Arthur, he immediately called 911, and waited until the
paramedics arrived. Then he followed them to the hospital.
Arthur's a widower, so Phillip has as much personal information about Arthur as anyone around here. He was still
at the hospital when the police arrived—apparently the
paramedics had told them that Arthur had some injuries
that were suspicious. Since there was nothing more that
Phillip could do for Arthur, they adjourned to the police
station. He was on the phone with me just as they arrived,

which is the only reason I know anything about what is going on."

"When was this?"

"About eleven."

"And you haven't heard from him since?" Meg asked. Elizabeth shook her head.

"Did he say *when* Arthur was attacked? I mean, yesterday? This morning?"

"Most likely this morning. The, uh, blood was still wet." Elizabeth shuddered. "Like your father, Arthur just couldn't stay away from the office."

Meg sat down and put her arm around her mother. "I'm so sorry. Can I get you something? A cup of tea, maybe?"

Elizabeth leaned slightly against Meg, which for her was a major display of emotion. "That would be nice, dear."

"I'll do it," Seth said, and headed for the kitchen before anyone would say anything.

Meg didn't want to say out loud what she was thinking: that her father might be suspected of attacking his business partner. But why would anyone think that? Still, she knew nothing about Arthur, or about her father's relationship with Arthur, professional or personal. And he had been associated with more than one recent crime, one of those violent. And if Arthur had been attacked this morning, he had no alibi. If she had been a police officer, or perhaps one particular Montclair police officer, she probably would have taken him in as well.

Apparently her mother had arrived at the same conclusions. "Oh, Meg, I'm afraid the police think Phillip attacked Arthur." And then she burst into tears.

Meg fought off her initial shock: she couldn't remember

ever seeing her mother cry, much less loud, sloppy, messy crying like this. She quickly drew Elizabeth closer. She could feel her whole body shaking.

Did Elizabeth believe Phillip had done this? Holding her sobbing mother, she couldn't be sure. Whatever was happening, it wasn't over yet.

15

Elizabeth recovered quickly, pulling back and wiping her eyes with a quick hand. "Goodness, I don't know what came over me. I'm very sorry."

Heaven forbid a Corey should show emotion. "Mother, you don't have to apologize for being upset. Your husband—my father—has just been hauled off to the police station under suspicion of who knows what, and you haven't heard a word from him. You *should* be upset."

"Oh, dear. Do you really think this is serious?"

"I'm afraid I do. Daddy told me that the police chief was going by the book with him, but it has been several hours now, and I know Daddy wouldn't want you to worry if he could prevent it." *Exactly like you're doing.* "I hate to say it, but I think my instinct was right. There's something going on here that we don't know about, and all the events of the past week are probably connected. We just don't know how yet. What can you tell me about Arthur?" Maybe a change to a more neutral topic would calm her mother down.

Elizabeth managed to pull herself together and sat back against the couch cushions. "I can't say that I know him well. He was with the same New York firm as your father, and when Phillip decided to leave and set up his own firm, he invited Arthur Ackerman to join him—they're close in age. I assume that meant that he respected Arthur's abilities, or needed his areas of expertise to complement his own. They've been working together for a few years now, but until they became law partners we'd never socialized."

Funny that the first description Elizabeth gave was of the man's professional abilities, not his personality. "Have you met him?"

"A few times, mostly at legal functions. His wife died a few years back, and he never remarried. He has a couple of children, but they live in other states. I'm sure Phillip had lunch with him now and then, in New York, but I wasn't included. I think Arthur specialized in municipal law—we didn't talk much shop the few times when the three of us were together."

As far as Meg knew, municipal law offered multiple opportunities for legal—or more like not-quite-legal—skulduggery. "Was he honest?"

"Meg! How should I know? I would like to think that Phillip would not have formed a partnership with him if he was not. To the best of my knowledge Arthur had more than enough money, and he didn't seem particularly greedy—he just wanted to keep busy, since there was little else in his life. That is, I admit, a judgment based on very little information."

"Did you like him?"

"What kind of a question is that?" Elizabeth said sharply, and then she slumped and waved her hand. "Never mind—I think I know how your mind works. Yes, I guess I did. He seemed like a kind, thoughtful man—I know, not the type you expect to see dealing with government agencies and their legal concerns. Maybe that was why he was effective: he seemed harmless. But he had a lot of valuable experience to offer."

Meg digested that for a moment. "Did he have any baggage? Anyone from a past job who wasn't happy with him?"

Elizabeth looked bleakly at her. "Meg, as I'm sure you know, your father and I don't talk business. I know what their legal arrangement is, between the two of them. I know what happens to the partnership if one or the other should die unexpectedly—I inherit Phillip's share of the assets of the firm, and Arthur has first right of refusal if I wish to sell that share. But Phillip has not said anything about Arthur's past history, nor would I ask. I realize that's of little help to you now."

Meg was stymied. How could her mother know so little about her own husband's professional life, which occupied the major part of his time and always had? How could she be ignorant of the character of her husband's partner of the last five years? Did she have so little curiosity? Or did she really not care? But for the moment all that was irrelevant. Elizabeth and Phillip had muddled along through more than thirty years of marriage, a marriage that would be judged successful by any outsider, and who was she to argue? She'd been married about three minutes. And she'd probably looked equally ignorant if asked about the details of Seth's business dealings.

Seth wisely chose this moment to step in. "Elizabeth, I think what Meg is trying to get at is, do you know of any reason why someone would attack Arthur?"

Elizabeth turned to him. "No, I don't. That doesn't mean there isn't one."

Seth nodded once. "So this is the harder question: do you think this attack was directed at Phillip rather than Arthur?"

Elizabeth looked startled at that idea, then stopped to consider it. "It could be that whoever did this expected the office to be empty, especially if it was early in the morning. I'm sure Phillip and Arthur made some provision for keeping an eye on the office—maybe someone who manages the building, who would stop by periodically. I didn't have the chance to ask if there were signs of a break-in, although it seems that anyone who wants to can get into anything these days without leaving much evidence. I don't know what state the office was in—messy or untouched. But to give you the narrowest answer to your question, if someone came upon Arthur from behind, unexpectedly, he could probably not distinguish him from Phillip. Both are men of a certain age, with fairly short silver hair, of similar height and build, and partial to nice suits. So if someone did not know them well, he could have lashed out, mistaking one for the other."

"But someone who knew one or the other would not have made that mistake," Seth said, almost to himself. "Did Phillip say he had an appointment this morning?"

Elizabeth shook her head. "No. As I told you, he gets

restless when he's away from his work for too long. You might even call his behavior compulsive. That's always been true. Add to that these other problems, and I think he wanted to get back to something familiar, that he understood—his comfort zone, his office. Just to center himself again. As far as I know he didn't expect to stay long, although he's been known to lose track of time. But the short answer? There was nothing unusual about his going in for a few hours, whether or not he was meeting someone."

"But why isn't he back by now?" Meg asked of no one in particular. Could he still be at the police station?

Her question was answered when she heard the sound of a car pulling into the driveway. Elizabeth was out of her chair before Meg could even react, and she hurried toward the kitchen and the back door. Meg and Seth exchanged glances. "Let's give them a moment," Meg said.

"Of course. At least we know he wasn't arrested."

"Or he was arrested and he's already out on bail," Meg shot back.

"Meg, you don't seriously think your father has anything to do with whatever is going on, do you?"

"Did he commit all or any of these crimes? No, I don't believe that. But is there something that he did that might have pushed someone to do him harm? Something that's been festering for a while, maybe years? That I can believe. Not that Daddy has ever done anything malicious or cruel, not deliberately, but he might have been oblivious enough to not think through the consequences of his perfectly legal actions, and that could be a problem."

"I see your point. So how do we fit the pieces together?" Seth asked. "We've got a fender bender in Amherst, the killing of the handyman, whether or not that was planned, and an attack on his law partner. Three incidents, and three different times and places. How would you connect the dots?"

"I don't know—yet. Let's see what Daddy has to say before we start theorizing. Maybe Arthur is a womanizer and somebody he'd rejected wanted revenge. Maybe he's a secret gambler. Maybe he's fronting for a drug-smuggling gang. Or maybe he woke up and explained everything and we're worrying about nothing." *Unlikely*, Meg thought.

Meg's mother and father came into the living room, arms entwined. Phillip looked exhausted.

"What happened, Daddy?" Meg asked. "How's Arthur?"

"Conscious, thank goodness, although that's of little help. He can't remember much of anything. The doctors said the specific memories might come back, or might not."

"But no lasting damage," Elizabeth was quick to add. "Can we all sit down?"

"Oh, sorry, of course," Meg said.

"Would you like a Scotch, Phillip?" Elizabeth said.

"Thank you, that would be very good." When Elizabeth had left the room, Phillip slumped back on the couch and rubbed his hands over his face. "I don't recognize my own life anymore."

Meg sat down in a chair adjacent to the couch and leaned forward to look at his face. "I know you've just been over all this with the police, but can you tell us what happened? What you saw?"

Elizabeth returned with a crystal highball glass holding an inch of brown liquid. Phillip took it from her with a smile. "Meg wants to review the case," he said. "Again."

"Why am I not surprised?" Elizabeth said as she dropped down beside him and took his hand.

"Look, I'm just trying to help," Meg said hotly. "If you want me to butt out, just say so and we'll be out of here." Seth laid a hand on her shoulder from behind, as if to hold her back. It worked.

Phillip didn't seem to take offense. "Sweetheart, I understand," he said, "and to tell the truth, at this point I'd be happy to have your help. The first two episodes, if you want to call them that, I could ignore as random events, but with what happened to Arthur I find now that I have to agree with your suspicions."

"I'm glad to hear that. Mother has been filling us in on what she knows about Arthur—"

Elizabeth jumped in. "Which was surprisingly little, I'm sad to say. Phillip, you've known the man for years—why don't I know anything about him?"

Meg stopped her—that was a subject for later. "Mother, please—you two can discuss that some other time. Right now, let me cut to the chase. Daddy, do you know of any reason, personal or professional, why anyone would want to do harm to Arthur?"

Phillip shook his head. "He's a good and decent man. I can't think of any reason."

Meg had expected that answer. "Then I assume you know what my next question is: do you think what happened to him was the work of someone who thought he was you?"

"Probably," he admitted. "Let me fill you in on what happened, or at least, what I know. I told your mother that I was going to the office just for a short while—I wanted to make sure there was nothing that required immediate attention, after my absence. I did not tell Arthur I was coming, because he had said he was taking some vacation time

himself, I think to visit one or the other of his children, and
I assumed he was still away. And since we were both going
to be gone, I gave Miriam—that's our secretary—the week
off as well. Our business has not been so busy that a call
can't wait a week. But I thought I'd check in anyway, see
if there were any messages. Mainly I wanted to get away
from this other mess. Obviously that didn't work." He took
a large swallow of his drink.

"So you went to the office bright and early," Meg said.
"Was the door open when you arrived?"

"It wasn't locked, but Arthur probably left it open—he's
often careless that way."

"I've never seen this office. What's it like?"

"Essentially three rooms: a reception area, where Miriam sits, but with seating for perhaps six to eight people,
and an office for Arthur and one for me. Oh, and a file
room, which isn't very large. Many of the files there date
back years, and we've asked Miriam to sort through them
and come up with some sort of plan to archive them."

"Okay, fine," Meg said, suppressing her impatience at
the pace of his story. "So when you walk in, you're in the
reception area with Miriam's desk. What did you see this
morning?"

Phillip shut his eyes briefly, and Meg thought he suddenly looked older than his years. "I saw Arthur lying on
the floor, facedown. There was a little blood on the back
of his head. Red, so fairly fresh. He wasn't moving. So of
course I went to him and checked for a pulse, and when I
found one I called 911 immediately, then waited for them
to arrive. I didn't attempt to move him because I didn't
know the extent of his injuries, and I thought I might do
more harm than good."

Arthur was facing away from the door when he was hit, Meg thought, *and he fell forward.* So he'd been surprised by someone? Someone who hadn't expected to find anyone there? And who had lashed out with whatever was handy? Would the police buy two panicky attacks associated with the same person?

"Could someone have hidden behind the office door and waited to attack?" Meg asked.

"It's possible," Phillip admitted, "although no one went dashing out when I walked in. He must have been long gone."

"Did you see a weapon?"

"I didn't think about that at first. But when the EMTs arrived, I think they had to kick aside one of those heavy brass bookends—you remember those, don't you? The reclining lions?"

"Oh, of course. You've had them in every office of yours that I've visited."

"Those are the ones. One was lying on the floor, the other was where it should be, on a shelf. It never occurred to me to tell the EMTs to handle it carefully, as evidence. My first thought was that Arthur had fallen and hit his head, so I wasn't looking for weapons. For all I know it's still lying on the floor."

"Did the police seal off your office?" Meg asked.

"They may have. I thought I should stay with Arthur, and I haven't been back to check. Nor do I know whether they searched the place."

Meg had a sneaking suspicion that if the police chief felt as much resentment toward her father as he had described, then the cops had probably been all over the so-called crime scene, looking for evidence that could implicate Phillip. She wondered how recently he had handled the lions—she had nicknamed them Castor and Pollux when she was about ten, because they were identical twins—but she wasn't about to bring up the fact that unless Miriam was a manic cleaner his fingerprints would be all over them. There were more important issues to think about.

"What state was the rest of the office in? Papers scattered around, file drawers hanging open? Did Miriam have a computer, and was it still there?"

"It was only after the EMTs had left that I realized there was some mess, but the police were already there. I didn't have a chance to see what had been tossed around."

"Throughout all the rooms?"

"No, only the reception area, I think. As I said, I didn't go through the entire office. I thought it more important to accompany Arthur to the hospital."

"Were there any papers *under* Arthur?"

Phillip shut his eyes again, but this time to better picture the scene. When he opened them he said, "I think not. So you're suggesting that they were tossed about after the intruder discovered Arthur in the office and knocked him out? That they weren't actually searching for anything?"

"It's possible, isn't it? Did the police take pictures of the scene?"

"Not while I was there, but they might have done so later."

Meg thought for a moment. "Okay, so Arthur unlocks the door and walks in, and startles this unknown person, who manages to get behind him and hits him with the bronze lion sitting on your shelf. Then he realizes what he's done, when Arthur goes down and he sees it wasn't you, and he decides to stage the space and make it look like an ordinary break-in. And then he ducks out, before accomplishing whatever he was after. Which could have been something in your files, or it could have been you personally. Was Arthur an early bird?"

"You mean, did he prefer to arrive early in the day? Yes."

"So the intruder could have been there before most of your building's tenants arrived, and planned to leave before they did. What kind of security is there in the building? Cameras? A guard?"

Phillip actually smiled at that. "Clearly you haven't seen the building. Arthur and I opted for lower cost and what we called 'period charm,' to put our clients at ease. It's an older building, nicely maintained, with a mix of small offices. But it has not been retrofitted with state-of-the-art electronic security devices. None of the tenants has ever seen the need for them."

"Street cameras?"

"Meg! I have no idea. If there are cameras outside the building that might have captured images of whoever came and went, I have never noticed them. Can we simply look at this without hoping to find convenient pictures of our criminal? Don't tell me you have such cameras on every tree in Granford."

That comment made Meg smile, if briefly. "I think we have to assume there are no pictures." There was a pause, and Meg looked at her watch. How had it become six o'clock? And she felt a stab of guilt: Seth and Elizabeth could have been playing gin rummy, for all the attention she had paid to either of them. "Look, guys, why don't we take a break? Get some dinner?"

"That's a nice thought, dear," Elizabeth said, "but I don't think I can face going out."

"Let me go find some takeout," Seth volunteered quickly. "If you'll tell me what you want and point me in the right direction."

"That's a wonderful idea, Seth," Elizabeth said. "Would Chinese do?"

Nods all around. "Let me give you something—" Phillip began, but Seth stopped him.

"I've got it. Just tell me where to go."

After discussing directions, Meg walked out to the car with Seth, leaving her exhausted parents sitting on the couch. "You are a saint, Seth. There are a lot of men who would have disappeared rather than sit through something like that."

"I'm not a lot of men. I think you're asking the right questions, and you're not sugarcoating them. Both your parents need to hear what you're saying. But we definitely need some food."

"Then go and slay the dragon, or the lo mein and egg rolls—whatever looks good. I love you, Seth Chapin."

"I know. That's why I'm still here."

16

Seth arrived a half-hour later with bags of food. They sat in the so-called breakfast room, because it was more intimate than the formal dining room and less crowded than the kitchen nook would have been. Everyone made an effort to avoid talking about Arthur or the attack or about Enrique or the state of Phillip's car, which made the conversations rather strained. Seth and Meg volunteered the details of their tour of Monticello, which her parents had never seen. Seth talked about antique tools, and Phillip listened politely, although Meg knew he had little interest in working with his hands. Elizabeth smiled when anyone was looking at her, but said little, her face falling back into worried lines when the others turned away—but Meg noticed. Her heart ached for her mother: she didn't deserve this. Maybe she'd gotten off easy thus far in her life, but to be thrust suddenly into not one but two murder investigations would be hard on anyone.

"I'll clean up," Elizabeth said when they'd finished eating. Meg was about to protest when she realized that having something to do would probably be the best thing for her mother.

"I think we'll go up, then," Meg said, glancing at Seth. He stood up and waited for her to do the same. "You both look done in. Get some sleep, will you?"

"Good night, sweetheart," her father said as he stood and kissed her forehead.

Meg hugged her mother, holding on a moment longer than usual, and then she and Seth left the room and crossed the hall to what Meg always thought of as the grand staircase.

"Do you think any kids ever slid down this bannister?" Seth asked on the way up the stairs.

"Boys, maybe. It's pretty high, and you could do some real damage to yourself if you slipped."

In bed, Meg, her head on Seth's chest, said, "I never realized how much my life would change when we got married."

"We haven't changed, have we?"

"Yes and no. Or maybe I should say, the unit that is now *us,* which is not the same thing as you and me. If we weren't married, I wouldn't dream of dragging you into this mess with my parents."

"I'm doing this for you, not for them. It's the transitive property of families."

"I appreciate it, and I'm glad you're here. I'm just worried that because it's now in the 'family' category, you think you have to be involved."

"You've been part of plenty of my family's problems. Now it's my turn. So, is there a plan for tomorrow?"

"We go talk to Arthur, if we can. Assuming he's willing, and up to it."

"Fair enough. Let's get some sleep."

Elizabeth was already downstairs in the kitchen when Meg came down. She looked better after a night's rest, but in the clear light of morning Meg realized how thin her mother's skin looked, like very fine suede. When had that happened?

"Coffee's made, dear," Elizabeth said.

Meg helped herself to a cup, then sat down across from her mother. "You look more rested. Is Daddy okay?"

Meg was startled when Elizabeth's eyes darted around the room. Making sure no one else would overhear them? "He's all right, but his doctor is worried about his blood pressure—it's too high. That was why we went up to Massachusetts early, before the wedding. We were taking a mini vacation of sorts, to try to slow down and relax. The first few days were lovely, and of course, so was the wedding, but obviously after that things didn't quite work out, and they're not getting better. But I don't see any way to tell your father not to stress out over what's happening. He thinks he's invincible and he's supposed to be in charge."

"He's cut back his working hours, hasn't he?"

"Perhaps by twenty percent? It's still far more than half of what it was, although he doesn't have to commute anymore—he goes into the city only now and then. I do want him to stay active and involved in something, but he

has few non-stressful interests. Or any interests at all, outside of work."

"I'm sorry. Does he mind that Seth is involved in this?
I'd hate to see them butting heads to see who is top dog.
Or ram. Sorry, mangled metaphor. If we could clear this
thing up—"

"It would be a godsend, darling, for both of us. I hope
you can. But do keep in mind that you have a life of your
own now, and it's not your responsibility to fix our messes."

"I know that. I want to help. Are you all right? I know
you've always looked out for Daddy because he won't do
it for himself, but you have to take care of yourself, too."

"I'm fine, dear. Just older, and slower. I take more naps
than I used to, and I forget details now and then, but my
doctor assures me that's well within the range of normal."

Phillip came bustling in, shaved, dressed and looking
energized. Seth followed. "Great news!" Phillip announced.
"Arthur feels much better, and has agreed to talk to us."

"Good heavens, Phillip," Elizabeth protested. "Won't
we overwhelm him if we all appear at once?"

Phillip looked deflated. "You might have a point."

"Why don't I stay here?" she said. "After all, I don't
know the man well."

"I'll keep you company, Elizabeth," Seth volunteered
quickly. Meg was surprised at first, but then remembered
that Seth had never even met Arthur, and he'd be just one
more body in the room. "You mind, Meg?"

"No, not at all. Maybe Elizabeth can tell you what needs
fixing in the house." Meg wasn't going to let him off the
hook too easily.

"Then it looks like you and me, Meg," her father said.
"You ready to go?"

"Daddy! I haven't finished my coffee, and I'd kind of like to eat breakfast. What's the hurry?"

Phillip relented and sat down next to his wife. "I just want to get on with things. And you kids must want to get home. I'm hoping that Arthur can give us enough information to point us in the right direction."

"You want some coffee, Daddy?" Meg asked, getting up.

Phillip glanced at Elizabeth. "Your mother says I should drink decaf, which I think tastes like dishwater, but I want to make her happy."

"The decaf is in the carafe on the counter there, dear," Elizabeth pointed out. "And there are cinnamon buns warming in the oven."

"I'll pour if you'll deal with the buns, Meg," Seth said.

Five minutes later they were all supplied with coffee and food and crowded into the nook around its round table. Meg decided to start the ball rolling. "I'm going to guess that Arthur won't have a lot of stamina, and the hospital may not want us to hang around too long. What's most important to ask him, while we have the opportunity?"

Phillip raised one eyebrow at her. "Well, obviously, did he see anyone? Or hear or smell someone behind him?"

"Good one, Daddy. If it was a woman, there might be perfume or soap. Do men still use aftershave? Or anything scented?"

"Don't look at me," Phillip said quickly. "But if this person was unwashed or a drunk, that might be noticeable."

"True," Meg conceded. "Next, we ask him what state was the office in when he arrived. Neat or messed up?"

"That's also a good point," her father said. "How about, did he see anybody in the hallway or elevator when he came in?"

"Yes, of course. Did he have time to check for phone messages?" Meg thought for a moment. "I know you've sworn that Arthur didn't have any enemies, but I'd like to hear it for myself, from him. I assume he's been practicing law as long as you have—he may have made enemies you know nothing about."

"Fair enough. How about if there have been any incidents in his life recently that he brushed off as mere annoyances at the time?"

"Of course, yes. Tell me, Daddy, is there any way this could be an attack on the both of you? Someone you defended or prosecuted together, in the past few years?"

"I hadn't considered that," Phillip said thoughtfully. "We should definitely ask Arthur if anything like that occurs to him. Well!" He clapped his hands together. "I'd say that's more than enough for this round. I'm not sure if the police have visited him yet, but I'll try not to cross any lines that might annoy them."

"Good idea."

Meg and Phillip left half an hour later. Before she joined her father in the car, she asked Seth, "You don't have any nefarious plans for my mother, do you?"

Seth tried hard to look innocent. "Who, me? Although I believe she mentioned something about baby pictures."

"Oh, God. I'm glad I won't be here." Meg shuddered.

"I can't believe you were an ugly baby."

"That's very kind of you. I don't think I was. More like ordinary. But remember, it's not only the baby pictures—it's everything up until I left for college."

"Then you'd better come back and rescue me."

"I'll try, but once my mother gets started, she's hard to stop." She kissed him lightly. "Thank you for staying with her."

"No thanks required. I like your mother, and I'd be useless at the hospital. It all works out just fine."

Her father honked the horn in the driveway. "I've got to go," Meg said. "I'm really hoping we find out something useful from Arthur."

"Good luck. See you later!"

In the car Meg asked, "Where are we going?"

"Mountainside Hospital—it's not far. You wouldn't know it, since you've spent little time here."

"And never needed a hospital, thank goodness. You called Arthur this morning?"

"I did. I'm not totally thoughtless—I wanted to be sure he felt ready for visitors, and I assumed you'd want to talk to him. The hospital will probably release him tomorrow—they're keeping him an extra day because it's a head injury, and he has no one at home to look after him."

"Poor man. What's he going to do?"

"He didn't volunteer that information. I'll check in on him, though."

More likely her mother would take over that task, and would probably deliver ready-to-eat meals that Arthur could heat up himself. "He lives in town here?"

"He does. He introduced us to the town, and then we found the house, and we've all been here ever since."

After a pause, Meg said, "Daddy, do you have any friends? I mean, that you've kept in touch with for years?"

His eyes stayed on the road. "Like from college or law school? Not many, I'll admit. We keep tabs on each other through the alumni news, but we seldom see each other. Is your situation any different?"

"Not really, I guess. I've lost track of a lot of the people I was close to once, although we might be Facebook friends now. But I'm so busy I don't have much time for social media."

"But you like your life now?" Phillip asked.

"I do. And I have new friends. Maybe I just feel guilty because I don't talk to you and Mother as often as I could."

"Don't you worry. We're happy you're leading your own life." Phillip pulled into the driveway of a multistory brick building that Meg deduced was the hospital, and he drove around the back to park. Inside they were quickly directed to Arthur's room, and Meg was relieved to see that he was housed in a general nursing area rather than one for critical care. He had indeed been lucky.

Phillip entered the room first. "Arthur, you look great!" he said, a bit more heartily than necessary. While they exchanged greetings, Meg studied the man in the bed. Her father's age, of course; fairly broad in the shoulder, from what she could tell. She couldn't begin to guess at his height, since he was lying down. His hairline was receding, and what hair remained was cut a bit shorter than Phillip's, but close to the same color, and Meg could see that from the back they could be mistaken for each other.

"I told you I had a hard head," Arthur said. "And this must be your daughter, Margaret." The man extended a hand to her.

"Meg, please. It's nice to meet you at last, Arthur, although I wish it could be under better circumstances. But at least it sounds like you got off with only minor injuries."

"That's what they tell me. Not even any stitches, just a couple of super-stick-ums. Well, you two, we should get down to business, before some dragon lady nurse comes along and tells me I need to rest. I assume you have questions?"

"Of course we do," Phillip said. "We went over them at breakfast, so we won't waste your time."

There was only one chair in the room, and Phillip went searching for a second chair for Meg, so they could both sit down. They sat beside each other on the window side of the bed. Phillip quickly and efficiently launched into the list they had discussed earlier, but most of Arthur's answers were less than helpful. No, he hadn't seen anyone, anywhere, even in the hallway. He hadn't expected to. He hadn't heard the person who hit him, and couldn't swear that he hadn't already been in the room, maybe hiding behind the door. No, he hadn't smelled the man—that question made Arthur laugh—although he was pretty sure it was a man. The only response of any value came when Phillip asked about the state of the office.

"Did it look as it always did, or did it look like it had been ransacked?" Phillip said.

"It looked the way it always did," Arthur said, surprised. "If it looked like someone had broken in, I would have shut the door immediately and called the police."

"If that's true, then someone else tossed papers and the like around after he hit you," Phillip told him. "Now we know that that happened after the fact. I regret that I didn't look to see what papers they were, but I was more concerned about you."

"I'm touched, Phillip," Arthur said wryly. "Does any of this help?"

"Yes, because now we know that the scene was staged. What did the police ask you?"

"Honestly, I can't remember. They realized they weren't going to get any useful answers from me on the scene, and then the doctors took over. Did they search the office?"

"I don't know," Phillip told him. "I haven't been over since this all happened."

Meg had watched her father in action, but there were still some important points he hadn't touched on, so she stepped in. "Arthur, I don't know you very well, so forgive me for intruding, but is there anyone in your life, past or present, who might want to harm you?"

Arthur smiled. "Meg, I have led a very bland, boring life. I cannot imagine that I have angered anyone enough to attack me. But thank you for asking—I'm flattered."

She couldn't help but smile back at him. "I would have said the same thing if it had happened to me, but I keep finding myself involved in crimes."

"Ah, yes," Arthur said, "Your father has told me about some of your experiences. But you're on your honeymoon now? Why are you wasting your time talking to me?"

Meg glanced at her father before replying. "I'd like to figure out what really happened before I leave. I've been hoping I can help, although that may be a bit presumptuous with two lawyers in the mix."

Before anyone could say anything further, there was a rapping at the door, and Meg turned to see a uniformed policeman. Behind him stood another man who was not in uniform but who radiated "policeman" anyway. Phillip had stood up quickly and squared his shoulders.

The Suit Man did not appear happy to see Phillip; Meg he ignored. "Corey," he said curtly.

"Chief Bennett," Phillip replied in the same tone.

"We're here to get Arthur Ackerman's statement. You can leave now."

Arthur sat up straighter in the bed. "Phillip is representing me."

The chief turned his cold gaze to Arthur. "You think you need an attorney?"

Arthur didn't back down. "No, but I am entitled to legal counsel. I want him here."

For a moment all the men tried to outstare one another, while Meg pretended to be invisible.

It didn't work. The chief turned toward her. "Who's she?"

"My daughter," Phillip said. "Margaret Corey."

"She can go."

Phillip looked at Meg and gave a small nod. Without a word Meg gathered up her coat and bag and left.

She had discovered one new fact: she did not like the police chief.

17

She stood in the hospital hallway, staring at the closed door and fuming. Whether or not Chief Bennett liked her father, he'd been just plain rude to her, and he'd more or less thrown her out. To be fair, there was no reason why she should be included in the statement or deposition or whatever it was, but he could have asked, not ordered. Was this his normal personality, or was it only her father that brought out that side of him?

What now? She had no idea how long this would take. Her father had driven them to the hospital, so he had the car keys in his pocket, and no way was she going to open the door and ask for them. Besides, where would she go? Sight-seeing? Shopping? That was ridiculous, while they were in the middle of a murder investigation. Yes, murder. To her mind, the attack on Arthur had clinched that. Enrique's death had been a murder, although it might not have been premeditated, no more than Arthur's attack was. It appeared they were dealing with a killer who didn't think things through or scout out his target locations before acting, and who was quick to resort to violence when things went wrong. *Great profile, Meg: your suspect is dumb, careless, and violent, and we don't know why he's doing this.*

She looked up and down the hallway. There were a few stiff plastic chairs along the wall opposite the rooms, probably for people just like her—overflow guests—so she sat in one. She rummaged in her bag, hoping she'd brought a book along. No such luck. She thought she'd call Seth, just to update him, but she wasn't sure cell phone use was allowed in the hospital, and decided to text him instead, concealing the phone inside her bag. She typed only "Police chief here for Arthur's statement. Daddy acting as A's attorney. No idea how long." She hit Send.

Seth texted back a minute later, but wrote only, "Up to third grade."

Great. Seth and her mother were dissecting her entire childhood while she sat here in an uncomfortable chair, having been exiled because she was (a) unnecessary and (b) Phillip Corey's daughter. Plus she'd been insulted, kind of. This was not going well. At least she didn't hear any yelling from inside the room, and she hoped her father was controlling his temper, for the sake of his blood pressure.

It was close to half an hour later when the door finally opened, and then only in response to a nurse who insisted that Arthur had suffered a concussion and needed to rest. Chief Bennett stalked out first, giving her a curt nod, which was at least a small improvement, and he was followed by the uniformed officer. Her father did not emerge, so Meg stood and joined him and Arthur in the room. "How'd it go?"

"As well as could be expected," Phillip answered.

"I really couldn't tell them very much," Arthur said, his tone apologetic.

"Arthur, I don't know that it matters," Phillip reassured him. "Chief Bennett is a very linear thinker. He sees each crime in isolation, but he's not looking to connect the dots to find a pattern. Or a single perpetrator."

"To be fair, Daddy, it's not obvious if you don't have all the details," Meg protested. "You told him about the Amherst incident?"

"Yes, but that was as an addendum to his interrogation about Enrique's death. I don't think he paid much attention to it. We were both tired, and close to snapping at each other by then."

"So there's no real reason for him to connect those dots. What now?"

Phillip looked blank for a moment, then he nodded at Arthur. "I think we should let this man get some rest now. Arthur, can we give you a ride home when they let you out tomorrow?"

"I hate to be a bother," Arthur protested.

"No bother at all. Just give me a call and one of us can get you home. Take care, now."

"Thanks, Phillip. Nice to meet you, Meg." Arthur raised a hand in farewell, and Phillip escorted Meg out of the room and toward the elevator. On the way he stopped at the nurses' station for a word, giving them his phone numbers if they needed to contact someone about Arthur. Since Phillip was now his friend, his business partner, *and* his attorney, it made sense. As Meg went past the nurses' station, she wondered how many police visits they had seen before, especially ones led by the chief.

Back in the car, Phillip quickly turned on the heater and they sat waiting for it to warm the car up. "What now?" Meg asked.

Phillip appeared lost in thought and didn't answer immediately. Finally he said, "Frankly, I don't know. Chief Bennett doesn't appear inclined to pursue Arthur's attack any further. He said there had been a spate of minor crimes in that neighborhood. He was going to send an officer to interview the other people with offices on that floor, but few people were there that early. He did say he would check whether the few stores along the street outside might have surveillance cameras, but I don't hold out much hope there. Have you found any in Granford?"

"Daddy, our crime rate is pretty low. I do know some of the larger fruit farmers around have installed cameras around the perimeters of their orchards. Hard to believe that people would steal apples, but it does happen. The problem is, if there are motion sensors, a passing deer or dog or even a large bird like a turkey can set them off, which is annoying. If they trigger only a camera, then what do you do with that information? Who has the time to look at pictures of a flock of turkeys? So most people don't bother."

"Here in Montclair we're too close to high crime areas to be so complacent," Phillip said. "Yes, our office is in an older part of town, but it's been gentrified, so it's not exactly a slum. But more to the point, Arthur and I believed that we had nothing worth taking. We don't keep any money in the office, and nothing of value. The only thing that's important are the files, and even those don't go back very far. Anything from the last few years is in electronic form, not paper, save for those pages that require signatures. And even that can be done electronically now, or so I'm told. And they're stored offsite—what is it you kids call it? The Cloud?"

"I'm not the right person to ask that, Daddy. Did you bring any older files with you, when you left your New York firm?"

"Only those that were not strictly proprietary. All open and aboveboard—the firm knew which files we took with us."

Meg sat back, relishing the warm air from the heating vent, and thought. "That's interesting."

Phillip turned to her. "Why do you say that?"

"Well, if Arthur remembers correctly, the intruder hadn't gotten around to looking for any files when Arthur walked in, but the intruder wanted the scene to look as though that was his goal, when he scattered some around. You really should go see if they were actually random—just papers pulled off a desk or something, not from a closed file."

"Why would this person fake this break-in? That doesn't make sense."

"Maybe he didn't want anyone to know what he was actually looking for, so he muddied the field. Look, if he had found what he wanted, he would have left the office and no one would be the wiser. Therefore, either he was interrupted when Arthur walked in, or he hadn't even started looking. So he makes a mess to convince the police that he broke in and was looking for something like money, and then he hightails it out of there."

"It's plausible. Maybe. I should go to the office and check out what state it's in, overall. The chief gave me permission, oh so graciously."

Meg grinned. "You're being sarcastic, I hope. Is he always that way?"

"Rude and cold? With me, at least. I can't speak to his interactions with other people. And since I don't currently handle criminal law, I haven't dealt with anyone in town who has crossed paths with him. But I think it's safe to say that he is a man who does not let go of a grudge easily."

"How many years has it been since the incident with his son?"

"Almost fifteen years, now. As I told you, it took place when we were fairly new to the community, and I thought it would be a good gesture. I couldn't have foreseen the outcome, but the chief can't or won't accept that. I even offered to sue the township where the jail was located, for negligence, but he declined, saying that he thought that might be a detriment to his job here. He'd rather just nurse his anger and blame me."

"Be that as it may, the question right now is what could be in the files," Meg told him. "You have all your files from the beginning of your partnership with Arthur, and they're in the office, but most of those are digital. You said you brought with you a limited number of files dealing with earlier cases from the New York law firm, in paper form. Do you keep them in the office? How far back do they go?"

"Yes, they're in the office, and they go back no more than five years before we opened our practice. What are you getting at?"

"I'm just trying to get a handle on what this person might have been looking for—if he was in fact looking for a file or files. You had five years' worth of earlier files, and digital records of your later ones, right?"

"Yes."

"And you can't think of anything in those that included anything controversial or dangerous?"

"No, I can't. But how would an intruder know that?"

"Exactly," Meg said triumphantly. "He wouldn't. It seems to me that he doesn't know what you have. He's looking for something, but he doesn't know where it is. He tried your home first, and then Enrique showed up, and the police, and then you. So he tried your office, early in the morning before you were likely to be there, if he even knew you were back in town. Only then Arthur walked in and interrupted him again. He must be getting really frustrated by now."

"And I presume you have worked the car accident into your scenario, too?" Phillip said.

"It's possible, don't you think?" Meg replied. "It fits if you include the car accident as part of the big picture. It was an inconvenience, but if that driver had wanted to do serious harm, he could have. Maybe he assumed you'd stick around Amherst until the car was fixed, which would leave him with a clear field."

"But we were gone for over a week! He had ample opportunity to break in then," Phillip protested.

"Maybe he knew only about the wedding, not about your taking some extra time away?"

Phillip smiled at her. "My dear, you have a devious mind. When did you start thinking like a criminal?"

"Only in the past two years."

"What does Seth think about all this?"

"You mean, solving crimes? I hope we're on the same page. It's not about playing sleuth, it's about righting wrongs. Granford is a small community, and everyone knows everyone else, often going back for generations. When a crime is committed there, it has a ripple effect, and it can hurt a number of people. Sometimes you have to reach back to past events to find out why any particular crime happened today. Which may be the case here. It seems to me that there may be something from your past, or your and Arthur's shared past, that is only now barging into the present. Your police chief does not seem to have the inclination to look that far."

Why? Meg wondered. Did that still go back to the problem with his son, years earlier?

"What do you suggest we do, my dear?" Phillip asked.

Meg couldn't remember if her father had ever asked her opinion about something that mattered, and she had to look at him to see if he was being sarcastic. The problem was, she didn't have a good answer. Best to get that out in the open now. "Daddy, I don't know. You and Arthur are thinking about your earlier cases. We're collecting evidence, some of which kind of contradicts the simplest solution—like the degree of damage to the car, or the fake mess in your office. We're trying not to tick off your local police chief, even while we're doing the work he and his department should be doing. Right now I suggest we go home and talk about what we want to do for lunch."

"A brilliant solution, Nancy Drew." Phillip started the engine and drove off toward his house.

When they arrived and tracked down Elizabeth and Seth, they were seated in the living room surrounded by photograph albums and boxes with more photographs, and both were laughing. Meg was glad to see that her mother looked much happier than she had at breakfast. "You two look like you're having a good time," she said.

"Oh, we are," Elizabeth told her. "I haven't looked at these in years, and Seth is such a great audience."

"Just looking for blackmail material, in case you get out of line," Seth said with a straight face.

"You wouldn't!" Meg shot back. "I could never show my face in Granford again."

"And therein lies my power," Seth said ominously. Then he smiled. "No, I probably wouldn't."

"We came back to see if there were any plans for lunch," Meg said.

"We have leftover Chinese in the fridge," Elizabeth told them, "and there are cold cuts and other sandwich fixings there, too. Or we could go out somewhere. We should probably take advantage of the decent weather, before it decides to start snowing."

"Sounds good to me," Meg said. "Where would you like to go?"

"Lunch at the club?" Phillip offered.

Meg watched for her mother's reaction, but she seemed to concur. "Great. I haven't been there for a while. Seth, that work for you?"

"That's fine."

"Do you play golf, Seth?" Phillip asked.

"No—I've never had the time to learn. Or a place to play."

"I don't play either, Daddy," Meg added, "unless you want to get into a putting match. That I can handle."

"We'll just have lunch, and then we can discuss what else we'd like to do," Phillip said decisively.

"I'll go change out of my jeans," Seth said.

Meg followed him up the stairs. When they reached their room, Seth said, "Anything of use?"

"Possibly. I met the police chief, like I said."

"And?" Seth asked, swapping his jeans for khakis.

"Stiff as a board and radiating hostility. Whatever he's got against my father, it's not going away, so I wouldn't expect much help from that quarter. Apart from that, a few tidbits from Arthur, but nothing that can't wait until after lunch. Anything you want to see in New Jersey?"

"Not that I can think of. But I never expected to spend time in New Jersey, so I didn't do a lot of research."

"We can talk about it at lunch. Come on."

They had a pleasant lunch at Phillip's golf club, but after they'd eaten, Phillip decided he really should go check on his office and begin the cleanup.

"What about Miriam, Phillip? Can't she help?" Elizabeth asked.

"I gave her the week off as well, don't you remember? There's no need to interrupt her vacation. And I doubt there is more than I can handle on my own, based on what I recall from when I found Arthur. Unless the police have managed to create further chaos. In any event I need to find out."

"I haven't met Miriam," Meg observed. "What's she like?"

"A bit younger than you, smart and efficient. I don't know why she wants to work for a pair of codgers like Arthur and me, but we're pretty flexible with her hours, so she can take a course now and then. She's studying to be a paralegal, so this is great experience for her. She's been with us for, what, a year now?" Phillip looked toward Elizabeth.

"That sounds about right," Elizabeth told him. "The woman who worked for you before Miriam retired, didn't she?"

"Yes." Phillip turned back to Meg and Seth. "We hired a woman who had worked with Arthur and me in New York. She had solid experience as a legal secretary. She needed the job, because the partners she had been working for left, and she wasn't young—probably sixty. She was pleasant enough, but she hadn't kept her technical skills up-to-date. She was helpless with the computer, and she wasn't very quick to learn. In the end Arthur and I had to let her go. Then we found Miriam, and she had us straightened out in a couple of weeks. I hope I don't mess up her filing system when I sort things out today."

Meg wondered if this former secretary might harbor a grudge, even if she'd been eased out gently. It wasn't easy to find a job—any job—when you were sixty, she'd heard, no matter how well qualified you were, and it didn't sound as though this woman had the current skills she needed for many jobs. "That was a year ago?"

"Arminda Colquit," Phillip said, "although she insisted that we call her Mindy, which I found a bit inappropriate for a woman of her age. If you're thinking she was angry at us for letting her go, you'd be wrong—she was the one who came to Arthur and me and said we needed someone with better technology skills. Miriam is a vast improvement, but she won't be back until Monday, so you may not have the chance to meet her."

Meg sent up a silent prayer that this whole mess would be wrapped up by Monday.

18

Phillip dropped Elizabeth, Meg, and Seth back at the house and took himself off to survey the damage at his office. Elizabeth declared she wanted to take a nap, which left Seth and Meg at loose ends. They retreated to their room. Seth said quietly, "Anything?"

"That I couldn't say downstairs? Or at lunch? Not really. Well, that may not be true. My father and I more or less agreed that the mess in the office had been faked to look like someone was looking for something, but it was kind of random. Arthur said nothing had been disturbed when he arrived, so things were tossed around after he was knocked out to make it look like a simple robbery. Or whoever it was, was frustrated when he didn't find any cash or valuables, assuming that was his original intent, and just started throwing things. That's what the police choose to believe, I gather. Goodness knows if they took any fingerprints, but most criminals these days know enough to wear gloves. Daddy didn't have time to check what was on the floor last time he was there, but he's going to take a closer look today. Do you seriously think this former secretary could have had something to do with it?"

"A sixty-something office worker beaned her former boss a year after she left? I have trouble believing that," Seth replied.

"Are you being sexist or ageist? Arthur may be Daddy's size, but he's a pussycat. I doubt he would put up a physical fight even if you came at him from the front. Which is not what happened anyway. Maybe she was looking for something incriminating that she could use as leverage," Meg suggested. "Like for a discrimination suit."

"You'd think she would have gone that route sooner, if she was going to," Seth countered.

"True. Unless, of course, she's been hunting for another job with no luck and has finally reached the end of her rope and had to take it out on someone."

"I can see that she might get desperate under those circumstances, but I can't picture her resorting to violence. Besides, she would know what was in the office."

"Not necessarily the more recent digital files," Meg said stubbornly.

"What else have you got?" Seth asked, ignoring her comment.

Meg gave him a dirty look, but she had to admit he was right. "Arthur claimed that he was pure as the driven snow and nobody wanted to do him harm. Having met him now and spent all of thirty minutes with him, I'm inclined to believe him. I think he's exactly what he appears to be. Which doesn't help us at all."

"And the police are all but standing on their heads to avoid looking harder at any of this," Seth said bluntly.

"Exactly. What do you suggest?"

"Talk to the police chief?"

Meg stared at him in surprise. "Seriously? Why would he talk to me? He isn't exactly fond of my father, and I assume that extends to me as well."

"He'll see you because you do have demonstrable experience with crimes," Seth pointed out, "and he should know that if he's done his homework."

"Oh, right. Sorry I didn't bring my press clippings with me. Seth, I'm an amateur, and I don't pretend to be anything else. Police don't like outsiders like me sticking their noses into police business, and I can't say I blame them."

"But you can offer some insights, and you've already said there were things he hasn't considered."

"I think the fact that I'm my father's daughter will outweigh my vast experience with crimes in rural Massachusetts. Seriously, wouldn't you resent it if a stranger from out of state waltzed into your office and started telling you what you were doing wrong and how you should be doing it?"

Seth smiled reluctantly. "Maybe. But do you have any better ideas?"

"Dammit, no. In Granford we know everybody, or at least you do, so there's a better chance of knowing who might have a motive. Here, I'm a fish out of water. I've never lived in this town. I haven't even lived in this state for years. I have no standing in this case."

"What do you lose by trying?" Seth countered.

"Apart from making a fool of myself? Not much, I guess. As long as I can avoid making things worse between the chief and Daddy. I should go alone, right?"

"Without me? I'd say so. This is your battle, and I'd just muddy the waters. Go. I may follow your mother's example and take a nap. Or find a good book. You, just do it."

"Seth, it's already Friday afternoon," Meg reminded him.

"Worth a shot anyway. If he's like most town police chiefs, and he has a fresh murder and an assault in his jurisdiction, he should be on the job working those cases."

"Maybe," Meg muttered.

"You looking for an excuse not to go?"

"Maybe," Meg repeated. Then she squared her shoulders. "All right, I'll try." Seth had a point, she had to admit. The chief might not be in at all; if he was in, the worst he could do was refuse to see her. The best case would be that he listened to what she had to say. "Give me the car keys."

Seth fished them out of his pocket and handed them to her. "Do you know where you're going?"

"Well, no, not exactly, but I figure it should be obvious if I just head for the center of town."

"Then go forth and conquer."

Meg did as promised, heading for the center of Montclair, and as she had hoped, the police department headquarters was easy to find. It was housed in a large and imposing older stone building on a corner; the main entrance was on the corner itself. She parked in the lot behind the building and marched up the stairs and into the reception area. A female officer stood behind a high desk; luckily there was no one else in the waiting area.

"My name is Margaret Corey. I'd like to see Chief Bennett," she said. "Is he in?"

The desk officer looked her over carefully, taking her time. "Is he expecting you?"

"No. But you can tell him this is in relation to the murder of Enrique Gonzalez."

A light dawned in the woman's eyes. "Corey—thought that name sounded familiar. You related to Phillip Corey?"

"He's my father."

"Huh. Let me see if the chief is free." She turned away to speak quietly into the phone. When she turned back, she looked surprised. "He says he'll see you. He'll be out in a minute."

Meg tried to remain composed while she figured out what she wanted to say—or ask? No, mainly she wanted to present her interpretation of what had been going on for the past week and try to convince the man that there was a common thread running through all the events. She recognized that it was presumptuous of her to even try to tell a police chief how to do his job, especially in a place where she did not belong, but she felt she had to try. She promised herself that she wouldn't be offended if he simply dismissed her.

Chief Bennett did not keep her waiting long, which was polite of him, and she took that as a good sign. He emerged from somewhere in the back of the building and said, "Ms. Corey? Follow me." He turned and walked back the way he had come, and Meg followed obediently, to a corner office toward the rear of the building. He gestured her into the room and shut the door behind them. "Please, sit down."

When they were both seated, Meg said, "I'm glad you're willing to see me today."

"Ms. Corey, as you must know, I've got two significant criminal cases on my desk—a murder and an assault that could have been deadly. I have to say I'm surprised to see *you* here. I hope you'll keep this short."

"I'll do my best. Look, I know you and my father are not on the best of terms."

"I would not let that affect how I conduct an investigation," the chief said, his voice cold.

"Of course not, and I wouldn't want to suggest that. And I'm not here to try to defend my father's past activities. But I have a theory about the Gonzalez murder and the attack on Arthur Ackerman, and I'd be grateful if you'd just hear me out."

The chief sat back in his chair, his expression neutral. "I'm listening."

Meg recounted the accident in Amherst, and admitted that at first she had dismissed it as an unfortunate but ordinary event. "I'll concede that in isolation, there's nothing significant about a minor fender bender in a dark parking lot. It's only when it's viewed in relation to what has followed that it becomes important."

"It sounds to me as though you're grasping at straws, Ms. Corey."

"I can see that it looks like that. But it was shortly after that that my parents returned home to find a body in their yard. That's certainly an extraordinary event, and the accident paled in comparison—although oddly enough, it provided an alibi for my parents. Wouldn't you say?"

"I can't comment on an ongoing investigation," the chief said, his tone neutral.

"I understand. To be honest, I was willing to consider those two incidents as unrelated, just a regrettable coincidence, until Arthur was attacked in the office he and my father share. Three cases of violence within a week, directed toward my family or their colleagues, seems beyond normal to me. Do you agree?"

Chief Bennett didn't answer her question. "Do you have more to say?"

Yes, plenty, Meg thought, but not much that she felt she could share with the police. "I don't want to overstep my bounds, but are you willing to entertain the possibility that these events are related, and that they're part of a campaign directed against my father?"

"Why would I do that? And what is the goal? He hasn't been attacked personally, has he?"

He made a good point. "No, he hasn't. But maybe this isn't about physically harming him or killing him. Maybe someone is looking for something, and the other people just got in the way. Both the death and the attack on Arthur could be viewed as unplanned—spur of the moment, committed by an amateur who had not expected to find anyone else on the scene. Maybe the car thing was a ploy to keep my parents away longer, and it succeeded—they ended up staying another night. In both cases the—may I use the term 'perpetrator'?—was surprised to find someone in his way."

Chief Bennett's expression didn't change. "You make it sound as though this attacker knows your father fairly well, and has been following his activities. Why else would he expect to have clear access to his home and office?"

"It's easy to keep track of people these days, isn't it? I'm sure my father and even my mother mentioned to friends and possibly clients that they planned to attend my wedding last week and would be out of town. My father asked Enrique to keep an eye on his house, and Enrique might have mentioned it to someone. And there's always the Internet. If my mother decided to put an announcement about my wedding in one of the local papers, it would be out there for anyone to see, and the logical assumption would be that my father and mother would be there."

"And someone assumed the house would be empty? If someone were checking your father's plans, at least digitally, then he should have guessed that your father would have made that arrangement with Enrique Gonzalez or someone like him to keep an eye on the house. They could have watched until they knew the coast was clear. Why didn't they?"

"You're right. Please, don't get me wrong—I'm not trying to present you with a perfect theory of all these crimes, tied up with ribbons. All I'm asking is that you keep an open mind about the idea that they may be connected. Maybe they're not exactly professionals."

"And the attack on Arthur Ackerman? How does that fit?"

"He had planned to be out of state visiting family, and must have told clients he'd be out of reach for at least a few days. He and my father gave their assistant the week off as well. This perpetrator could have known from any number of sources."

"Why would this perpetrator have been in the office?"

Meg had to admit to herself that was the weakest link in her theory. What could anyone have wanted so badly from her father that they would kill someone, even if it was an accident? "I don't know. As I said, maybe he was looking for something he believed my father had, either at home or at the office."

The chief sat back in his chair and regarded her steadily, but not unkindly. "Ms. Corey, I understand what you're trying to say. I admire your desire to defend your father.

But you've given me next to nothing tangible to follow up on. There is little physical evidence to support your story."

"Did you look at the bronze lion bookend at the office after Arthur was attacked?" When the chief looked blank, Meg said, "It's one of a pair that my father keeps on a bookshelf in his office. I understand it may have been kicked out of the way when the EMTs arrived and removed Arthur. But my father told me that when he arrived, it was lying in the middle of the floor, close to Arthur. It may have been used to hit Arthur—it's certainly heavy enough. An intruder could easily have grabbed it as a weapon."

"Just as he grabbed a convenient brick to kill Enrique?" the chief said, sounding skeptical.

"Yes, in much the same way."

The chief didn't answer for a few moments, staring at the pen he was flipping between his fingers. Finally he said, "Ms. Corey, it might surprise you that I'm aware of your activities in your hometown, and your involvement in more than one other crime. The one involving Congressman Sainsbury in particular. I can use Google as well as any other person. That's why I agreed to talk to you at all. I believe you're intelligent, and that you mean well. But aren't you too close to this? Aren't you biased in favor of your father?"

"Possibly. But the same charge could be leveled at you, against my father."

The chief stiffened. "Ms. Corey, as I've already said, I would not compromise a case for personal reasons. I encourage you not to let your imagination run wild for those same reasons." He stood up. "Now, I have other matters to attend to. I'll see you out."

Meg stood reluctantly. He was ending this meeting, but

at least he'd listened. Maybe. "Thank you for talking with me, Chief. I appreciate it."

The chief escorted her to the front door. They shook hands cordially, and he watched her leave the building. It was already getting dark, and Meg trudged toward her car, frustrated. Had she accomplished anything? It didn't seem likely.

Back at the house, her mother was still in her room, either asleep or hiding, with the door closed. Her father apparently had not yet returned from cleaning up the office. Meg sighed; now there would never be any sort of forensic evidence. She and Seth sat in the kitchen with coffee, and she updated him on her meeting.

"He agreed to see me, which was the first surprise," Meg said.

"What's the man like?" Seth asked.

"As I told you, stiff. Formal. Serious. I don't think he smiled once while I was there. Okay, we were discussing a murder and the attack on Arthur, but he wasn't being terribly sociable."

"But he listened?"

"He did. He let me talk, and I explained as clearly and briefly as I could. I told him my own theory."

"How did he respond?"

"He's got a very good poker face. I can't say I impressed him—I have the feeling that he thinks I'm trying too hard to clear Daddy's name, for personal reasons, which is a fair assumption, I guess. I asked him to at least consider what I had said, and to keep an open mind. He did say one thing that surprised me: he looked me up online. He read about my connection to the congressman."

"That's interesting. At least that gave you some bona fides—you're not just the flaky daughter."

"Maybe," Meg said glumly. "I'm running out of ideas. Even if he does dig a little harder, there's still precious little to find. I'll be the first to admit that my case is weak."

"Are you ready to give up?" Seth asked.

Meg sighed. "I don't know. I'm beginning to think maybe we should. I don't know what we hope to accomplish, or *can* accomplish in a short time. Unless somebody comes up with something, all I see are dead ends. Do you want to go home?"

"Yes, but not if you feel there's something left to try. It's not like we have to get back to our jobs right this minute."

"Well, we can decide tomorrow. So, we ate out for lunch. Did Mother mention anything about dinner? Should we make something?"

"Let's see what's in the freezer," Seth said.

"Another thing I love about you, Seth Chapin. You just roll with the punches. Solve a murder? Sure. Make dinner? No problem. You are a very steadying influence."

"I hope I'm more than that!" he protested.

"Definitely, Mr. Chapin."

19

The freezer yielded frozen beef chunks—at least, Meg thought it was beef, but it could have been lamb or kangaroo for all she knew—so they decided on a stew for dinner. Uncomplicated comfort food, substantial and warming. She and Seth worked companionably in the spacious kitchen.

"It's amazing having this much room to work in, isn't it?" Meg commented.

"It is, but don't let it give you any ideas. Does your mother enjoy cooking?"

"I think so. She was never a fancy cook, but we always ate well. Are we making dessert?"

"Let's get the stew put together first," Seth said wisely.

So they peeled and chopped, and set a large Dutch oven filled with sautéed beef pieces and onions and stock and red wine on the stove top over low heat to cook slowly. Meg pushed her hair out of her face. "I guess we need to stick close to make sure it doesn't cook too fast—I don't know this stove."

"I'm not going anywhere," Seth said. "So, dessert."

"Did you find any apples in your searching?"

"I believe I did—check the drawer in the fridge."

There were in fact apples there, although Meg sneered at the pedestrian Delicious variety, which in her opinion were good for neither eating nor cooking. But she wouldn't have known that two years earlier, so who was she to judge? "What are we making?" she asked Seth, who was seated at the dinette watching her.

"We? I'm labor—I'll do the peeling. After that you're on your own."

"Gee, thanks," Meg said, reaching for her mother's well-worn copy of *Fanny Farmer*. In the dessert section the book fell open to a familiar apple crisp recipe, which Meg recalled fondly from her childhood. Comfort food indeed. She handed several apples to Seth. "Here. Peel."

The stew was simmering and the apple crisp was in the oven when Elizabeth came into the kitchen. She still looked tired, but less anxious. "Something smells wonderful. I'm sorry I abandoned you this afternoon, but I was exhausted."

Meg stood up and hugged her mother. "Don't apologize. You've had a rough week."

"And you're supposed to be on your honeymoon, sweetheart. Hello to you, too, Seth," Elizabeth added. "Now, if you'd just booked a plane and left for Bermuda or Cancún like normal honeymooners, you wouldn't have gotten dragged into all this."

"Mother, can you see either of us sitting on a beach and sipping whatevers? That's not our style. We wanted to see Monticello, and that's what we did."

"Well, I still feel badly that things turned out like this. What did you find to do this afternoon? Apart from cooking, that is?"

Meg and Seth exchanged glances. "I went to talk to Chief Bennett," Meg finally said.

Elizabeth's expression changed quickly to concern. "Why would you do that?"

"Because I think he isn't seeing the whole picture of what's happening."

"Did he actually talk with you?"

"He did. Yes, I was surprised, but I think he was trying to be fair. Look, can we wait until we're all together before I go into the details? You do think I should tell Daddy I went, don't you?"

Elizabeth perched on one corner of the banquette. "I suppose you have to. But I wish you wouldn't dig yourself in any deeper, Meg. This isn't your problem."

"Why is it not my problem?" Meg protested, a bit louder than she had intended. "You're my family, for God's sake." Seth, who'd been washing the last of the dishes they'd used, laid a restraining hand on her arm, and Meg held her tongue until she was calmer before addressing Elizabeth again. "Mother, as a family we've always led a very, well, untroubled life. I can't remember fights and crises. I'm not complaining, but looking back it seems almost unnatural. Fighting is normal—it means you care about something, rightly or wrongly. The absence of fighting suggests to me that you don't care." *Or you're worried more about appearances*, she added to herself.

"Margaret, of course we have feelings. You must know that we cared about you. We wanted to create a stable environment to raise you. But neither your father nor I was particularly demonstrative. Did you feel unloved?"

"No, of course not. But this isn't about me, don't you see? Did you and Daddy never fight, even behind closed doors?"

"Well, yes, occasionally. Meg, why are you bringing this up now? You can't rewrite history. Your father and I have had a reasonably happy life. I hope you had a happy childhood. You've grown into a strong, smart woman, and I'm—we're very proud of you."

"I had a fine childhood, but that's not the point. Right now I feel like shaking you. A dead man was found in your backyard—someone you knew. Daddy's partner was attacked and his office trashed. You can't just treat this as a small inconvenience and brush it off. It's not that simple."

"It's not your problem," Elizabeth repeated stubbornly.

"But it is! You're my parents! I can't just drive off into the sunset and leave all this dangling, not if I think I can do something about it."

"And you seriously think you can?" Elizabeth challenged her.

"I can try," Meg said. "And in case you hadn't noticed, I can be as stubborn as you."

Elizabeth shut her eyes for a moment, then shook her head. "Apparently I can't stop you. Have you spoken about what you're doing to your father?"

"Not since I talked with the chief. He's still at his office, isn't he? I was thinking we could talk at dinner, or after."

"He won't be happy about it, you know."

"Yes, but I'm tired of being the good little girl and keeping quiet."

Elizabeth produced a small, sad smile at that. "I always thought you were a bit too good. I guess you finally outgrew it."

They heard Phillip's car pull into the driveway, and the slam of the car door. Phillip came stomping up the stairs and into the back hallway. "Damn, it's cold out there. Is that dinner I smell?"

Elizabeth got up to greet him with a peck on the cheek. "The children cooked. Isn't that nice? When will it be ready, Meg?"

Meg checked the clock. "Half an hour. Shall we eat in the dining room?"

"If you'd like," Elizabeth said.

Seth, who had wisely kept silent through the exchange between Meg and Elizabeth, stood up. "I'll set the table, if Meg will show me where things are."

"No problem," Meg said. "Come on." She led him down the hallway to the dining room. "You didn't say a word," she said in a low voice.

"What did you want me to say?" he replied. "I like your mother, and I agree that your family has a tendency to smooth over the surface of things. But that's your battle to fight, not mine."

"And your family was different, or at least your father was."

He smiled at her. "Yes. There was a lot more yelling, mostly from my father—my mother always played peacekeeper. I tried to keep my mouth shut, but Stephen usually got in his face. Meg, do you really think you and I can make a difference in the next couple of days?"

"With the murder and the assault? I . . . don't know. But

I want to be sure we're not missing something. If you want, we can set a deadline. It's Friday now. Say, if this isn't resolved by Monday, we head home?"

Seth looked relieved, Meg thought, and she felt a pang—this wasn't anything he would have wished for. But then, neither had she.

"I think that would be the best thing to do," Seth said slowly. "I'm sorry, Meg. I know it's got to be difficult, to walk away."

"It is. But I owe you something, too. And we do have our own lives to think about. I'm sorry you have to sit there and listen to all this stuff. Ancient history."

"It's part of what made you who you are, Meg." He folded her into his arms, and Meg leaned against him.

Damn, this couple thing is complicated, Meg thought. She wanted an equal partnership with Seth, but nothing was that simple—no matter how hard her mother tried to create that appearance. She and Seth meshed well, and he was a great sounding board, and truly grounded in what mattered. Even so, she still felt guilty thrusting him in the middle of her parents' problems—particularly since her parents didn't appear to want their help at all. "Thank you," she said.

"For what?"

"For just being who you are. For staying around. I don't think I'd have the nerve to challenge my parents without you here to back me up."

"You underestimate yourself, love. But I agree with you. Pretending this isn't happening or that it's insignificant won't make it go away, and your parents have to understand that."

"Exactly."

* * *

Somehow the table got set, and it was barely half an hour later that they were all seated around the big table in the formal dining room. On the driveway side, multipaned French doors occupied the center of the wall, but showed only darkness outside. Meg realized that she couldn't see lights from any of the other houses on that side of the street, which meant that the occupants of those houses couldn't see inside her parents' house either. The high hedges worked; no one would have noticed Enrique's comings and goings, nor those of anyone following him. She should take a look out back, to see if the same was true there. Since the patio was nestled in a sheltered corner, it was probably equally invisible. There would be no help from the neighbors.

Meg hoped to get through dinner without any unsettling discussions. They all deserved some pleasant family time. Seth and Phillip conferred over a choice of wine, and Phillip brought two bottles of red to the table. Meg set candles in the center of the table, lit them, then dimmed the overhead lights.

When they were all seated, Elizabeth looked around the room. "I'd forgotten how lovely this room could be. It's been a while since we've sat in here, or at least, with company. The room—and the house, of course—was built for a more genteel era, and for people with substantial means. Which meant at least one servant. Did you know that there's a foot button under the table to call the cook from the kitchen?"

"The world has changed a bit, hasn't it," Meg agreed. The stew was savory, the wine was mellow, and Meg let herself relax into the moment.

"You never told us the details of your trip back to Madison, Meg," her father said. "Did you find it much changed?"

"It's hard to say, Daddy. Obviously some of the stores have changed, but not the basic layout. It doesn't seem any larger than it did. I took Seth by the high school, but I didn't feel any need to go in and reminisce. And we went to look at our old house—which has really changed! They've dressed it up a lot, but I gather that end of town is pretty upscale now, so maybe they were trying to keep up. That's the first house I really remember—I was, what, four when we moved there?"

"It was a nice place to live," Elizabeth said. "Good schools, convenient commute for your father—although longer than from here—and good people."

"Were you sorry to move, Mother?"

"Yes and no. We'd spent some happy years there, but once you'd gone off to college there was no reason to stay, so we found this house. What about you, Seth? You've lived in one town all your life, and from what you've said, you have many generations of ancestors who did the same. How do you feel about that?"

"At the risk of sounding provincial, I've always thought it was an asset. My father ran a small business, and he knew his clients and their homes well. That kept him in business. I've inherited that, although I've shifted my emphasis away from plumbing. But the bottom line is, it's home. I feel a sense of 'belonging,' if you will. I hope Meg will feel that, too."

"I already do, in a way," Meg said thoughtfully. "Part of it by proxy, through you, but part of it because—well, this may sound silly, but I kind of feel the presence of all those generations of ancestors, and I've got nearly as many of those as you do, Seth. You know, I always remembered that one trip we made to Granford years ago, Mother. The house and the place made an impression on me, although I thought the two old ladies were kind of weird."

Elizabeth laughed. "I think they were, a bit. They had grown up in that house, and lived in it all their lives. No offense, Seth, but I think they demonstrated the downside of staying in one place. They were cut off from the world. You've certainly reached out farther."

"I hope so," Seth said.

"Oh, Daddy," Meg interrupted. "Did I tell you I ran into Joe Caffarelli in Madison? He's running the sporting goods store, the one that his father started. He told me he'd been clearing out some of his father's papers and discovered that his father had been a client of yours."

Phillip looked over their heads, searching his memory. "Caffarelli . . . oh, right, I think I remember. Small store, on the main street? I think I heard from someone that he'd passed away. Is the store still in the same place?"

"It is. I'm not sure it's changed at all, except for a coat or two of paint. I didn't think you handled that kind of client."

"Generally I didn't. But we were new in town—it must have been oh, the late eighties? I used to run into Joe Caffarelli or his wife at your school functions, since, as you mentioned, his son was in your class. After one event we got to talking and he said he needed a lawyer and wondered if I could recommend anybody. I said I was new to the area and didn't know many local people, but I'd be happy to take a look at his problem and see if there was anything I could do. I didn't expect it to be complicated."

"Did it turn out otherwise?" Meg asked.

Her father's expression changed, as if a curtain had dropped. "I can't discuss client cases with you."

"Daddy, this was almost thirty years ago, and your client is dead. Isn't there some sort of statute of limitations or something?"

"I suppose there's no harm to be done," Phillip said grudgingly.

"Well, now you've got me curious. Was there something unexpected about the case?"

"It involved my only brush with the Mafia," Phillip said.

20

"What?" Meg erupted.

Phillip held up the second bottle of wine. "If I'm going to tell this story, it may take some time. Would anyone like a refill?"

"Let me," Seth said. He took the bottle and made a circuit of the table. Elizabeth placed her hand over her glass and shook her head.

When Seth had resumed his seat, Phillip said, "Seth, have you been aware of much Mafia activity in your part of Massachusetts?"

"I can't say that I have. I'd guess that there's more going on in Boston, maybe Worcester. I know there are drugs around, so there may be some connection there, but it could as easily be some other group bringing them in. My general impression is that our part of the state isn't important enough to bother with."

"That's possible. Our situation, when Meg was young, was rather different. We'd lived in the Boston area, so I knew a bit about what was going on, but when we moved to New Jersey we found ourselves in the midst of a real hive of Mafia activity. Well, to be entirely accurate, by the time we arrived the FBI and other agencies had begun cleaning house, so in a way it was the end of an era for the Mafia, but there was still plenty going on. Did you realize that the show *The Sopranos* was based on a New Jersey mob family?"

"We don't watch much television, Daddy," Meg said impatiently. "So all the hype was real?"

"Sad to say, yes. All the gruesome headlines, all the stories about hits and bodies dumped who knows where— most of those actually happened. My law firm had nothing to do with all that, but it was hard to ignore if you read the New York or Newark papers or watched the news."

Meg tried to remember if she'd been aware of any of that and came up blank. Apparently she hadn't been tuned in to local news when she was in high school. She did recall that there were plenty of Italian surnames among her classmates, but it had always seemed ridiculous, not to mention bigoted, to assume that they were involved in illegal activities. She wanted to think she had taken the high road by ignoring the idea, but it was more likely that she'd just been oblivious. "So how did you get sucked in, and where did the Caffarellis fit?"

"It was very small potatoes, my dear. Joe Caffarelli— the father—had opened his sporting goods store a few years earlier. It was doing pretty well, since he supplied all the uniforms and equipment to the local schools. But then he started having issues with his suppliers. You have to remember this was all before the Internet, so you still had to talk to real people to place orders and such, not just fill out forms on a computer."

"So why did Joe need help?" Seth asked.

"As I said, he'd been in business for a few years, and for most of that time had had no problems. Suddenly his suppliers started giving him trouble. Orders were misplaced or delayed, or what was delivered was wrong. But for a small business, it made an impact. Joe took pride in the service he provided to local communities."

"Was this more than one supplier?" Meg asked.

"A couple—not all of them. But the ones giving him trouble were both in New York. You would think that the orders would be simple, but something wasn't right. Joe thought for a while that it was his fault, or he sent in the wrong order, or the vendor had changed accounting systems, but after a while it became clear that the vendors were acting deliberately. So he asked me if there was anything I could do."

"You mean, like sue them?" Seth said.

"Let's say, threaten to sue them. Send them a letter on official law firm stationery and put the fear of God in them."

"Did that work?" Seth asked.

"No, which surprised me. Joe had told me he thought his difficulties were due to ordinary human error on the part of the vendors, but when they ignored my letters I began to wonder if there was something more going on. After giving them a reasonable amount of time to respond,

with no results, I went back to Joe, and that's when he filled
me in on the whole picture. He hadn't known all the details
when he first talked to me."

"Dessert?" Elizabeth interrupted, standing up. "Why
don't I put on some coffee?" Without waiting for an answer
she disappeared toward the kitchen.

Meg watched her quick retreat, then turned to her
father. "Has she heard this story?"

"I'm . . . not sure. As I've told you before, I've always
been scrupulous about not talking about my clients at
home. Joe was my client then, so I would not share any
confidences. But she had to have been aware that I was
working with Joe, through the mothers' grapevine. Madison was not a large town. I think she deliberately turned
a blind eye to any hint of even mildly illegal activity in
our new home."

"So you never discussed this?"

"No, most likely not. And, as you well know, we remained
in that community until after you graduated from high
school."

"Yes, I know that. So what happened with you and
Joe?"

"We arranged meetings with the vendors, one at a time.
Both said more or less the same thing. Or maybe I should
say, they *didn't* say the same thing. I wish I could have
taped the conversations, because they'd be classics in
doublespeak by now."

"I'm not following," Seth said.

"I don't blame you, my boy. I had trouble figuring out
what the message was myself."

"And what was that?" Meg asked.

"The details are a bit fuzzy now, but as I recall, the gist

of it was that Joe was not ordering from the right vendors, or he was not ordering enough, or maybe it was the shippers who were unhappy, but the bottom line was, he needed to spend more money to get anything at all. Plus they disavowed any knowledge of the missing or incorrect orders and demanded full payment from Joe. That alone nearly crippled his business."

"So he paid? And kept on placing inflated orders?" Meg said, outraged.

"He felt he had no choice, if he wanted to stay in business. Meg, he didn't tell me all of this, and it took me several years to put the pieces together. As it turns out, Joe was connected to one of the families, but he didn't want to have anything to do with them. He wanted nothing more than to be an honest businessman in a small town, and raise his family. But the family wouldn't let him do that."

"By family, I assume you mean Mob family?" Seth asked.

"Yes. You have to remember those were difficult times for the Mob. The feds were looking hard at them, and making significant arrests. A lot of their own were turning informer in exchange for lighter charges or sentences. So those running the show were trying hard to hang on to what they had. My guess was—and I never discussed this with Joe—that his family wanted to make an example of him. The income from his tiny business couldn't have been important, but what mattered was keeping him in the fold and toeing the line with the bosses."

"But his business survived?" Meg asked. "After all, it's still there, and his son is running it now."

Phillip nodded. "It did, but barely. Look, the people in town liked Joe, and liked doing business with a local store.

Joe had to raise prices a bit, but they accepted that. Joe told me he'd decided not to pursue his case any further. He thanked me for my efforts and tried to pay me for my time, but I told him I didn't want any money from him, and I was sorry that I hadn't been able to help."

"So you two stayed on good terms?"

"Yes. There were no hard feelings. As I said, it was much later when I realized I couldn't have made a difference, because Joe's problem was not about standard business practices. But I never heard the details from him, just an apology for wasting my time. And after another couple of years, the whole crime scene changed. And that is the sum total of my interaction with the New Jersey mob."

"So they never sent thugs after you to threaten you?" Meg asked, not sure if she was joking.

"Of course not. Even back then, the Mob had become a business, with a bottom line to watch. A lot of the thugs had law degrees or MBAs and wore suits."

"Meg?" Elizabeth's voice floated out from the kitchen. "I could use a hand."

Meg stood up. "Excuse me. Apple crisp coming up."

In the kitchen, Elizabeth had plates and cups laid out, waiting. "Should we use a tray?"

"Sure. Mother, were you hiding from our conversation? You looked unhappy when it came up."

"You mean, about the Mob? Maybe I was. I didn't want to know back then."

"Why? If you don't mind my asking," Meg said.

"You have a right to ask, I suppose. Because I was new to the community and you were young, and Phillip was commuting and working long hours at his new firm so I was often home alone, and I just didn't want to add anything else to my plate. Of course I knew the Mob existed in New Jersey, but I didn't go looking for trouble. Your father told me something vague about Joe's case when Joe dropped it, and I didn't ask any questions. And to the best of my knowledge, that was the only time your father crossed paths with organized crime. Most of his work in those days was with giant corporations with an ever-changing cast of characters. Shall we go back in?"

"Let's." Meg loaded up a tray with four plates of apple crumble. Her mother picked up the coffeepot, and together they marched into the dining room. A second trip took care of the cups, sugar, cream, spoons, and forks.

When they had distributed desserts, Meg said, "So, it's still a small world. On my first trip back in decades, I run into exactly one person I knew back in the day, and it turns out that his father was your client. What're the odds?"

"You really haven't kept in touch with any of your other high school friends, Meg?" her mother asked, and the talk turned to safer matters.

When they'd finished eating, Seth volunteered, "I'll clear up. You all can go get comfortable."

Elizabeth stood up. "I think I'll go up. But, Meg? You can stay and talk with your father. Phillip, she's had an interesting day, and I'm sure she'd like to tell you about it." Before Meg could respond, Elizabeth had left to go up the stairs.

Meg was ticked off at her mother's not-so-subtle nudge, although she realized she had no right to be—she needed to talk with her father about her conversation with Chief Bennett. Seth had conveniently absented himself to the kitchen. She had nowhere to run. "Let's go sit in the living room," she said, leading the way.

Her father followed. "Do I infer that there is an agenda here?"

"I keep forgetting you're a lawyer. You're used to looking for small clues in ordinary conversations."

Phillip sat on the long couch. "And?"

Meg sat in an adjacent overstuffed chair. "I talked to Chief Bennett today."

There was a spark of anger in Phillip's eyes, but when he spoke his tone was level. "What did you hope to accomplish?"

"I wanted to tell him that I thought the three events of the past week could be connected."

"I hope you didn't claim that that was my opinion."

"No, I didn't. You might be surprised to learn that he was aware of my involvement in some of those events in Granford."

"You said events, plural. More than I already know about?"

Meg nodded.

Her father cocked his head. "Interesting—we'll have to talk about those sometime. But your history may explain why he agreed to see you. How did he respond?"

"Carefully. He was polite but no more. He listened to what I had to say, but he did not volunteer any information. I was in and out of there in less than half an hour."

"And do you feel better now?"

Meg studied his face for any hint of sarcasm. "Not really. Look, Daddy, I'm not on some crazy crusade. I'm not using this as an excuse to avoid being alone with Seth—we're good, and he supports what I'm doing. And I know that I have to end this at some point, but I'm not quite there yet. Just for the record, do you see any possibility, however remote, that your fleeting contact with the Mafia back in the eighties has anything to do with what's happening now?"

"No, I do not. Put that idea to bed."

"Fine, I will. See? We've already crossed one thing off the list. What's left?"

"Meg, I really don't know," Phillip told her.

Meg felt deflated. "So we still have no clear reason why Enrique died and Arthur was attacked. And that 'we' includes the police. I told the chief I thought someone was looking for something. although that something may exist only in his imagination."

"I've already told you, Meg—I keep very few files on any of my older clients, and I can't quite see any of the corporate titans I knew in the past running around bashing people now. I can't imagine what anyone would be looking for."

"But somebody killed Enrique and hit Arthur—you can't deny that. And I refuse to consider those two things as unrelated. It may be harder to fit the accident with the car into the picture. Say whoever it was knew that you'd be away from home, and that both you and Arthur would be out of your office. But Enrique's murder and the attack on Arthur happened only this past week. Maybe the intent was to disable your car and make you stay away longer while it was getting fixed. He didn't expect you to stick to your original schedule, rather than wait for your car."

"But what does this person want?"

"I don't know. But let's say that he didn't know he wanted it until very recently. That's why his planning was sloppy. Of course, he expected both you and Arthur to be away, but if he'd known that, he could have gone into this house and your office at any time earlier. Therefore something changed and he had to act quickly, which didn't work out so well."

"What's your point, Meg?"

"Who knew you both would be gone? Did you tell anyone that Enrique would be looking after your house?"

"No, I didn't see any need to. People in the neighborhood are used to seeing him here, so they wouldn't be alarmed. Meg—"

Meg held up one hand. "I'm not done yet. Who has keys to both your house and your office?"

"Arthur has both. Enrique had the house key. A couple of neighbors do, too. As for the office keys, only building management as far as I know, in addition to Arthur and me. And Miriam, obviously, since she works for us, but we gave her the time off, too. We're not the first occupants of that suite, so there could be others floating around. Maybe that break-in was a mistake, and whoever it was, was looking for a former tenant."

"After five years? And that wouldn't explain the break-in here."

"Meg, do you have a theory? Or are you just throwing facts around and hoping they land in some kind of pattern?"

"Door number two," Meg said, ruefully. "Something's very wrong here, but I don't know enough to make things fit. But can you understand that I can't just walk away until we know something more?"

"I suppose. But I reserve the right to throw you out in the near future. Go home and be happy with Seth—I can cope with whatever this is."

"Soon, Daddy, I promise."

21

"You came up late last night," Seth said, rolling over in bed to face Meg.

"I'm sorry—my father and I were talking and I lost track of time. You were asleep when I came upstairs. Weren't you?"

"Yes, I was."

"I'm sorry. Not exactly a romantic honeymoon, is it? I know this wasn't exactly what we'd hoped for—well, except for the first part, which was nice. But I'll be the first to admit that camping out at my parents' house doesn't fit anyone's description of a good time. You are far too understanding. I don't think it would make much difference in figuring this out if you dragged me out of the house by my hair and threw me in the car."

"You can actually picture me doing that?" Seth said in mock horror.

"No, not exactly. But a girl can dream, can't she?"

"I'll keep that in mind."

"Are there any sounds of breakfast-making coming from the kitchen?"

"Not that I've noticed. Why?"

"I have an idea about how we can pass the time . . ."

An hour later they meandered down the stairs and into the kitchen, where Elizabeth was just putting the coffee on. "Good morning, Meg, Seth. Did you have a nice chat with your father, Meg?"

"Yes, we did, after you kind of forced us into it. I'm embarrassed about how little I know about what Daddy was doing when I was growing up."

Elizabeth laughed. "Good heavens, don't apologize, Meg! Children aren't supposed to be interested in what grown-ups do. They have their own lives. If you had paid attention, what do you think it would have changed? Would you be a lawyer now, rather than a farmer?"

Meg filled a cup of coffee for herself, then held up the pot toward Seth. He nodded, so she filled a second cup, then joined him at the banquette. "Probably not. Maybe I never felt sure enough of myself to even picture myself telling people what to do, or even defending people. Working with numbers seemed safer."

"But you manage a crew now, don't you?" Elizabeth joined them at the table.

"With Bree's help, yes. I'm still learning. And of course, I'm older now, and I've hit a few speed bumps along the way, so my perspective has changed." *And maybe I really have gained a bit more self-confidence.*

"What about you, Seth?" Elizabeth turned to him. "Your father was a single contractor, right? And you've followed in his footsteps?"

Meg waited to see how he would answer that. She had never met his father, and knew of him only through Seth and his mother Lydia. Her general impression was that Stephen Chapin had been a rather irascible man who didn't play well with others. Seth was nothing like that, and seemed to be universally well liked, at least within Granford.

"Elizabeth, I took over my father's business out of necessity, when he died, but I found I do enjoy being my own boss, especially now that I get to work with old houses. I hire subcontractors as needed, but I have plenty of people I work with. I certainly don't try to do everything myself."

A phone rang, startling everyone. Elizabeth listened for a moment, and then they could hear Phillip's voice coming from the other end of the house, and she relaxed again. *Was she expecting more bad news?* Meg wondered.

A couple of minutes later, Phillip came into the kitchen. "You'll never guess who that was."

"So we won't try," Elizabeth said. "Nothing bad, I hope?"

Phillip poured himself some coffee, finishing off the pot, and Elizabeth rose to make another. When Phillip sat in the place she had vacated, he said, "That was the hotel in Amherst. They've identified the person who hit our car."

"How?" Meg asked. "I thought they didn't have cameras, and there were no witnesses."

"Yes to the first, but as for the second, the hotel sent out a discreet e-mail to all the guests on the parking-lot side of the building that night, asking if anyone had noticed any-

thing out of the ordinary. They received an answer yesterday. Someone had heard the crash and looked out the
window, and there was enough light in the lot to enable him
to identify the make and model of the car, and that it was
a local license plate."

"Why did they wait so long to report it?" Meg demanded.

"They were traveling themselves, and not checking
their e-mails regularly. But there's more. As luck would
have it, a car matching that description was stopped that
same night by the Amherst police and the driver was
arrested for operating under the influence. His car was
damaged. They only just put the pieces together and realized it was the same vehicle."

Meg wasn't sure whether to feel disappointed or
relieved. "So it looks like the incident in Amherst isn't
related to what happened here in Montclair?"

"So it would appear. Are you disappointed, Meg? I
know you've been having a fine time weaving your own
theories." Phillip looked surprisingly cheerful. "Pancakes,
everyone?" He didn't wait for an answer but stood up and
started rummaging in the kitchen cupboards for the
ingredients.

Elizabeth sat down again and shook her head, smiling.
"It won't do you any good to say no," she said in a stage
whisper. "He loves his pancakes."

Breakfast was a relaxed meal, uninterrupted by any
more phone calls. There was nothing to be done about
insurance claims or murder investigations. Did Phillip
think that by eliminating one support for her logic about
the crimes, the rest would simply disintegrate? Meg wondered. The other two pieces were far more serious—and

in one case, deadly. But she was reluctant to spoil the cheerful mood in the kitchen.

After breakfast Meg and Seth cleaned up—her father had always been a messy cook, and that hadn't changed. "So the fender bender in Amherst had nothing to do with what happened to Enrique. Or it did, but not by anyone's plan," Meg said, scrubbing the griddle.

"Yes," Seth said, as he dried a plate and added it to the stack on the counter.

But Meg couldn't let it go. "My father said that he and my mother had intended to stay in Massachusetts a few days longer last week, until the problem with his car happened. He was *not* expected to be here last week, by whoever killed Enrique."

"All right," Seth said cautiously. "You're assuming they didn't expect to find Enrique here either?"

"Whoever it was may not have known about Enrique." Meg turned off the water and faced Seth. "But whoever it was—this person who *wasn't* in the parking lot in Amherst— if he knew my parents and Arthur would be gone, he could have searched the house and the office at any time. Why'd he wait so long?"

Seth shook his head. "Meg, I can't tell you that. How many people knew your father would be gone?"

"Arthur, of course, but he was supposed to be gone for the same period. The secretary, Miriam. Anyone my mother might have told. If it was summer I'd say a golf buddy, but I don't think anyone's playing this time of year. Or maybe I should say, my father is not among the manic few who insist on playing year-round. Do you know, there are some people who actually get orange balls so they can play in snow?"

"No, I did not know that, and I'm sure my life was just fine without that factoid. I do not play golf. I have no intention of playing golf at any future time in my life. Can I discard that bit of information?"

Meg swatted his arm. "Fine, laugh at me. All in all I doubt they'd have told many people. It's not like the good old days when the comings and goings of the upper crust would have been reported in the local newspaper's society column."

Seth came closer and laid his hands on Meg's shoulders. "Let it go, Meg," he said gently. "Your father can figure this out without your help. Why don't we find something more pleasant to do?"

She grinned at him. "We already did that this morning. You'll need to come up with something else."

"All right. Jigsaw puzzles? Your mother and I already combed through your childhood pictures—and I warn you, she's promised to send me copies of some of the more compromising ones. Ah, I know! Yearbooks. You have a high school yearbook here somewhere?"

Meg shut her eyes momentarily. "Have you ever seen a yearbook that makes anybody look good? But, yes, my mother loves to save things like that. It's either in the room we're in or in the office upstairs."

"Let's go find it," Seth said firmly. Meg followed him up the stairs.

It took no more than five minutes of searching— Elizabeth might have a sentimental streak, but she was nothing like a hoarder, and kept her possessions in good order. Meg was the one who found it. "Here it is." Seth reached for it, but she pulled it back quickly. "Do you promise not to laugh? And to never share it with anyone you know?"

"Hey, you can look at mine any time you like."

"It's not the same thing," Meg retorted. "The hairstyles when I was in high school were not kind to girls. You probably looked exactly like you do now."

"A few pounds lighter, but I get your point." He raised his right hand. "I promise that whatever we find in that yearbook will not be used against you in a court of law—or anywhere else. Now can I see it?"

"I guess," Meg said with a sigh. They settled themselves comfortably in the window seat, nestled against each other. "I assume you want to see my individual portrait photo first?"

"Of course. Show me."

Grudgingly Meg took the book and paged through it until she came to the seniors page with the *C*s. "There," she pointed.

"Ah," Seth said, and pulled the book toward him. "Cute."

"Would you have gone out with me then?"

"Meg, I didn't go out with anyone back then. I might have hung out with a group of pals that happened to include girls, but that was about it. Besides, I didn't have a lot of spare time, since working for my father kept me busy."

"Poor baby. So there was no girl you worshiped from afar?"

"Nope. I figured it was hopeless. I was smart, but my father was a plumber. I didn't really fit in with any particular group."

Meg thought briefly about asking when and how Seth

and his wife—correction, *first* wife—had connected, but decided it might spoil the mood. Wow, she was a second wife. She'd never thought about that. Seth had never brought it up, exactly, but Meg guessed that he was the type who had imagined he'd be married to only one woman. Meg had met the ex, Nancy, briefly, and had trouble picturing them together.

Meg reclaimed the yearbook and turned back a page. "Here's Joe Caffarelli. His haircut is a hoot, isn't it? I guess he's lost a bit of hair since."

"So do we all," Seth said.

They held the book between them and leafed through it. Meg pointed out favorite teachers, the few clubs and activities she'd taken part in (mainly for college application purposes), and various candid shots, which turned out to be mainly of cheerleaders and football stars. The whole thing made Meg feel sad—it seemed so long ago now. They'd all been so full of hope and plans back then. How many of those plans had come to pass? Her life certainly didn't match what she had expected then. College, yes. First job, check. But now? Things had taken an unexpected turn.

"Wait a sec," she said, as Seth turned another page. "Go back to the other page."

Seth did, then looked at her. "What?"

What had caught her eye . . . "There, in the junior hockey team—Miriam Caffarelli."

Seth didn't speak for a moment. "Were there many Caffarellis in your school?"

"No, just Joe's family. I'd guess this is his younger sister."

"And her name is Miriam?"

"So it seems. I didn't know her then. Heck, I barely knew Joe, and only because he was in my class. And Miriam is such an old-fashioned name—I'd guess that she probably went by some nickname, like Mims or Miri."

"And you're thinking . . ."

"You know what I'm thinking," Meg said flatly. "We have to show this to my father." She stood up, grabbing the yearbook from Seth as she went, holding the place with her finger. "Come on."

They found Phillip in the study on the same floor. He looked up when they entered. "Hello again, darling. Did you have any plans for the day? Or were you thinking of hitting the road?"

"Neither, just yet. Can I show you something?"

"Of course. What is it?"

Meg laid the yearbook, open to the page she had held, on the desk in front of her father. Then she pointed to the one picture of the hockey team. "See anyone familiar?"

Her father looked at the page, bewildered, and then he focused more intently. "This Miriam Caffarelli here—you're guessing she's my secretary?"

"What do you think?"

He turned his attention back to the photo. "It's possible. My Miriam's got a different last name—Miriam Del Monte."

"She could easily be married."

"Yes, that's true."

"Do you have a copy of her job application? A CV?"

"At the office. Not here at home. You think she's related to Joe?"

"I don't remember any other Caffarellis in town."

Phillip sat back in his swivel chair and looked up at her. "And what conclusion do you draw from this?"

"That's it's one more coincidence in this whole mess. And I don't like it."

22

"What do you propose to do about this, Meg?" Phillip asked.

"Tell me more about Miriam. How did you come to hire her?"

"Sit down, please." Phillip gestured toward a couple of straight-backed chairs opposite the desk. Meg and Seth sat. When they were settled, Phillip leaned back in his chair again and steepled his hands. "As I've told you, I went into private practice with Arthur just over five years ago, after working at Blackwell, Hyzy, and Cates for something like a quarter of a century. Arthur and I had talked about doing this for some time, and had discussed what our goals were. We're not young, and we wanted a lighter and less demanding client load. We found a small office—which, it occurs to me, you haven't seen yet—and we moved into it and set up shop."

"Has private practice met your expectations?" Seth asked, ignoring Meg's glare at his interruption.

"By and large, yes, Seth. We take what clients we choose, and we turn away some. I think it's worked well for us."

"And Miriam?" Meg demanded.

"When we went out on our own, we brought one of our secretaries with us from our former firm. I've told you this before, Meg. A lovely woman, and she was used to working with us, but her skills had not kept pace with the times, and she decided to retire. We were sorry to see her go.

"So we needed to find a replacement, although we had ample lead time for the transition. I think we went through a local agency, and asked for someone with some legal experience and a general interest in the law. There were several strong applicants, and Arthur and I interviewed a number of them. We wanted to find someone who would stay around for at least a few years."

"Did Miriam come through that agency?"

"To tell the truth, I think she was referred to us by a client," Phillip said. "We asked among our friends, if they knew anyone who was looking for a position, and she could have heard of the opening through one of them."

"Do you remember that interview?" Meg asked.

"Darling, we talked to perhaps a dozen people, and I haven't thought about it since we hired Miriam. She has been a dependable employee, and she's smart and hard-working. We've had no complaints about her performance, and we were satisfied with our choice."

"Did she ever mention Madison?"

"Not that I recall. Where we had lived in the past would not have come up in a job interview. Where we had worked would. We told her that both Arthur and I had worked at a large New York firm, but we were looking to take a step back. As I think about it now, I believe Miriam admitted up front that she had little office experience, but she was taking classes to become a paralegal, and she had strong computer and office management skills. Arthur and I agreed to take a chance on her, and it's worked out well for all of us."

"What do you know about her personal life?"

Phillip gave a brief laugh. "Surely you know that a prospective employer is not permitted to ask that sort of question?"

Meg nodded impatiently. "Sure, but you've been working with her for a year now, right? Don't you ever talk about things unrelated to the law and the office? Is she married? Does she have kids? Where does she live?"

"Meg, I think you're overreacting about this. Don't you agree, Seth?"

"Humor her, Phillip," Seth told him. "This will go more quickly if you do."

Seth's comment irked her—it sounded condescending, which was unlike him.

"Daddy, do you agree the photograph in the yearbook looks like Miriam?"

"Perhaps, but it's an older photo and the girl Miriam Caffarelli was much younger then."

"And the coincidence of the surnames?"

"I haven't ruled out the possibility. But what does it matter?"

"Daddy, you're saying you don't know about husband or kids?"

Phillip took a deep breath to compose himself. "I have no information about either. Miriam has never made nor received many personal phone calls at the office, nor has

she asked for time off unexpectedly, which I would antici-
pate if she had young children at home or at day care. But
I have not asked about her interests outside of work. We
have discussed the legal classes she has taken. But that has
been the full extent of our personal interaction. She has
been an exemplary employee."

"She knew you'd be attending my wedding?"

"Of course she did. Arthur and I discussed it, and we
saw no reason why Miriam couldn't take the time off while
we were gone—with pay. She had vacation time coming
to her, in any case. We have always tried to be fair employers. And this is perhaps our slowest time of year, just before
the holidays."

"Did Miriam have any issues with Arthur?"

"Meg, you have no idea how silly a question that is.
Arthur is a very kind man, although he does have a mind
like a steel trap when it comes to legal issues. He gets along
with everyone, especially Miriam."

"This isn't helping," Meg said, almost to herself. "Any
noteworthy or controversial cases that you're working
on now?"

Phillip sighed. "Arthur and I opened this firm so we
wouldn't have to deal with that kind of case. Our client
base is stable. We don't make an extraordinary amount of
money, but we're comfortable. I hate to burst your balloon,
but everything has been going just fine."

"Do you mind if I talk to Miriam?"

Phillip cocked his head at her. "I probably can't stop
you, can I? Today is presumably her last day of vacation,
but under the circumstances it seems appropriate to call
her and see if she can meet with us tomorrow. Perhaps at
the office?"

"If she's willing. I'd like to see your office anyway. Do you know if Arthur will be in the office on Monday?"

"I haven't spoken to him since I gave him a ride home from the hospital, but he seemed to be well on the road to recovery then. I assume he'll be there."

Meg glanced at Seth. "Would it be rude to ask him to join us today?" Meg hated the way she sounded: pushy and petulant. Did her father take her seriously? Or did he actually believe she was wrong and was only humoring her? She really didn't know if she believed her own reasoning, but she couldn't seem to let it go. "The sooner we can get this cleared up, the sooner we can get out of your hair."

Phillip smiled. "My hair is happy to have you, Meg. Let me make some calls."

When Phillip had left the room, Meg stood up abruptly. "I need some fresh air. I'm going outside." She stalked away without anyone following, and that included Seth. Did she want him to follow? No, she decided, at the moment what she wanted was time to think. Alone.

She grabbed the first heavy coat she came to in the hall closet and went out the back door to the patio. The place where Enrique had died. It was ample in size, partly covered with an old-fashioned metal awning. The outdoor cushions had been taken in for the winter, but the bare seats were still there, under the awning. She dropped into one of those, facing the lawn with its brown patches, and sulked.

This is why I don't come visit my parents often, she said to herself, silently. *I'll always be their child, and they'll always be my parents. There's no way they can see me as an equal—the deck is stacked against that. It's not even personal. But that doesn't explain why I'm so upset. So, Meg, why?*

All right, I'm upset because I'm scared. There's a threat out there, but I don't know where it's coming from and Daddy and Mother refuse to acknowledge it. They think I'm overreacting. Am I? A man is dead, and another was hospitalized. There's no reason to think this is over, because we don't even know why it started. Someone was looking for something. They didn't find it on their first try at the house because they ran into Enrique, and it's been pretty much continuously occupied since, so no one's been back here to continue the search. Which is not the same as saying they won't be back. Whoever it is tried looking at the office after that, and ran into poor Arthur in the way. This mysterious searcher wasn't very smart, and was definitely unlucky. And is most likely getting frustrated.

She had a new thought. *This person is an amateur, who didn't think through the basics, like, make sure no one is around. If you want to break in, do it at night, when it's unlikely you'll run into anyone. If you're worried about a flashlight showing, shut the blinds. But both the house where I'm sitting and the office are unlikely to be observed after dark anyway.*

What about the alarms? Meg asked herself. Maybe he had known about Enrique and was waiting for him to disarm the alarms when he arrived, so he could get in. Maybe the intruder hadn't meant to kill him but had planned to sneak in behind him and wait until Enrique left, before searching. But Enrique had turned back or something and startled the guy. The weapon—a brick—suggested he had been killed outside. Maybe the intruder had meant to knock him out and had hit him too hard, then panicked when he realized what he had done.

Or she. Meg regretted she hadn't asked her father some basic questions about Miriam's build. In the yearbook photo she had looked pretty average, but she could have changed since. Would she have been strong enough to drag Enrique's body out of sight? She probably wasn't strong enough to stuff him in her car and dispose of him elsewhere. Had Enrique ever met Miriam? If he had, her presence wouldn't have alarmed him at first. She could have said Phillip had asked her to get something from the house, and that would have sounded believable. Why kill him? It didn't make sense.

And what would Miriam want in the house?

"Meg?"

Meg hadn't even heard Seth approaching. She realized she was freezing, and wrapped the borrowed coat more closely around her before turning to him. "Hi."

"Are you all right? You look like you want to bite my head off."

"I won't, I promise. But I don't know if I'm all right. I know I'm scared, and frustrated, and a bit angry at my parents for dismissing what I believe are real concerns. For them, not for me. Us."

Seth moved a second chair closer to hers. "They're your parents. It comes with the package."

"Am I being unreasonable? No, don't answer that, because I probably am. But something is wrong here."

"Is that all that's bothering you?" Seth said quietly.

"I . . . Seth, is that going to be us in twenty, thirty years?"

"Meg, their relationship has worked for them for over thirty years," Seth pointed out.

"But that's not what I want for us!" Meg burst out. She stood up and started pacing. "Every marriage is different—I get that. But we should be able to argue, and to share, and to lean on each other. I don't want to be them."

"That won't happen, Meg. We won't let it. If you see any signs of that, feel free to tell me." He stood up and pulled her close. "You're freezing."

"I don't care. I needed to get away from everybody and clear my head. I feel so mad that there's nothing I can do right now, so I have to wait until tomorrow, and smile and play the dutiful daughter. And both Mother and Daddy treat me like I'm twelve."

"Maybe they're scared too, and can't admit it—to themselves or to each other. Face it, an unexplained death can be terrifying, especially when it's in their own backyard, in this case literally. Maybe they're in denial."

"Maybe," Meg said, her voice muffled by his coat. "So what do I do?"

"Stick to your guns. If you believe what you're saying, follow through. I'm with you all the way."

"Thank you. I wish I knew what this person was looking for. Since they checked the office, it must have something to do with a legal case, but Daddy says he hasn't been involved in anything controversial for a while, and neither has Arthur. What's so important that someone resorted to violence to get it? And why now? What's changed?"

"Meg, I can't possibly answer any of those questions, particularly if you can't."

"You can be an objective observer, a sounding board," Meg pointed out. "You don't have a history with any of these people, so if some part of their behavior looks wrong to you, it probably is. You could go have a man-to-man chat with my father—maybe he's holding back because he thinks he's protecting the poor little womenfolk."

Seth smiled. "Maybe. But is he really that macho?"

Meg had to smile in return. "The term 'macho' has seldom been applied to my father, by anyone that I know of. Gentlemanly, maybe. Courteous. And just a wee bit sexist."

"Meg, you've asked him whether he knows anything about any of this, and he's told you no. You're going to have to find out more, if you want him to listen to you."

"How?" Meg shot back.

"Google New Jersey Caffarellis?" he said, after a pause.

Meg considered. "Well, it's a start, if I can finagle some computer time. Since it was our honeymoon, we didn't bring our laptops along, remember? In any case, it beats sitting here in the cold worrying."

"I would agree with that. Can we go inside now?"

"Yes," Meg said firmly. "We have work to do."

23

Meg went back inside, followed by Seth, and after hanging up the coat she had borrowed, made a beeline for the kitchen. She was colder than she had realized: her hands were shaking and her nose was running. But at least her head was clearer. "You want some tea?" she asked Seth.

"Sure." He settled himself at the banquette and watched her move around the kitchen. "Love that stove," he said, pointing to the massive six-burner cooktop with double ovens.

"It's really something, isn't it? But I don't think we'd have room to move if we tried to fit it into our kitchen. Besides, we'd never cook for enough people to make it worthwhile."

"True. Did we time our wedding to avoid hosting Thanksgiving?"

"Not necessarily," Meg said, rinsing a teapot with hot water. "I didn't mean to dump it all on your mother. And there's still Christmas," she warned him.

"Mom's used to handling Thanksgiving. But maybe we should step up for next year."

"Fine—as long as we don't invite more people than we can fit into the dining room." Meg quailed at the thought of preparing a major meal for a dozen people, but no doubt the old house had seen its share of Thanksgiving dinners in the past, and who was she to complain? "Do you think your mother and Christopher are serious?"

"Is that question related to Thanksgiving?" Seth asked.

"Sort of. They've been spending time together lately, not that they tell us about it. What do you think?"

"Maybe," Seth said cautiously. "It's not exactly the kind of thing a son talks about to his mother, at least not these days. In the old days I could have taken Christopher aside and demanded to know what his intentions were, or just told him to back off. But I both like and respect Christopher, so I have no grounds for objection, if that's what makes Mom happy. And she deserves to have someone in her life, if that's what she wants. Besides, it would be handy to have the resident orchard expert right next door."

"They might decide to move to Amherst together, you know."

"Aren't you jumping the gun just a bit? They haven't even told us they're dating."

"I know, but I'm looking ahead. Then there would be two empty Chapin houses over the hill, and we have to figure out what to do with them." The water boiled, and Meg poured it over tea bags in a china teapot. "As for the working relationship with Christopher, I wouldn't want to bypass Bree and undermine her authority. She knows enough to reach out to Christopher when she needs help. Will it make you uncomfortable, now that we're married, having her living in the house?"

"Yes and no. She's been there longer than I have, but some throwback side of me wants to toss her out of our cave. She knows she could move to what's been my house."

"That seems like a lot of house for just her, but on the other hand, she's not exactly the type to want roommates, and I doubt she wants Michael to move in with her."

"Why not?" Seth asked.

"I don't think they're particularly serious about each other. And I think Bree is a lot more ambitious than Michael, which could be a problem down the road. We'll have to talk with her when we get back. If we ever do."

Elizabeth walked quietly into the room. "I thought I heard voices down here. We must be on the same wavelength—I was just going to make a pot of tea, but you've beaten me to it. What have you two been up to? Are you completely bored yet?"

Meg carried the teapot, clad in a cozy, to the kitchen table, and then retrieved cups, spoons, sugar, and milk. "Getting there—no offense intended."

Elizabeth held up a hand. "None taken! I know how busy your lives are, and I'm sure you're chafing to get back and get on with things. How did the new bathrooms turn out?"

"I didn't send you pictures? Shoot, I must have forgotten—I was a little distracted. It's great, having choices for a change. And I love the old bathtub! I wish I'd had it when I first started working in the orchard—my whole body ached for months."

"I can imagine," Elizabeth said. "Will Bree be staying on at the house?"

"Seth and I were just talking about that. We really haven't had that discussion yet, what with everything else that was going on before we left. One more thing on the to-do list."

"Meg, you know we won't be offended if you want to leave soon," Elizabeth said carefully. "You have your own lives to live."

Meg glanced at Seth before answering, choosing her words. "Please don't take this the wrong way, but it seems to me that you and Daddy are playing ostrich about what's been going on. With Enrique and Arthur, I mean."

Elizabeth looked at her tea, and added some more milk. "Is that the way it appears? You may be right. We've led such quiet lives, and it seems so unreal that someone we knew was murdered here, on our own property, and a friend was attacked at the office. Maybe we are trying to ignore both events, which I can hardly defend. I know you've had much more experience in such things."

"Not by choice, believe me."

"But you've jumped right in and confronted them," Elizabeth replied. "I admire that."

Meg smiled at her mother. "It's not like I had a choice. In one case I had to prove myself innocent, and in another I had to turn around and do the same for you. Not that I distrust law enforcement, but they do try to make the simplest solution work before they look any further. We're lucky to have a friend on the Granford police, one who has an open mind."

"But you didn't stop after just those two situations, dear, did you?"

Meg sighed. "Not exactly. I always believed that New England was a peaceful place, but I've discovered there's a lot going on beneath the surface. And memories are long—sometimes going back centuries. Old crimes don't just disappear, they go underground, waiting."

"Nothing so interesting here," Elizabeth said sadly.

Are you sure? "Mother, what do *you* think is going on?" Meg asked.

Elizabeth looked up at her then. "Meg, I honestly don't know. I know it's not right to ignore what's happened, but I can't begin to explain it."

Impulsively Meg laid her hand on her mother's. "I hate to think of leaving you two when you don't know what you're facing."

"That's sweet of you, but I don't know if you can help. Thank you for trying, though."

"We want to help, Elizabeth," Seth said.

"I know, I know. I feel so useless!" Elizabeth replied.

Maybe it was time to change tactics, Meg thought. "Have you met Miriam?"

"Your father's secretary—or should I say, assistant? Yes, a few times, when I stopped by the office. Why do you ask?"

"I just wondered what you thought of her?"

"Well, she's about your age, so she's not just starting out. She seemed pleasant and competent. Your father's had nothing but good things to say about her."

"You're both women. Didn't you get anything personal from her? I know Daddy wouldn't think of such a thing."

"I've spent very little time with Miriam, dear. I believe

she's married—well, since she has a different name from the one in that yearbook of yours, that would be logical."

"Do you believe that Miriam is the office Miriam?"

Elizabeth nodded. "Yes, I do. I can see the resemblance to the old picture. Maybe she heard about the opening through the Madison connection. But I wouldn't say she's made any effort to hide it. I think, as Phillip said, it simply doesn't come up."

If there was a connection there, and if Miriam had had an ulterior motive in getting the job, she still hadn't made her move, and she had been in the job a year. If she'd wanted no more than to go through Phillip Corey's files, she would have had plenty of opportunities before now, starting with her first week on the job. Phillip and Arthur had apparently given her complete access to all the files in the office, which went back to when they'd started the practice. And Miriam knew the schedules for both her father and Arthur. She had keys to the office, and she could well have known about Enrique and used him to get into the house, or, heck, she could have borrowed Daddy's keys and had copies made.

"Meg, I think you're seeing villains behind every bush now," her mother said. "If Miriam had wanted to find something, she could have done it at any time. She has free run of the office, and she's been digitizing the back files for a while now. There's nothing hidden there."

"I know—I was just thinking the same thing. Does Daddy keep any files in the house?"

"I don't know, to be honest. Nothing current, I'm sure. There may be some old boxes in the attic here. When we moved, years ago, we had a company come in and deal with all the packing, so I can't say that I looked at or labeled every box. I can't say how far back they might go. Why on earth would it matter?"

"Mother, I'm just trying to look at all possibilities. The bottom line is, someone broke in here and into Daddy's office presumably because they were looking for something they believed he had. If it was only this house, it could have been a simple robbery—it's an upscale neighborhood, and this house is pretty well concealed, at least in back. But the office break-in? I assume there's nothing of particular value there—apart from the files. No money, no valuables. Why break in there?"

Elizabeth shrugged helplessly. "Meg, I don't know."

Meg glanced at Seth, then back at her mother. "Do you think we could look in the attic, see what's up there?"

"You should ask your father, but I have no objection—as long as you don't leave a mess."

"Don't worry. And I'll talk to Daddy first." Meg stood up quickly, but then stopped and kissed her mother on top of her head, which appeared to startle Elizabeth.

Seth followed Meg into the hall. Meg turned to him and said, "If Miriam is actually Joe's sister, that suggests that what we're looking for dates back to the years we all lived there. Yes, Joe and Miriam were kids then, but it's possible that something happened then that didn't seem important at the time, but that does now. Does that make sense?"

Seth shrugged. "In a way. At least it narrows the search. We're looking for boxes of files from your father's legal activities for the years that he and your family lived in Madison. Wasn't he with the New York firm then?"

"Yes, but he may have taken on some cases of his own.

Like what he did for Joe Caffarelli. There could have been others."

"Your father seems to be a methodical person. He might have made some copies of documents or notes from his prior job and kept those, or, as you say, he could have handled other cases that didn't involve the law firm. Didn't Joe Caffarelli mention that he'd just cleared out his father's files himself? And he found a file on his dealings with your father?"

"He did. But Miriam's been working for him for a year, long before Joe went through his old files. And she was just a kid when Daddy was trying to help Joe. It seems more likely that she might have remembered the name, and when the job opened up she decided to apply for it. Look, all I want to do now is dot another *i* or cross another *t*. If there's nothing there, then we'll know. Let's tell Daddy we'll be looking around the attic."

"Boy, you sure know how to show a man a good time. I'm really looking forward to rooting around in dusty old boxes in a freezing attic."

Meg swatted his arm. "Hey, you'll have the pleasure of my company."

They found that Phillip had retreated to his study on the second floor again. Did he and her mother ever spend time with each other? Meg wondered. "Hi, Daddy. Seth and I thought we'd look through the attic and see if there's anything of mine left there. I've got more room in my house now, and I could take it off your hands if you don't need it."

"Ah, darling, I don't spend much time poking around up there, so I'm not sure what odds and ends have accumulated. If there's any furniture up there that strikes your fancy, you're welcome to take that with you. We have more than enough as it is."

"Thank you—I'll see what we find. Do you and Mother have any plans for the day?"

"Not really, other than enjoying spending time with you two. I need to get ready to get back to work tomorrow, and I'm sure Arthur will be a bit slower than usual."

"We're coming with you, if that's all right."

"Do I have a hope of stopping you?" Phillip softened his comment with a smile. "Things are likely to be quiet. As I think I've said before, no one wants to start litigation before Christmas, so my calendar is fairly clear. I assume you want to introduce yourself to Miriam."

"Yes, I do. Ready for the attic, Seth?"

"You're fascinated by attics, Seth?" Phillip asked.

"Actually, I am, since I remodel older buildings. I haven't had a chance to get up close and personal with many from this era—the 1920s, right?—and I'd be interested to see how construction techniques have evolved. But the truth is, I'm just muscle for Meg—I get to move stuff around and carry it down if she finds anything she likes."

"That sounds familiar. Well, I'll let you go. And don't be surprised if Elizabeth and I take a nap later—one of the perks of growing older. Or we could watch your New England Patriots playing."

"Okay. We'll try not to make too much noise upstairs, Daddy. See you later."

Meg led the way up to the third story. "The guest room and bath are down at that end." She pointed to the end opposite the stairs. "The maid's room is at the front, there—it has its own bath. And the attic—what there is of it—is at the back." She opened a closed door, and a chill gust of musty air greeted them. The space was unheated, but not unpleasantly cold. It had a solid floor, but the rest of it was unfinished, and poorly lit. They stepped into the room, and Meg pulled the door closed behind them, then turned to survey the scene. "This is really very tidy, which makes our job easier, I guess. I'm impressed that they've gotten through thirty-plus years of marriage without accumulating more stuff. Or maybe they've dumped a lot of it along the way."

"I don't see much from earlier generations," Seth commented. "What about your grandparents? Didn't they leave anything behind?"

"Apparently not. I never knew them, you know."

"Why?" Seth asked. "I can't imagine that."

"A variety of reasons, I guess. Died young, moved away, hated each other on first sight. We didn't discuss it. I probably know more about them from my genealogy research than I ever heard from my parents. Anyway, Mother kept the family jewelry, which was pretty modest, and a few odds and ends like sewing boxes or china, and some photographs, but I don't remember any furniture or big stuff—oh, except for one wing chair. There"—she pointed again, to a neat stack of Bankers Boxes grouped together in a corner—"that looks like the best candidate for Daddy's legal records. You want to split them between us?"

"Fine with me. Remind me what I'm looking for?"

"We're assuming that anything from Daddy's current practice is kept at his office. He set up that practice about five years ago. So anything older than that but not the product of the New York firm is the best bet, I think."

"And what do I do if I find something? Mark it? Pull it out?"

"Damn, I should have thought this through better—I would have brought sticky notes. For now, just leave the covers in place but stick them on end, and I'll look at them. Is that okay?"

"This is your idea—I'm just along for the ride."

"Then let's get going before it's too dark to see up here."

24

They worked in silence for a while. At least the contents of the boxes were neatly arranged and labeled, which helped, and the outside of the boxes bore the approximate dates of the files. Meg had no idea what she was looking for, apart from her suspicion that it was something that had happened at least fifteen years earlier and it might involve someone from Madison. Joe Caffarelli had mentioned that her father had helped his own father out, when they'd first moved to the town around thirty years ago, but that case had come to nothing, according to her father. Would he have bothered to keep any records of that?

After half an hour of digging through files, Meg reached the conclusion that her father had kept every scrap of paper that had anything to do with any legal matter. One box contained nothing but instruction manuals and guarantees from a range of appliances she was pretty sure he hadn't owned for years. She doubted that he'd done the filing himself, but he'd instructed someone to take good care of the files, and he'd moved the records to Montclair with him. So if there was something of a legal nature to be found, that had precipitated the recent events, it would probably be here somewhere.

Seth had pulled out his share of boxes and lined them up in chronological order. "Got something," he called out.

Meg straightened up, stretching her back, and went over to join him. "What?"

He handed her a slim file. "Labeled 'Caffarelli, 1987.'"

"That would have been not long after we moved to Madison." She took it from Seth and looked around for a place to sit and check it out, but the attic offered few comforts.

"You want to take it downstairs and read it?" Seth asked.

"No, I think we need to finish up here first, while there's light. There can't be too much more to go through. But I'll put this by the door so it doesn't get lost."

After another half hour they'd been through all the boxes, with no new discoveries, and shadows were collecting in the corners. "I guess that's it," Meg said reluctantly. "I hate to pin all my hopes on that one file, but I don't see anything else that fits."

"So let's look at it and decide if it's relevant," Seth suggested.

"In a moment. You see anything up here we want?"

Seth scanned the room. "I don't see much of anything. Sad, kind of. You should see my mother's attic—she must have at least four generations' worth of stuff up there."

"It makes me a little sad, too, I guess. There are no memories here. I know—there's not much point in keeping useless stuff, but handling something that one of your ancestors owned or even made makes them more real, somehow. Like shaking hands with them across the years. Apparently I didn't inherit that feeling from either of my parents—maybe somebody up the line somewhere. Okay, let's go downstairs and see what we've got."

Seth picked up the sole file on the way out the door, and Meg made sure the lights were off before she pulled the door shut behind them. Out in the hallway she couldn't hear any sounds of activity, so she and Seth made their way quietly to their bedroom and sat on the bed. He handed her the file.

"Okay, what've we got?" he asked.

Meg looked at the battered old file. "I'm almost afraid to look. If there's nothing there that matters, I don't have a Plan B. Which means we go to Daddy's office in the morning, meet Miriam, if she's willing, say hello and good-bye to Arthur, and head home, I guess."

"You've done what you could, Meg."

"I know. It just seems unfinished." She opened the file and started reading.

It didn't take long. There were typed summaries of some conversations with the elder Joe Caffarelli, and copies of formal correspondence, as her father had said. But far more interesting were the handwritten notes her father had included. They were a bit cryptic, but knowing what she knew, they told a bigger story. When she was finished reading, she carefully closed the folder and sat staring at the cover, trying to think.

"Well?" Seth asked.

She looked at him them. "My father lied to us."

"What do you mean? When?"

"When he told us about his dealings with Joe Caffarelli, in Madison. There's not much detail in the file, but here's how I'd reconstruct what happened. We know that Joe senior was related to a Mob family, at a time when that mattered. He tried to distance himself, but they wouldn't let him. The overtures were more or less as my father described them—they wanted some kickback from the sports store in exchange for expedited shipping and such. I think Joe was just exploring the options, legally, to see if he could put them off. That's why he came to my father, rather than an unfamiliar law firm. But he wasn't entirely honest with my father then."

"But your father said he knew about the Mafia connection," Seth said.

"Yes, he did. He wasn't blind or stupid. He offered Joe a strictly by-the-book opinion, and sent those letters he mentioned and got no response. And then Joe told him, 'thanks, but we're done.'"

"So Joe accepted the inevitable?"

"Maybe. As my father suggested, maybe he figured out that to stay in business he had to go along with the plan. The store was pretty small potatoes then. And Daddy and Joe parted ways, apparently amicably.

"But the story doesn't end there. My father kept his eyes open or his ear to the ground or whatever you want to call it, and he realized that in the late eighties the sports business was just an opening wedge. He guessed that Joe got sucked in deeper. You have to remember, drugs were relatively new then. A sports store which sold to a lot of area high school and amateur teams would provide a lot of access to potential customers. So even if Joe looked the other way, maybe there were employees he was urged to hire, or suppliers that included something extra in their shipments. I don't know, and my father didn't say much, because I doubt he had much proof. But he did leave a few handwritten notes in the file, and one of them says 'drugs' with a question mark."

"Okay, say your father knew there was something going on. What could or should he have done back then?"

"I don't know. He had no proof, or at least there's none here. He'd just moved to town, and he had a child in school—me. In theory he could have gone to the FBI or the state attorney or something like that, but I get the feeling he liked Joe Caffarelli and he didn't want to get him into any more trouble than he was already in. So in the end he did nothing, apart from watching. But I'm pretty sure he knew what was going on."

Seth thought for a moment. "Say that's true. Why would anyone be so interested in that file now and want to get their hands on it? Has something changed?"

"Maybe," Meg said. "Here, look at this." She handed him a page of handwritten notes.

"What am I looking at?" Seth asked, bewildered.

"It's my father's notes on a conversation he had with Anthony Del Monte, at some social event. Off the record."

"Why is that important?"

"Because Anthony Del Monte is the New Jersey attorney general, who made a name for himself prosecuting organized crime cases back then. And it looks like he was in bed with the bad guys."

"That's a big jump to a conclusion, Meg. What part of these notes says anything like that?"

"I know it's thin, but often there's information in what is *not* said. Daddy asked him about a hypothetical case, and Del Monte blew him off, politely, of course. Probably not surprising, taken by itself."

"From these notes, it looks like he said 'thanks for stopping by' and showed Phillip the door. That's not exactly incriminating. He must have been a busy man."

"I get that. But look at his name."

"Del Monte? Why?"

"Because that's Miriam's last name."

Seth stared at her. "Ah. So now you're suggesting that Miriam is not only Joe Caffarelli Senior's daughter, but she's also married to a relative of the attorney general? But that doesn't prove much by itself, other than that they all knew each other."

"Seth, we now have a whole series of coincidence stacked up. How many coincidences does it take to make a fact?"

"Mark Twain probably had something to say about that. What's your point now?"

"One, the attorney general is now running for governor."

"And you know this why?" Seth asked.

"Because since I grew up here, my brain is tuned to pick up the words 'New Jersey' wherever I hear them. And there haven't been all that many governors in my lifetime."

Seth shook his head. "And there's another point?"

"Miriam was helping her brother clear out their father's old files very recently, and maybe what they saved on their end, that corresponds to this one here, triggered some old memories and looked like it could be trouble, which Del Monte didn't want at this particular juncture. So Miriam took it upon herself to see if she could find and eliminate whatever information my father had saved, just in case. But things got a little out of hand, with Enrique and then Arthur."

Seth sighed. "Meg, you know I love you. I respect your intelligence. I know you aren't given to fantasy. But you have strung together a series of 'what-ifs' and 'maybes' that defies probability. Your thesis here is that Miriam is Joe senior's daughter. I'll buy that. She's married to a politically connected guy whose father is running for governor—it should be easy enough to verify that. Somewhere along the line she saw something or remembered something about her father's past that set off alarm bells, and she decided she needed to remove any evidence of it, if such evidence even existed, so that her hypothetical father-in-law wouldn't get blindsided by it. And there she was, by design or your favorite word "coincidence," in the perfect position to check out all of your father's files. She knew what was in the office files, so she decided to look here at the house and unfortunately ran into Enrique, who she killed. Then she decided to take another pass at the office in case she had missed something, and had the further bad luck to run into Arthur and walloped him, too, but at least he survived her attack. Does that about cover it?"

"Seth, I don't know whether to laugh or cry. Yes, those are the high points, except that I think for the last steps she needed an accomplice, and her husband—the candidate's son—is the likeliest contender for that role."

"I'm glad you added some muscle to the scenario, in case it turns out that Miriam weighs a hundred and ten pounds and is only five feet tall. Do you have the ghost of a plan about what to do next?"

"Talk to Miriam tomorrow?"

"I agree that we should, but we need to talk to your father first, about that file we found."

"And if he continues to lie about the file? The one he conveniently forgot he had? To pretend it was an innocent claim that went nowhere?"

"You've got me to back you up."

"Do I need that?" Meg asked.

"I think so. Look, I never got along with my father, and I sure as hell know he didn't listen to me about anything relating to his business. I wasn't allowed to have an opinion, even when I knew I was right. So the bottom line is, I let him bully me simply because he was my father." When Meg started to protest, he held up one hand. "I'm not saying your father is bullying you, but as you've already pointed out, in some part of his mind he still sees you as his little girl. Not an adult, running a business, and solving crimes. And that's just the way it is. So if we talk to him together, I'm the objective third party, and that means he'll listen to me in a different way."

Meg smiled. "Yes, because you're male. Part of me wants to stamp my foot and say 'me do it!'. And another part of me is grateful that I married such a smart man. Let's do this."

They went down the stairs to the second floor. Her parents' bedroom door was closed, but Meg peeked into the adjoining office and found her father sitting there in the near dark. He looked up and saw her, with Seth behind her.

"Did you find what you were looking for?" he asked quietly.

"You knew what we were doing?"

Phillip sighed. "Ah, Meg, I may be getting older, but

I'm not stupid. You've got a bee in your bonnet about Enrique's death, and you can't let it go. You were always a stubborn child. But I will admit you started me thinking, and then I started putting two and two together. What did you find?"

"The Caffarelli file, with your notes."

Phillip nodded. "That's what I suspected. And why do you think that's important?"

Meg glanced at Seth, who nodded as well. "Here's what I think happened. Let me run through it before you comment, okay?"

"I'm listening."

Meg outlined her current thinking, setting out the steps that had led her to her conclusions. She tried not to apologize for the flimsy theories, but just stated the evidence as she saw it. Her father watched her face silently and did not interrupt, as he had promised. Seth stood near the door, like a statue.

When she finally wound down, she said, "I know this seems improbable, but it's the only thing that makes sense to me. You're the lawyer, Daddy. Tell me where the holes in my story are."

"I can't. Because I think you're right."

25

That was the last thing Meg had expected to hear. "Really?"

"Yes. You must think I'm an old fool. *I* think I'm an old fool. I saw only what I wanted to see. I truly hoped that Enrique's death was simply a robbery gone wrong and had nothing to do with our family. Meg, I actually resented you for what I saw as trying to spoil a happy visit, and I apologize. I know you and Seth have given up part of your own time together to try to sort this out, even though I did nothing to encourage you. But I'm still incredulous that Miriam could have played any part in this. She's a lovely girl—woman. She's smart and hardworking. She's the ideal employee, I would have said. Now you're suggesting that she's been scheming against me for as long as she's worked for me?"

"I don't think this started that long ago—there must be something recent that triggered it all. And she wasn't scheming against you, Daddy. She was looking out for her own family's interests, if what I guess is right. I can't speak for what she hoped to prove. Maybe she hadn't known about the Mob connection and didn't want to believe it, and was looking for proof. Or maybe her husband was behind it—he wanted to clean things up before his father announced his candidacy for governor, and make sure nothing would come back to bite him."

"You think his father is involved in any part of this?" Phillip asked.

"Why are you asking me? I don't even live in this state. I don't know the man or his track record, public or private. But I'd be willing to believe that if it came out that he was involved with the Mafia, even at arm's length, it would not help his political career. Do you think he was, back then?"

Phillip shook his head. "I don't want to speculate any more than you do. But there is another piece of information that you need to know, that isn't in that file you have there. His son is a loose cannon. He has a criminal record, and he's prone to violence."

The scenario keeps getting more and more complicated, Meg thought. *At what point does it collapse due to its own absurdity?* "Why do you know this, Daddy?"

"Because his son Ricky was one of the men who beat up Chief Bennett's son while he was in the holding cell after his arrest and left him permanently damaged. But Ricky was never accused of that, because Tommy Bennett—the son—couldn't remember anything, and the others in the cell swore they hadn't seen a thing—to hear them tell it, he beat himself up. So that was dropped, but the damage was done. I'm going to guess that Ricky's been involved in other incidents that have turned out the same way as well—kept off the record."

"Are you saying the dear Dad Del Monte has pulled strings to keep his son out of trouble?"

"I think it's a strong possibility, Meg. But as in so much of this castle in the air that you've constructed, I have no proof. And it would be dangerous to fling unsubstantiated accusations around, particularly with an election coming up."

"So this Ricky—he's Miriam's husband?"

Phillip sighed. "I don't know that for a fact, but I'll concede that it seems likely. If it's true, then they've been married for some time. All her work references were for Miriam Del Monte."

"Well, if she's close to my age, that's not surprising. I'm the outlier on the marriage age curve." Meg shook her head to try to clear it. "This just keeps getting worse. Joe Senior didn't want to work for the Mob but he was forced into it, simply because he was born into the wrong family. In a way he did you a favor by dismissing you as his attorney when he saw he couldn't win. His daughter may or may not have known about his involvement, but she—or her delightful husband—are worried that there might be something in those files of yours that could spell trouble for Anthony Del Monte. So Miriam enlisted her husband, Ricky—or maybe he enlisted her—to track down the files. It's clear that you like and respect Miriam, so I'll cut her a break and say she isn't capable of hitting people with heavy objects. That leaves her husband, Ricky, who is a known hothead, and he's the one who panicked and killed Enrique and clobbered Arthur."

"You don't have to spare my feelings, Meg, because I may well have misjudged Miriam. But it does seem more likely that Ricky was the one wielding the brick. Miriam could still have been the brains behind what they tried to do."

"Which means you are still at risk. And if he finds out what we know, he's capable of coming after you again. Can we find a legal way to stop him?"

"Meg, I'd love to think so, but we're sorely lacking in evidence. I'm sorry I have to keep repeating myself."

"Will Chief Bennett help?"

"I don't know. I don't begin to know how to approach him with something like this. Oh, and keep in mind, if we're right about this and make a public stink about it, the possible future governor of the state will be an enemy. Assuming, of course, he survives the double scandal of old Mafia ties and a psycho son he's been protecting for years, and gets elected."

"Let's worry about one thing at a time." There was one more point that troubled Meg. "Daddy, how much does Mother know about any of this?"

Phillip looked away. "I've always tried to protect her. She's long since stopped asking about my work. She knew I was helping Joe, at the beginning, but I told her he'd dropped the issue and that was the end of that. I never told her about the suspicions I had about Joe's involvement in . . . other things. For the record, no one from that—what should I call it? Way of life? Illicit side?—ever approached me about any other matter, personal or professional. Which made it easy for me to forget all about it, until now." Phillip seemed to realize suddenly that Seth was still in the room. "What about you, Seth? What do you think of this mess?"

Seth responded carefully, after a moment. "I think it's

possible that Meg is right about what she's laid out to you. But as you pointed out, we have nothing tangible that we can take to any authorities, just conjectures and guesses. If I get a vote, I'd say we talk to Miriam tomorrow, without accusing her of anything, and see what she says. If she stonewalls us, we haven't lost much—"

"Except possibly a good employee," Phillip interrupted.

"Yes, there is that, if she takes it the wrong way. She may get up and walk out on us without confirming or denying anything. But I don't have any other ideas."

"Do we tell Mother what's going on?" Meg asked.

Phillip shrugged. "What's to be gained? It would only worry her, and if this comes to nothing, that would have been needless. If we learn anything useful from Miriam, we can fill her in then."

They passed the rest of the day without bringing up anything about Miriam or murder, although Meg felt like her worries had to be painted all over her face in neon colors. But her mother didn't pry—did she prefer *not* to know if something was wrong? How had she so easily dismissed Enrique's death? Did this show hidden depth of strength on Elizabeth's part, or no depths at all? Meg was no longer sure.

They were clearing the table after dinner when Elizabeth asked, "Have you decided when you'll return home?"

Meg and Seth looked at each other. "We thought we'd stick around another day or two, if that's all right. We want to go see Daddy's office tomorrow, and meet Miriam, and maybe then we can decide."

"That sounds like a nice plan, dear. Dessert?" And no more was said.

* * *

The next morning Meg was rummaging through her suitcase, as Seth watched. "I really need to do some laundry," she said.

"Won't it keep until we get home?" Seth asked.

Was that a complaint, buried in his question? "We could leave tomorrow," she said tentatively. "After we've talked to Miriam."

"And what if she says she has no idea what you're talking about? Or even if she admits to everything? What will you do then?"

"Turn it over to my father and the police, I guess. I can't stay here and badger my father's secretary, even if I think she's an accomplice to murder."

"I'm glad you recognize that, Meg." Seth jumped quickly out of bed. "I'm going to grab a shower," he said, disappearing into the bathroom.

He was not happy with the situation, Meg acknowledged. Neither was she, but now that she'd gotten things rolling, she couldn't just walk away. Or was that just her rationalization? And she wasn't being fair to Seth. Throughout their jumbled honeymoon he'd been a rock, not demanding anything from her, letting her find her own way through this series of unexpected events. But he deserved better. This was *their* life, and he should come before her mother and father now.

She joined him in the shower. "I thought we could save some time if we showered together," she said into his ear.

"We'll see," he said, and then said no more.

When they went downstairs, Phillip was already dressed and finishing his coffee. "Do you want to go with me, or take your own car?" he asked as soon as he saw them. Meg saw that he had somehow become energized by the idea of confronting Miriam and resolving at least one part of the puzzle.

Meg glanced at Seth. "We should probably take two cars, but we can follow you, since I don't know the way. Do you want some time alone with Miriam?"

"Not necessary. Look, I'm not going to tell you what to say, Meg. I like Miriam, but if in fact she is implicated in what you described, I can't defend her actions. On the other hand, if I think you're being unfair, I'll step in. Agreed?"

"Of course."

"Phillip," Elizabeth interrupted gently, "could they at least eat breakfast first?"

Phillip seemed startled by the question. "What? Oh, well, of course. We've got plenty of time."

It was nearly half an hour later when they were finally ready to leave the house. Meg hadn't had much appetite, worried about the coming encounter with Miriam. She was effectively accusing someone she had never met of murder, and that didn't sit well with her. She found her mother staring at her with a concerned look more than once as she munched toast and drank coffee.

Phillip was plainly champing at the bit. "Ready? I'll go warm up the car. I'll wait until you two are lined up behind me before I go, all right?"

Meg and Seth nodded like obedient children, even though they had already found their way down a few hundred miles of the East Coast without mishap. Her father's subtle reminder that she was still the child here? Mixed messages again.

The ride to the office took only a few minutes. Phillip

drove to a small parking lot adjoining the building and parked, then waved them into an adjoining space. Meg watched him as they pulled in: he looked more excited than worried. Did he still trust Miriam? Meg wasn't sure. He led them into the building, a four-story, solidly built older structure, and well maintained. The brass in the elevator was polished, and the elevator moved smoothly if slowly up the few floors to Phillip's floor. When they emerged, Meg saw a corridor lined with similar doors, most with gold lettering of some sort, along a well-lit, clean hallway. Meg wondered briefly if her father was happier here than he had been in the corridors of corporate power in New York—she'd have to ask him, when she had time.

The Corey & Ackerman door was unlocked when Phillip reached it, with lights showing inside. Phillip opened the door and let Meg and Seth enter, then followed. "Miriam! How was your vacation? Is Arthur in?"

Meg studied Miriam quickly. Fairly slender, nicely dressed; her desk was tidy. But there were dark circles under her eyes, and she glanced briefly at Meg and Seth before turning back to Phillip. But Meg had seen a spark of fear. "Great, Mr. C. I got a lot done around the house. Is this your daughter?" She turned back to look at Meg, the smile still pasted on her face.

The resemblance to Joe Caffarelli was unmistakable. *One question answered.*

"It is," Phillip said, "with her new husband. Miriam, may I introduce Meg and Seth Chapin? This is their honeymoon, and they've been kind enough to spend some of it with Meg's mother and me before heading home to Massachusetts."

"Nice to meet you," Miriam said mechanically. "I've

been hearing about your wedding plans for months now. Everything go okay?"

"It did," Meg told her, trying to work out how to approach what she really wanted to ask. "It was a small wedding, in a local restaurant, but all our friends were there. That was what we wanted. Are you married, Miriam?"

"Sure am. Going on fifteen years now. This your first visit to your dad's office?"

"It is. I don't spend much time in New Jersey these days. I went to college in New England and I used to work in Boston, and then I ended up running an apple orchard at the other end of the state. I had a lot to learn when I started, so that keeps me busy. Seth owns the property next to mine, and we invested in a new batch of trees together. And then we got married."

"Wow. I can't keep a geranium alive." Miriam turned back to Phillip. "Arthur left a phone message saying he was on his way. What's this all about?"

Phillip glanced at Meg before answering. "Miriam, we appreciate your coming in on the weekend, but after what's happened—the death of Enrique Gonzalez, and the attack on Arthur here in the office—I have a number of questions, and I think you may somehow be involved."

Miriam wisely didn't comment, but stared apprehensively at Phillip. There was a moment of awkward silence. Meg realized that since she'd asked for this meeting, it was up to her to fire the opening salvo. Or toss out the first pitch. Or something. *Quit stalling, Meg!* "Miriam, did you happen to grow up in Madison? Because you look a whole lot like a guy I went to school with. Joe Caffarelli." She stopped and waited for Miriam's reaction.

It came quickly. Miriam's eyes widened. She looked

like she was turning over answers in her mind, and Meg wondered which way she'd go: denial? A quickly fabricated story? Or the truth?

Then Miriam slumped in her chair. "He's my brother." Then she looked at Phillip. "I'm so sorry, Mr. C. How much do you know?"

Phillip said gently, "I think we'd better take this someplace more private." Then he led them all into his office and closed the door.

26

Getting everyone settled took a few silent minutes, and Seth had to retrieve one of the chairs from the waiting area. The time appeared to allow Miriam to get her story straight. *Is that good or bad?* Meg wondered.

And then she realized that she and her father hadn't really worked out a strategy for this discussion. He was the lawyer, and Miriam's employer, but she was the one with both answers and questions. Still, she was relieved when Phillip made the first move.

"Miriam, you've been working for Arthur and me for a year, and we've been more than pleased with your work. But there have been some recent incidents involving both my family and this office—serious incidents, in one case fatal—and it seems possible that you may have been inadvertently or deliberately involved. My daughter Meg has raised some questions about these incidents that I can't answer, and I'm hoping you can help us."

"She's the one with questions?" Miriam sputtered. "Why her?"

Meg answered her directly. "Miriam, for reasons I don't really understand, I've been involved in a couple investigations in the town where I live. Maybe I'm just oversensitive to crimes these days, but I would appreciate it if you'd tell us what you know. If you aren't involved in these recent events, I'll be the first to apologize."

"We'd like to help you, if we can," Phillip added.

Meg watched as Miriam's expression changed and changed again. She almost felt sorry for her. If she was right, Miriam was torn between loyalty to her family and doing what was right, for an employer who had been nothing but kind to her. Miriam couldn't know how much the rest of them knew or suspected. She looked at Phillip, who nodded at her, signaling her to go ahead.

Miriam looked down at her hands. "Yeah, you got it right, Meg. Joe's my brother, and he told me he'd run into you this week, big surprise." She looked up then. "Mr. C, Dad always respected you, so I grew up knowing who you were, and that you'd tried to help him. He felt bad that he had to shut you down on his case, but that was business. And I knew who Meg was back then in school, too—one of the smart ones, going places. You've got to believe me when I say I applied for the job here because I knew about you from before, from my family."

"But you didn't mention the connection to my father?" Meg asked.

Miriam shrugged. "I didn't see the point. I didn't even know if Mr. C would remember it—it was a long time ago.

And I was happy he wanted to hire me because I was qualified. It's been good, working here. Hasn't it?" she appealed to Phillip.

"It has, Miriam," Phillip said gently.

Miriam turned back to Meg. "You know about Ricky and his dad?" she asked. Meg nodded. "I like Tony—that's my father-in-law. He's a good guy, and he'd make a good governor. And he's respected in the state, so he's got a real shot at getting elected. Then when Joe and I were going through some old stuff of our dad's, we found his file on what he asked you to do, Mr. C. There wasn't much in it— nothing that made you look bad. You did what you could for him. But my brother filled me in on the whole story. I guess Dad shared it with him, but not me because I was a girl and younger and he didn't think I needed to know. Joe told me about the 'family'"—Miriam made air quotes when she referred to what Meg assumed was the Mafia—"and how they leaned on Dad, made him do things he didn't want to, just to stay in business. It got worse after he told you to shut down, Mr. C. They wanted more than money."

"Miriam," Phillip said, "we have some guesses about what that might have been. But even if we've guessed correctly, I don't see how that led to the attacks. Can you explain that?"

"I asked Tony about it, because he'd been involved in those Mafia trials back around then. I'd never thought much about what he did then—he defended the accused, and he got them off, which nobody thought could happen. That was before he got to be state attorney, but it helped him get there. But I figured he had to know what was really going on with his clients then, so I asked him for the story on my Dad and his business, and he told me that he'd learned that it wasn't just a shakedown for some money from Dad. That the guys pressuring him wanted a foothold in the sports community, so they could sell drugs to the kids."

"And he never did anything about it?" Meg asked, incredulous. "Reported it to someone?"

"You've got to remember what it was like back then, Meg."

"I wasn't paying much attention when all this was happening, and then I left the state. Fill me in," Meg told her.

Miriam nodded. "Okay. Tony was in the middle of a long, hard trial that was getting a lot of press attention, even national, because mostly nobody took on the Mob. A couple of junior wiseguys hassling my dad was peanuts in comparison to that. And there weren't any records of anything about it, just talk. So, yeah, he let it go. There were probably a lot of things like that, that people kind of swept under the rug—not just Tony. The prosecutors had to pick their battles, you know?"

"So why was finding that file of your father's so important?" Meg asked.

"I didn't think it was, but it mattered to Ricky. My husband, Tony's son. You know about Ricky?"

Phillip spoke up. "I told her that Ricky has had some trouble with the law, although usually he has escaped penalty."

"Yeah, right," Miriam said contemptuously. "Ricky's got a temper, and he doesn't always stop to think. Tony tries to keep him close these days, so he doesn't get into any more trouble. But I made the mistake of telling Ricky about Dad's files, and he gets it into his head that maybe that could come back and bite Tony in his campaign, and maybe he should do something about it. I told him there was zip in those files, and he asks, 'What about that lawyer? Maybe he's got records on what went on. You work for him—you can find out.'

"Mr. C, I didn't want to drag you in. You and Arthur have been good to me. But Ricky wanted to do *something*—I don't know, impress his dad, or something like that. I told him I knew what was in the office files, and I hadn't seen anything that old, so he said, 'What about their house?'. And I said, 'How am I supposed to know what he keeps there?'. And he said, 'We can get in there—they're out of town, right?'. See, I'd told him about your wedding, Meg, and how your dad had given me time off since he and Arthur would be gone. So Ricky knew the house was empty, and he could get in and out without anybody knowing."

"But he hadn't counted on running into Enrique," Phillip said.

Miriam hung her head. "That's your gardener guy? Yeah. Told you Ricky doesn't think things through. He didn't expect to find anybody there, and then this Enrique pops up and Ricky panics and hits him with the first thing he finds. And Enrique goes down and hits his head, and that's that. Ricky panics and says, 'Let's get out of here.' By the time he calms down and remembers he never got to look for the file, you were back, Mr. C, and there were cops all over the place, and we never tried to get back in."

"Was Ricky ever inside the house?" Meg asked suddenly.

"Yeah, for a couple of minutes, and then suddenly Enrique shows up out of nowhere—he had a key, I guess. So Ricky goes after the guy and had to shut him up. But Ricky never got very far in the house before that, just around the first floor, poking at things."

So Mother was right—someone had been in the house, Meg thought. "Where were you, Miriam, while this was happening?"

"I was . . . inside, I guess." She couldn't meet Meg's eyes. "Ricky said I had to come with him to identify the file. But we never even got as far as the office."

"So you betrayed me, Miriam," Phillip said, his voice cold. "You and your husband broke into my house, and Enrique died."

"I'm sorry! I know it was wrong, but Ricky said it would help his father, and I figured if I went in with him it would go quicker, because I knew what I was looking for. You'd probably never even notice—it was an old file. We didn't expect to run into anybody else."

"That's not an excuse," Phillip told her. "Why did you have to break into the office? You know the files here better than anyone."

"Yeah, but Ricky was really manic by then. He couldn't go back to the house because there were too many people around, so I guess he was hoping it was in the office and I'd missed it. So we went. We didn't expect to find Arthur there, Mr. C! He told me he'd be gone all week."

"You could have killed him, too, you know." Phillip did not appear to be in a forgiving mood. "You and your husband together have committed multiple criminal acts. And I'm not going to accept the flimsy excuse, 'he made me do it.' You're a grown woman with a mind of your own. I had no proof, Miriam," Phillip said more slowly. "I liked your father. I thought he was a good man, and he didn't deserve to get into trouble. Your father never admitted to anything— he may have thought he was protecting me by not involving me. He asked me to help him with the letters, and then at some point he backed off. It took me a while to understand why, but I hadn't lived in New Jersey long then. I decided after the fact that he had figured out what was really going on, so I put the file away and didn't think about it again. I didn't even remember I had it—until Meg found it in the attic."

"So if Ricky had just left this alone, none of this would have happened?" Miriam asked.

"I'd say so, Miriam. And I never made the connection between you and your father-in-law. Del Monte is not an uncommon name. Unlike Caffarelli."

"Miriam, why did you think my father's dinky case with your father back then could possibly be important now?" Meg asked.

"I didn't, but Ricky did. He thought there might be records of the guys who were stiffing my dad. Companies, shippers, whatever, who had Mob ties back then, even if it wasn't widely known. And if one of those names was connected to one of the defendants in one of Tony's cases—who kept on with business as usual while that trial dragged on for, like, years—and could be linked to Tony, it could be a problem. Something his opponents could use against him. So it seemed like a good idea to get rid of the file—if it existed—just in case. That's what Ricky thought. And he thought it would be easy to get in and out without you ever knowing."

"But surely you must know I would never use something like that for political blackmail or dirty tricks," Phillip said.

"Yeah, I know, Mr. C. And I know you're not exactly political, right? But, see, it was out there, and that made it a threat. Or that's how Ricky saw it."

"Let me ask you one thing: is Anthony Del Monte an honest man?" Phillip asked.

Miriam nodded vigorously. "Yeah, I think he is."

"Was he involved in this attempt to retrieve the file?" Meg asked.

"No! He doesn't know anything about it. He wants to run a clean campaign, based on his record. Yeah, he hung out with some sketchy characters back in the day, but he was doing his job, giving them the best defense he could. There was nothing underhanded about what he did. No bribes, no witnesses who conveniently disappeared. He won fair and square, mostly by making the other team look like a bunch of idiots. Didn't make them happy, so it took him a while to climb back up the ladder. But he did it the right way."

"Is he getting any help from the Mob now?" Phillip asked.

"For his campaign, you mean? No. Sometimes he takes on clients from the old days—although mostly now it's their sons or even grandsons—but only if they have a good case, and he'll tell them to their face if he thinks it's hopeless. He's clean. Really."

It was at that moment that they heard the front door of the office open. "Anyone home?" Arthur called out.

"In here, Arthur," Phillip replied.

Arthur opened the door to Phillip's office and stopped on the threshold "When you asked me to meet you here today, I thought it was to be just the two of us. I assume this is Seth Chapin?"

Seth had gotten to his feet. "I am. Good to meet you, and to see you looking so fit."

"You're looking well, Arthur. No aftereffects?"

As her father talked, Meg studied Arthur. He looked

much better than he had the last time she had seen him. He'd been lucky, or at least lucky compared to Enrique.

"I'm ready to get back to work. The house is too quiet. What have I missed?" Arthur gazed around the room once again. "Meg, it was nice of you to come visit during your honeymoon. I'm glad to say I'm fully recovered. But what's going on here? Don't tell me you're just having a friendly chat."

Phillip sighed. "Find yourself a chair, Arthur, because this conversation concerns you, among other things."

Arthur didn't protest, but merely went into the front room and retrieved a second guest chair—but not before locking the door to the outer office. He set the chair down firmly as the others shifted to make room, then sat in it. "What's this all about?"

"Your attack, for one thing," Phillip began. It took the combined efforts of both Meg and Phillip to bring Arthur up to speed on what they had come to suspect, and what Miriam had just confirmed. Miriam remained silent throughout the explanation, until the end.

"I'm really sorry, Arthur," she told him. "You didn't deserve what happened. And like Mr. C says, I can't blame it all on Ricky."

27

"Your husband Ricky?" Arthur asked.

"That's him." Miriam struggled to find words. "Look, I know this sounds dumb, and maybe I was too stupid to see it. When I married him right after high school, I thought he was exciting. You know, kind of a bad boy? And I wanted something more than working for my dad in the sports store, but he couldn't afford to send me to college. Ricky's dad was kind of cool, and I thought maybe Ricky was going places. But he didn't." She seemed to stall again.

"Do you have children?" Meg asked, hoping to break the logjam.

Miriam shook her head. "We were waiting 'til we were more settled, and then . . . well, I decided that Ricky wasn't exactly father material."

"Did that bother him?" Meg asked.

"Maybe. I think he would have been happy if I'd stayed home with a couple squalling kids while he went out and did important guy things. But I made sure that didn't happen."

"What does he do, professionally?" Phillip asked.

"I know it sounds stupid, but I really don't know. He gets paychecks—or direct deposit these days—from a high-end auto repair and detailing place. He spends his days out of the house, but anytime I ask him about work he changes the subject. His dad wanted him to go to college, even junior college, but Ricky just plain wasn't interested. Maybe if he'd tried he would have done all right, but back then he really wanted to stick it to his dad."

"But he and his father are on good terms now?" Meg asked.

"As long as nobody brings up certain subjects, like race, and privileged rich people."

"What about the Mafia? And politics?"

"We don't talk about the Mafia. If you want my opinion, I'd guess Ricky has been, well, what you might call 'muscle' for them, but only small-time. He liked to beat on people, but he's not smart enough to be a hit man, and there aren't a lot of job openings for that these days anyway. You've got to be connected, and he isn't, or not in the right way, and that really ticks him off. That's why Tony is trying to keep him close these days, gave him a campaign job to keep him out of trouble. Like that worked," Miriam said bitterly. "I think Ricky likes the idea that his dad could be a big man in the state, bigger than he is now, and some of that would trickle down to him, so for a while he tried to clean up his act. But Ricky doesn't have a lot of skills that would be useful in a campaign, unless somebody needs a driver. And he's lousy at sucking up to people, being charming. Forget about him asking them for money or any other kind of support. Tony keeps him on a short leash, in case he goes off on someone and screws things up. I feel kind of bad for Tony—he doesn't deserve a kid like Ricky."

"Does he ever talk to you about Ricky?" Meg asked.

"Sometimes. I don't tell him everything, but I think he guesses a lot. He's smart."

Arthur had been following the discussion carefully, and now he spoke for the first time. "Miriam, from what you've said, it sounds like your Ricky is responsible for one death, plus the attack on me." Meg noted that Arthur didn't mention that Miriam was an accomplice.

"Look," Miriam began, "I think what happened is this. Sometimes Ricky can be pretty shrewd, especially if he sees an advantage for himself. I think he decided he could do his father a good turn and clear up that old mess, only that meant he had to find the evidence and get rid of it. Thing is, he doesn't think well in the moment—he just lashes out. Which is what happened with Enrique, and with you, Arthur."

"Let me get this straight," Phillip interrupted. "You were willing to participate in an illegal break-in?"

Miriam wouldn't meet his eyes. "Well, yeah, at your house. But I figured you'd never find out. And I've got a key for here, so that's not breaking in, right?"

"Miriam, your husband killed an innocent man," Phillip said coldly. "You knew it, and yet you did nothing."

"And of course you didn't think to call the police at the time?" Arthur asked. "Perhaps Enrique could have been saved."

"How was I supposed to explain what we were doing there? Ricky told me to shut up and let him think. Then he calmed down and decided that we could get rid of the body, but maybe we should find the guy's car or truck or whatever and use that, and nobody would know he was ever there. So we kind of covered him up out back and figured nobody would notice him, and we'd come back later when we found the truck. Ricky got the guy's keys out of his pocket, and we went off looking for the truck, only we never did find it and Ricky worried someone would see us wandering around the neighborhood. But by the time we got back, you were there, you and your wife, in some rented car, so we split. When we drove by the next day there were cops there. We figured somebody had found the body, so we just kept going."

Phillip's face looked like it was carved in stone. "Just to be clear: You and your husband decided to break into my house to look for a file you weren't even sure was there? And when you were interrupted by an innocent man, who was authorized to be there, you killed him?"

"Ricky did. Accidentally!"

Phillip waved his hand dismissively. "And you told no one, not even anonymously. And rather than end things there, you decided to come to the office, where you assaulted Arthur?"

"He wasn't supposed to be here! Arthur, I'm really sorry." Miriam turned to him, pleading.

Arthur was not about to let her off easily. "Miriam, you could have explained your way out of it when you ran into me. You could have given me an excuse that you wanted to work on something at home, or even something dumb like you needed to water the plants. You could have introduced your husband. Instead, you hit me?"

"Ricky did it," Miriam replied, her tone desperate. "I was in the office going through the files, and Ricky was hanging out in the front room waiting for me, behind the door, I guess. When you walked it, he just grabbed something and *bam*, you went down."

"That seems to be Ricky's response to a lot of things," Phillip said. "Hit first, think later. Is the man on drugs?"

"Maybe. I don't know. I don't ask. Mostly I try to keep out of his way."

"Did you check to see if I was still alive?" Arthur asked.

"Yes! I was scared. And then Ricky said we had to get out of there, fast. So I threw some random files around, to make it look like you'd walked into a break-in, and we left."

"Leaving me on the floor, unconscious, with a possible skull fracture that could have killed me, not knowing how long it might be before anyone found me?"

"Well, yes. But Ricky—"

"Do not blame your husband, young lady!" Arthur thundered. "You bear a portion of the responsibility for Enrique's death and my injuries."

Miriam stared at him openmouthed. Meg guessed that she'd never seen him angry before.

"Quite right, Arthur," Phillip said in a calmer tone. "The question is, what do we do now?"

"We take Miriam to the police and she will tell them what she has just told us," Arthur said, not giving an inch.

Miriam sprang out of her chair. "No! Ricky'll kill me!"

Phillip stood up as well. "I agree with Arthur on this. Your husband has committed serious crimes that we all are now aware of, and who knows how many others—I doubt that these were the first violent incidents he's been involved in. You are an accomplice—and please don't insult my intelligence by saying you didn't know what he was going to do. You knew what he was capable of. Arthur and I will accompany you to the police station, and you can hope that a full explanation and assisting the police in finding your husband may earn you a lighter penalty."

Miriam looked like a caged animal, her eyes darting around the room. Seth stood up quietly and blocked her path toward the door. It didn't take her long to realize she had no options beyond going with Phillip and Arthur and confessing to the police. Finally she said, in a dull voice, "All right. I'm sorry, Mr. C, Arthur—all of you. I never thought things would go this far. And, yeah, I should have known that Ricky had gone over the edge. I just didn't want to see it. You can keep him away from me, keep me safe, can't you?"

"The police can help you with that. Get your purse and coat, and we'll go directly there."

Miriam complied wordlessly, and the older men led her to the outer door. Before they left, Phillip said, "Meg? Why don't you and Seth go back to the house now? I'll meet you there later. You don't need to come to the police station—I think you've given us all the information we need."

Meg felt exhausted. "Okay. See you later."

Seth waited until the door closed behind the small group, then took the chairs back to the outer office. Meg didn't move from her original seat, so he came back and sat in the adjoining chair. "You were right," he said.

"Looks that way," she answered. "Do you think Miriam was telling the truth?"

Seth sat back and stared at the ceiling. "How should I answer that? Is she trying to throw her husband under the bus to save herself? Maybe. But I think even if she pins the blame on him for starting this, no one's going to believe she hit not one but two men, both of whom were larger than she was, and disabled them. I think any jury would buy that her husband did the dirty work. He can protest all he likes. But I'm pretty sure she'll face charges for something."

"Can Anthony Del Monte step in and fix this, do you think?"

"Meg, I'm not sure how New Jersey law works, but there's a murder and an assault. How's he going to make those go away?"

"An insanity plea for Ricky?"

"Not having met the delightful Ricky, I'm not going to guess how he'll come across. I'd be willing to bet he's known to the police, one way or another. He can't slide out of all his crimes, no matter who his father is."

"What happens to Miriam?"

"You're asking me? I'm a plumber-slash-carpenter. I don't have a law degree. She's a personable youngish woman who tells a good story. If I had to guess, I'd say she'll get off but not completely. She went willingly with her husband. For all I know, she'll plead battered wife syndrome—she was under Ricky's thumb. Ask your father, when the dust settles."

"And Tony Del Monte? Will this destroy him, too?"

"Maybe. Miriam says he didn't know what was going on, but his name is going to be linked to this anyway, and that can't be good for his political campaign."

Meg was silent for a few moments, trying to find a coherent thought in her head, and failing. "Seth, how can any woman follow her husband blindly into doing something wrong? How could she be that desperate?"

"You mean, you wouldn't kill for me?" he replied.

Was he joking? "I don't think so. Does that mean I love you less than Miriam loves her Ricky?"

"I wouldn't say that. Only that you have a clearer sense of right and wrong than she does."

"Her father runs a small-town sporting goods store. Mine was a high-powered corporate attorney. I went to college, and she didn't."

"And that gives you a stronger moral compass? Did you miss the Great Recession altogether? A lot of smart, educated, employed bankers did their best to fleece a lot of the American public and thought nothing of it. Why do you want to blame yourself for any of this?"

She was about to make a glib comment, but she stopped herself. Seth was right—she was deflecting to cover up what she really felt. "I guess I feel guilty for starting this whole thing. We didn't have to stop here. We could have gone straight home. It's almost insulting of me to imply that my father couldn't have sorted out his own legal problems here."

Meg swallowed. "I guess the real question is, why did I think I had to be involved?"

"Because you believed, probably rightly, that the police would have written off the two events as two interrupted burglaries, and Ricky would have gone on hurting or killing people. You were right—you saw the situation more clearly than the police did. And because they're your family, Meg. That's a one-two punch, and you didn't have a choice."

"I'm sorry you had to get dragged into this," Meg said.

"If you're in it, I'm in it. Come here." He stood up and extended his hand.

Meg took it, and he pulled her up and into his arms.

28

Eventually Meg looked at her watch, and was surprised to find it wasn't even noon.

Seth noticed. "You hungry?"

"I don't know. I can't remember breakfast. I guess I'd just rather go back to the house and wait to see what the police have to say."

"It may take a while, so we might as well eat now. We can fill your mother in on what Miriam told us when we get back. Unless you don't want to?"

"It's okay. It'll save time in the long run. And maybe we can think about going back to Granford?"

Seth smiled. "I thought you'd never ask."

Since they were already downtown in Montclair, they decided to walk until they found someplace to eat. To her own surprise, Meg found that she had missed the physical activity of managing the orchard—she was used to working long, hard hours, then falling into bed, tired. Sitting in a car traveling hundreds of miles wasn't at all the same. She felt restless; it was time to get on with her life, now that her father's problems had been sorted out. She hoped.

They found a self-consciously retro diner, ate, walked back to the car, then drove slowly to the house. As they drove along, Meg realized how little the town meant to her. She had no attachment to it, apart from her parents. She wouldn't be sorry to leave, and she doubted she'd be coming back. Maybe she and her parents could meet in neutral territory somewhere.

When they walked into the house, it was quiet. "Mother?" Meg called out.

"Up here," Elizabeth's voice came from somewhere upstairs.

They went up the staircase; at the top, Seth peeled off to the room they were staying in. Meg found her mother standing in the middle of the front bedroom, the nominal first guest room, surrounded by boxes and suitcases. "After you went looking through the attic," Elizabeth said, "I realized how long it had been since I'd gone up there. It could really use some sorting—and dumping. This is just the start." She waved her hand at the jumble of things she'd brought down.

"Daddy's not back?" Meg asked.

"No, I haven't heard from him or seen him. I expected you all back by lunchtime, but when you never showed up, I just kept working up here. What's going on?"

Meg sighed, trying to remember how much of the story Elizabeth knew, and how much she hadn't heard. "Let's go downstairs and sit down, and I'll fill you in."

Elizabeth gave her a quizzical look, then followed her down the stairs. When they were settled, Meg began telling the story yet again. How many times had she done this now?

Elizabeth let her talk, without interrupting. When Meg finally ran out of steam, her mother said, "I didn't know. I guess I didn't want to know. You'll find out, over time, that you and your husband fall into routines, patterns that you're both comfortable with. And the longer that goes on, the harder it is to break out of them. Your father and I have been married a long time, and I guess at some point, I stopped asking questions. I knew there were things about his work that he couldn't tell me about, and it got too confusing to figure where the boundaries were, so I gave up. I had hoped that when he opened his own office, there'd be more time for us, together. And I think he's trying—that's why we were taking some extra time around your wedding, just the two of us. Which was lovely, until that problem with the car . . . What happens now?"

"As I told you, Daddy and Arthur took Miriam straight to the police station. She said she'd tell the whole story to the police, although she might have changed her mind after she'd had time to think about it. Or changed her story. If she's still admitting that she had some hand in the break-in here that led to Enrique's death, I would think they'd have to arrest her, but given her father-in-law's prominence, I doubt she'd spend much if any time in jail right now."

"And of course they'll be looking for her husband."

"Yes. Again, having a powerful father may come into play there, too. I hate to say it, but if he's out on bail, you might want to check your security at the house here."

"You really think he's dangerous?"

"From all I've heard, yes. He's got quite a temper."

Finally they heard the sound of a car in the driveway. Meg and Elizabeth stood quickly and made for the kitchen, and Seth came down the stairs and followed them. They stood in a cluster, waiting for Phillip to appear.

Phillip came through the back door and stopped at the sight of them gathered together in the kitchen. "I should have texted or something to let you know I'd be a while—isn't that what the younger folk do these days? It certainly took longer than I expected. Did you fill in your mother, Meg?"

Meg nodded silently.

"Phillip, is everything all right?" Elizabeth asked, anxiously.

"Let's sit down and I'll bring you up to date. But I'd really like a Scotch first. Any other takers?"

The rest of them shook their heads. "I'll make a pot of tea," Elizabeth said brightly, and set about boiling water. Meg began collecting the other utensils, while Seth followed her father down the hall to the dining room and the liquor cabinet.

It was more than ten minutes later that they finally assembled in the living room, Scotch and tea in hand. Meg glanced briefly at Seth—had he gotten any advance word from Phillip?—but he gave a small shake of his head.

"All right, Daddy, you've gotten our attention," Meg said. "Is this how you manage trials? By keeping people waiting?"

"Do you know, sweetheart, I've taken part in very few trials. My goal has always been to settle before things reached that stage, and overall I've been quite successful. But you're right—I know you're eager to hear the results of our visit to the police station."

"Did Miriam stick to her story?" Meg demanded.

Phillip nodded. "She did."

"Wait—did you sit in on her 'confession'?" Meg made air quotes. "Isn't that unusual? You didn't say you'd represent her, did you?"

"No, dear, I don't do criminal law, and I would recuse myself in any event, since I'm personally involved in this case. But the chief kindly let me observe. She made her one phone call, in this case to her father-in-law. I'm sure he'll find her a competent attorney."

"But she didn't wait until she had one present?"

"No. She waived that right. To tell the truth, I think she was afraid. If she waffled or refused to speak now, she may believe that her husband would find a way to silence her. I think she wanted to be sure her story was on the record, with witnesses. As it was, she barely had time to give the outlines when someone arrived to post bail for her. Which was amusing, in a way, because the police hadn't even decided what to charge her with, much less think about bail."

"So what happened?"

"The man turned out to be from the state attorney general's office, and he persuaded the police that she should be released on her own recognizance, because she wasn't a flight risk and had no prior record, and, implicitly, because of her political connections. Her husband, Richard Del Monte, was not mentioned in this discussion. They let her leave, but not before they had printed her statement and had her sign it."

"Do the police know where Ricky is?" Meg asked anxiously.

"They are looking for him as we speak. He was not at his home, but Miriam went to his father's house."

"What happens now?" Seth asked.

"I can't say, but I think our part in this is done. They already have our statements about what little we know about Enrique's death, and I had nothing to add." Phillip turned to his wife. "Elizabeth, do you have a home number for Enrique's family? I'd like to volunteer to cover the costs of his funeral. The police will probably release his body shortly, now that they know what happened."

"Of course. I'll find it for you. I'll also follow up on the insurance claim for the car, now that we know what happened there as well."

"Be sure to get copies of the accident report," Phillip said, back in business mode.

"Of course, dear," Elizabeth said. "How is Arthur?"

"I'd say he's about eighty percent, physically. He's angry, no surprise, mainly because Miriam abused his trust. We both liked her."

That was all well and good, Meg thought, *but both of her employers had been clueless about the personal demons she was wrestling with.* "Can she go home? I mean, will that be safe? Or maybe she still has family in Madison that she can stay with?"

"We didn't discuss that, dear. It's up to the police now to protect her. Obviously she won't be coming back to the office."

Yes, burgling the home of one of your bosses and bashing the other one over the head would make that difficult, Meg said to herself, but refrained from saying out loud. "So we're done, right? Maybe there's someplace we could go for dinner, to get away from all this?"

"An excellent idea, Meg. Elizabeth? Is there any place you'd prefer?"

"Your club should be quiet tonight," she said, and

Phillip volunteered to call for a reservation, and headed for his office. Elizabeth followed a few moments later, claiming she wanted to shower before going out.

That left Seth and Meg alone in the living room. "Home tomorrow?" Meg said.

"That sounds good to me," Seth replied.

The sound of the doorbell echoed through the hallway. "I'll get it," Meg called out, not sure either of her parents had even heard it. She went to the front door and was surprised to find Chief Bennett standing on the other side.

"Is your father here?" he asked, without preamble.

"Yes, he's upstairs. Please, come in—it's cold out there." After the chief had walked in, she shut the door behind him. "Let me go get him."

She hurried up the stairs and found her father in his office. "Daddy? Chief Bennett is here."

Phillip stood up abruptly. "What can he want now? We just left him." He brushed impatiently past Meg and went down the stairs.

The chief was still standing in the hallway, looking uncomfortable. Seth had come as far as the living room door to greet the chief but still hung back, and Meg joined him.

"Chief Bennett, what's this all about?" Phillip demanded. "Is Miriam all right?"

"Luckily, yes. I wanted to let you know that Richard Del Monte has been taken into custody. He did not go easily."

Phillip responded quickly. "I didn't expect otherwise. Where did you find him?"

"As you know, Miriam Del Monte was released from our custody, and she was taken to her father-in-law's house.

Anthony Del Monte was there when she arrived. He was informed that the police were looking for his son, although no arrest warrant had been issued yet. Then the police left. Anthony Del Monte apparently thought the best solution would be to talk with his son and his daughter-in-law together, and convince Ricky to turn himself in, so he called Ricky on his cell and asked him to come over. Ricky did. It should be no surprise to you that when he heard what Miriam had done, he lost his temper and physically assaulted his wife. His father tried to separate them, and when he was unsuccessful, he called the police, who arrived quickly and took him into custody. Miriam escaped with only a few bruises."

"Thank goodness," Phillip said quietly.

"As you might guess," the chief went on, "Anthony Del Monte will not be able to smooth this incident over, and no doubt it will appear on the news shortly." Chief Bennett hesitated a moment. "There's one more thing, Phillip," he said. "You know I've held you accountable for what happened to my son?"

"Yes, you made that clear at the time. I understood how you felt."

The chief nodded, once. "What you may not have known is that Ricky Del Monte was the person who attacked Tommy in the holding cell. But even then Ricky was outside the reach of the law, because of his father and . . . other connections. No one would testify against him, so no charges were ever brought." He took a deep breath. "So I have to say that I'm glad he's finally been arrested, on a far more serious charge, although I wouldn't have wished such an ending on his father. But it was wrong of me to put the responsibility for what happened to Tommy on you, and Richard Del Monte will finally pay the price. I apologize if I took out my anger on you."

"Bill, I'm a father, too. I can certainly understand what you felt then."

"Ironic, isn't it, that your daughter was the one who started this ball rolling?" Chief Bennett turned to Meg. "I did listen to what you told me, Meg, even though I thought your conjectures were improbable. But you were right—clearly you're your father's daughter." He regarded the group again. "That's all I came to say."

"Thank you for telling us, Bill," Phillip said. "Let me see you out." The two men walked out the front door together.

After the door had closed, Elizabeth came down the stairs, wearing a terry-cloth robe and still toweling her hair. "I heard voices, but I wasn't decent. What did I miss? Where's Phillip?"

"He's saying good-bye to Chief Bennett, outside," Meg told her. "The chief came by to say that Ricky Del Monte lost it when he found out what Miriam had done, and attacked her. His father called the police, and he was picked up at his father's house."

"So is it over now? The police know what happened with Enrique and Arthur? What about Miriam?"

"She wasn't harmed, but we don't know if she'll be charged, or with what."

Phillip returned, shutting the front door behind him after a gust of cold air followed him in. When he spotted his wife, he said, "They told you?"

She crossed quickly to him and hugged him, then stepped back. "They did. Oh, Phillip, what a sad mess! That boy should have gotten help years ago, and now more people have suffered. What will the police do with Miriam?"

"I would guess that the police will go easy on her, given the circumstances. I'll help if I can, but I can't lose sight of the fact that she betrayed both Arthur and me, and put us all at risk. She knew what her husband was capable of."

And that made her as guilty as he was, Meg thought to herself.

29

Dinner at the club was a subdued affair, each of them lost in their own thoughts. Over coffee—everyone had declined dessert—Elizabeth said to Meg, "Not exactly the honeymoon you and Seth had planned, was it, darling?"

"No, but it's kind of typical of our luck, Mother," Meg replied with a rueful smile. "Seth, I think you deserve some kind of medal—for patience, for not whining, for letting me do what I thought I had to. Right or wrong."

Seth glanced at his companions around the table. "I believed you *were* right. If I had thought you were wrong, I would have told you. But you answer to your conscience, not to me."

Meg laid her hand on his, fighting tears, and said, "Thank you."

Elizabeth and Phillip gave them a long moment before bringing them back to the real world. "Will you be leaving now?" Elizabeth asked, a touch sadly.

"I think we need to. We've been gone, what?"

"Just over a week," Seth reminded her.

"Wow, it feels a lot longer than that." Meg shook her head. "Mother, Daddy—we should plan a vacation where we can just enjoy one another's company. Just not during harvest season—"

"—or if there's a drought," Seth picked up the thread—

"—or if we're planting a new orchard, or, heaven forbid, starting up a cider operation."

Her mother laughed. "Just send us your calendar for the next year, and we'll try to squeeze in a visit somewhere."

"We'd like that."

The next morning Meg and Seth set off early, after a round of tearful good-byes. *Partings are always hard,* Meg reflected, glad that she was going back to her own home— with her own husband. She remained quiet, save for necessary driving instructions, until Seth reached the highway. "So we've survived ten days of marriage, and there's been only one murder."

"Something to remember when we're old and gray," Seth agreed. "We're going to avoid the New York traffic, right?"

"If I pay attention to the exits, yes," Meg told him. "After that it's easy." After a few more miles, she began again. "You know, I meant what I said last night—you were a rock."

"Mostly I kept my mouth shut," Seth said.

"Don't put yourself down. You were behind me all the way. Can I ask you a question?"

"Of course."

"After spending an admittedly stressful week with my parents, what do you think of their marriage?"

Seth didn't hurry to answer. "As you have pointed out on more than one occasion, they're kind of formal with each other. I'm kind of surprised by your mother, now that I know her better—she's an intelligent, capable woman, but she's never worked?"

"For pay? Well, she did before she married—you heard all that the last time they were in Granford. Are you asking tactfully if Daddy insisted she stay home?"

"Did he?"

"I don't think so. He made plenty of money, so she didn't *need* to work, but I don't think he would have been upset if she had chosen to, especially after I was old enough to look out for myself. She certainly came of age in a post-feminist culture that would have encouraged her to work. Her choice, but I know I couldn't stand that lifestyle, even if you were fantastically rich."

"So you became a farmer and married a plumber? Is that some kind of delayed rebellion?"

"I hope not! I like what I do. I like doing it with you. Isn't that enough?"

"Of course it is. And the same goes for me. Works out well, don't you think?"

"I do. Now, why does that sound familiar?" Meg asked, suppressing a giggle.

Once assured that Seth knew where he was going—not that she had had any doubts—Meg dozed intermittently as they drove northward. Luckily the weather had cooperated with them, which might be the only part of the last week that had worked out as intended. Well, Monticello had been all that she had hoped for, but after that things had sort of fallen apart. Still, they'd wrapped up not one but two crimes in a record five days. Maybe she and Seth were getting better at this. But she hoped with all her heart that they wouldn't have to put their experience to work again, in Granford or anywhere else. Poor Miriam. No, poor Enrique, who hadn't deserved to die because one young man thought breaking the law when it suited him was acceptable, and when he was thwarted, lashed out violently. She had no pity for Richard Del Monte, and only a bit for his father, who had ignored his son's obvious problems for too long, and who now had to live with the results.

The final time she opened her eyes, it was growing dark, and she recognized the back road from the Massachusetts Turnpike to their end of Granford. "How long was I out?" she asked Seth.

"An hour or two—it's after five. Almost there."

"Thank goodness. Can we figure out what normal is now?"

"I hope so."

Seth made the turn by the big farm stand, then another turn a couple of miles farther, and then they were approaching her house—no, *their* house. Bree must be home: there were lights on in several of the windows, and the house looked warm and welcoming in the dusk. They crunched over the gravel of the driveway, pulled to a stop, and Seth turned off the engine. "Home."

"It is." She leaned over and kissed him, then quickly disengaged her seat belt and jumped out of the car, slowing only when she realized how stiff her joints were when she stood up. It didn't matter. She strode to the back door, fishing out her keys as she went, but the door was already unlocked, so she walked into her kitchen, with Seth close behind. They were greeted enthusiastically by Max, who couldn't seem to figure out which one of them to jump on, so he tried both of them on for size several times. Lolly, in her favorite place on top of the refrigerator, stood up and stretched, but waited for them to come to her. And Bree was standing by the stove, which was covered with pots issuing good smells. "Welcome back," she said. "Still married?"

"So it seems," Meg told her. "How'd you know we'd be home today? I kept forgetting to tell you when we were coming, but things kept happening so we weren't really sure until last night. Anyway, thanks for all this!" She waved her hand around the kitchen. "We're tired and hungry and I'm sure Seth has had enough driving for a while."

"Your mom called to let me know you were on your way, so I could shoo out all the guys from the orgies. Kidding! And I figured you'd be hungry."

"Can we wash up before we eat?"

"No hurry."

"Is all the plumbing still working?" Meg asked, glancing slyly at Seth.

"Of course it is—your husband installed it, didn't he? He's good."

"I know. Let me go and clean up, and then we can come down again and tell you all about everything. Unless Mother already unloaded the story?"

"Nope," Bree replied, "she said you'd have plenty to tell me but she'd let you do the telling. There wasn't a murder involved, was there?"

"As a matter of fact, there was," Meg said. Before Bree could close her gaping mouth, she and Seth fled upstairs.

Five minutes later they were seated around the kitchen table with wineglasses in hand. Max had his head laid on Seth's knee, and Lolly had settled under Meg's feet, which suited her fine since she didn't plan to move for a while. Bree dished up and then demanded, "Okay, spill it. And start from the beginning."

Telling the tale of the accident in Amherst, which had turned out to be nothing more than an accident, and the discovery of Enrique's body, and the attack on Arthur Ackerman, and the unraveling of the connections—between the past, the Corey family's time in Madison, combined with the history of the New Jersey Mob; then fast-forward to the present and Phillip's secretary and the state attorney who had hoped to run for governor—took the better part of an hour, allowing for interruptions from each other and Bree's incredulous questions and second helpings of dinner. When they had finished, Meg felt like a limp balloon. And it was only seven o'clock.

"So, did we miss anything while we were gone? Any word from Lydia or Rachel?"

"I'll bet you two have figured out that Lydia and Christopher are kind of together now," Bree said.

"Yes, we noticed that even in our rose-colored fog. How'd you figure it out?"

"Hey, I'm not stupid—I saw them together. Enough said. By the way, Lydia said Rachel is fine, Maggie has gained a pound, and they're looking forward to seeing you when you're ready. You'd better warn her to set aside a chunk of time, if you're going to tell her what you told me."

"Duly noted," Meg said.

"Any natural disasters?" Seth asked. "You know, floods, blizzards, earthquakes?"

"Nope. A few snow flurries. All good. I've held off on the pruning, but that can wait for January."

"You mean we actually have free time?" Meg said, laughing. "Well, I can get an early start on running the numbers before year-end. You want to take some time off, now that we're back? Go visit family or anything?"

Bree suddenly looked nervous, and had trouble meeting Meg's eyes. "Well, there's one thing I have to tell you . . ." She stopped, as if searching for a way to go on.

Please, no more crises! Meg sent up a silent prayer. "What?"

Bree cleared her throat. "I've had a job offer, or not a job, exactly, but sort of a senior internship."

"Okay," Meg said cautiously. "Doing what?"

"Helping with an orchard. In Australia. Christopher told me about it, and so I applied, and they made the offer while you were gone. They're doing some really interesting stuff with creating new varieties of apples."

"And what did you tell . . . whoever this is?"

"I haven't yet, because I thought I owed it to you to talk with you first. But I'd have to leave by the end of the month, if I'm going."

Nothing is ever easy, is it? Meg reflected. "Bree, you have been a godsend, helping me with the orchard these past two years. I wouldn't have made it without you. But I can't stand in your way if this is what's right for you."

Bree smiled. "Great, because I think it would be really cool to work in Australia, at least for a while. But the good news is, Christopher said he'd help you find someone to fill in for me. And it's the slowest time of year, so you'd have plenty of time to bring this person up to speed."

"Then go, with my—our—blessing. You're not leaving tomorrow morning or anything like that, are you?"

"No, ma'am. I'll be around for a week or two. And thanks—I didn't want to feel guilty about leaving you on your own." She stood up and said, "If it's okay with you, I'll go upstairs now. I can clean up in the morning."

"Shoo! We can handle it."

After Bree disappeared, Meg turned to Seth. "Well, never a dull moment in Granford, is there?"

"You aren't upset?" Seth asked.

Meg shook her head. "Not really. I don't want to hold her back, and I know we can cope, one way or another. You want to take Max out while I do the dishes?"

"Works for me. I'll see if I can tire him out."

"And when you two get back, we can go to bed."

"Now there's an invitation I can't refuse."

Recipes

Cooking in winter in New England has always been a challenge, although the number of fresh ingredients available in markets has increased steadily. But it's still cold, so warm and spicy dishes are welcome.

Carrot Ginger Soup

2 tbsp olive oil

1 lb carrots, chopped small

1 lb turnips, cut into half-inch chunks

1 large onion, diced

1 large apple, preferably a green variety, peeled, cored, and diced

4-6 cloves garlic, minced

2 tbsp fresh ginger, grated

> 3 large sprigs thyme (strip the leaves off the stems)
> 1 tsp curry powder
> 4 cups water or vegetable broth
> Salt and pepper to taste

In a deep pot, heat the oil over medium-high heat, and add the chopped carrots and turnips. Cook until they brown on one side at least.

Stir in the chopped apples, onions, and garlic and reduce the heat. Cook until the onions are translucent but not browned. Add a half teaspoon salt.

Stir in the thyme leaves, curry, and grated ginger, then cook for two minutes until fragrant.

Add the water or broth, bring to a boil, then turn down the heat and simmer for about 10 minutes, checking to make sure the vegetables are tender (the carrots and turnips might take longer). Add salt and pepper to taste.

You can leave the soup chunky or puree it. An immersion blender is a good option if you want to thicken it while leaving some texture.

Serve it with a hearty bread—homemade if you have it—and you've got a satisfying supper for a chilly night!

Steamed Chili-Garlic Cod

This is a tasty recipe that's great for a cold, damp winter's night. Flash-frozen fish is widely available even in winter. If you keep the ingredients on hand, you can have a quick dinner!

    2 8-oz cod (or other white fish) fillets
    4 tbsp Asian sweet chili sauce (also known as Thai
       chili sauce)
    2 tsp rice vinegar
    4 tsp soy sauce
    4 garlic cloves, thinly sliced
    Lime slices (optional)

Preheat the oven to 400 degrees.

For the glaze, in a small bowl mix the chili sauce, rice vinegar, and soy sauce.

Cut two sheets of parchment paper, large enough to wrap your fillets. (Note: it's hard to get two fillets that are exactly the same size. Don't worry about it.) Dab a bit of the sauce on each piece of parchment paper, then place one fillet on each sheet and brush with the glaze. Top with the garlic slices (and the lime if you're using it).

Fold the parchment paper over the fillets, crimping the edges to seal the packets. Place them in a baking pan.

Bake 12-15 minutes in the preheated oven (depending on the thickness of your fillets). Remove the pan from the oven, place the packets on a plate and open them carefully (watch out for the steam!).

Drizzle any of the juices from the packets over the fillets and serve with rice.

Apple-Cherry-Marzipan Pie

This is a rich and delicious twist on a traditional apple pie.

CRUST
8 oz (1/2 pound) unsalted butter, chilled and cut
    into pieces
1 lb plain white flour
1/4 cup white sugar
Pinch of salt
Water (about 5 tbsp), chilled

Place the butter and flour in the bowl of a food processor and pulse until the mixture resembles crumbs. Add the sugar and salt and pulse again.

Place the water in a cup or pitcher (you can add an ice cube to keep it cold) and add slowly until the mixture holds together to form a dough. You may not need all the water, but the dough shouldn't be crumbly.

Knead on a floured surface just long enough to combine. Wrap it in plastic wrap or put in a plastic ziplock bag and chill in the refrigerator for 20 minutes.

FILLING
Zest of 1 lemon
Pinch of ground cinnamon
1/3 cup white sugar
4 tbsp cornstarch
6 apples, peeled, cored, and cut into half-inch slices
    (Cortlands work well—just make sure you use a
    good cooking apple)

7 oz marzipan, cut into small cubes
1 cup dried cherries or dried cranberries

Preheat the oven to 375 degrees.

In a bowl, combine the lemon zest, cinnamon, sugar, and cornstarch.

Flour a board and a rolling pin. Remove the pastry from the refrigerator. Divide into two portions, one half the size of the other (the larger will be for the bottom). Roll out the larger piece and fit it into a 9" pie pan (the pastry should overlap generously), pressing it against the sides of the pan. Place in the freezer to chill for 10 minutes.

Arrange a layer of apple slices in the pie dish and sprinkle with the marzipan cubes and cherries or cranberries. Repeat in layers until the pan is nearly full at the edges and heaped in the middle.

Roll out the smaller piece of dough to make a lid that fits over the apples. Crimp the edges of the bottom crust over this to seal. Make a hole in the center of the crust to let the steam escape.

If you like, beat an egg yolk with a little water and use as a glaze over the crust.

Bake for 40-45 minutes, or until the pastry is golden-brown (test to make sure the apples are soft). If it's getting too brown after 25 minutes, cover the top with foil to keep the edges from burning.

Sheila Connolly

GOLDEN MALICIOUS

• *An Orchard Mystery* •

Apple orchard owner Meg Corey dreads the labor of manual irrigation to stave off a drought, but that's nowhere near as bad as when she finds a dead body at an old saw mill's forest reserve while taking a much-needed break.

And the body isn't the only frightening discovery she makes. A mysterious insect infestation seems to have migrated to the area—one that could bring serious harm to local woodlands. And it's up to Meg to find out what's behind this sudden swarm of trouble.

PRAISE FOR THE ORCHARD MYSTERIES

"A winner for cozy mystery fans."
—Lesa's Book Critiques

"[A] fascinating whodunit."
—*The Mystery Gazette*

sheilaconnolly.com
facebook.com/BerkleyPub
penguin.com